The Graveyard Position

The Graveyard Position

A Novel of Suspense

ROBERT BARNARD

This edition first published in Great Britain in 2004 by
Allison & Busby Limited
Bon Marché Centre
241-251 Ferndale Road
London SW9 8BJ
http://www.allisonandbusby.com

A catalogue record for this book is available from
the British Library.

10 9 8 7 6 5 4 3 2 1

ISBN 0 7490 8326 3

Printed and bound in Great Britain by
Creative Print + Design, Ebbw Vale, Wales

Novels by Robert Barnard

Death of an Old Goat
A Little Local Murder
Death on the High C's
Blood Brotherhood
Unruly Son
Posthumous Papers
Death in a Cold Climate
Mother's Boys
Sheer Torture
Death and the Princess
The Missing Brontë
Little Victims
Corpse in a Gilded Cage
Out of the Blackout
Disposal of the Living
Political Suicide
Bodies
Death in Purple Prose
The Skeleton in the Grass
At Death's Door
Death and the Chaste Apprentice
A City of Strangers
A Scandal in Belgravia
A Fatal Attachment
A Hovering of Vultures
The Masters of the House
The Bad Samaritan
No Place of Safety
The Corpse at the Haworth Tandoori
Touched by the Dead
Unholy Dying
Bones in the Attic
Mistress of Alderley
A Cry from the Dark

Short Story collections

Death of a Salesperson
A Habit of Widowhood

Writing as Bernard Bastable

To Die Like a Gentleman
Dead, Mr Mozart
Too Many Notes, Mr Mozart
A Mansion and Its Murder (US only)

ROBERT BARNARD was born in Essex. He was educated at Balliol College, Oxford, and after completing his degree he taught English at universities in Australia and Norway, where he completed his doctorate on Dickens. He returned to England to become a full-time writer and currently lives with his wife in Leeds, Yorkshire. The couple are currently collaborating on a Brontë encyclopaedia. In his spare time he enjoys opera, crosswords and walking the dog. In 2003 Robert Barnard was the recipient of the prestigious CWA Cartier Diamond Dagger, an award in recognition of a lifetime's achievement in crime writing.

for
PETER AND SHEILA
Partners in Crime

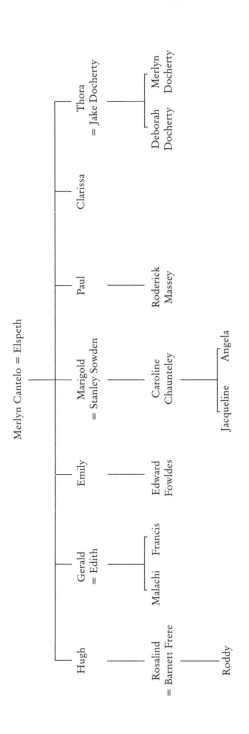

The organist was playing yet another slow, amorphous piece, and for the mourners who had taken their pews early, enough was becoming enough. You couldn't expect the relentless cheerfulness of Rossini, but times had changed since the era when you only got the musical equivalent of a thick black-out curtain at funerals.

"So very un-Clarissa," said her niece Rosalind Frere. "Particularly in her earlier years." She gave another of her surreptitious quick glances at arrivals through the main door. "Oh, there's whatsername. Caroline Chaunteley. She never went near Clarissa in her last years, that I do know, though Clarissa was awfully kind to her when she was young ... as we all were."

"Nobody went near her in her last years," said her husband Barnett.

"That's not fair! I went as often as I could. We're not a drop-in sort of family – we keep ourselves to ourselves... I did my best, though she was obviously failing, physically as well as mentally."

"You said she threw a meat pudding at you."

"Well, it was more a sort of gesture, showing she wanted to." The levels of Rosalind's truthfulness were well-known to her husband, who merely raised his eyebrows.

"Oh, here's the coffin," said Rosalind brightly.

The music had changed inconspicuously to something with a muffled, march-like beat and the coffin began up the aisle, borne by a mixture of undertaker's men and relatives.

"Oh look, there's Cousin Malachi. They've put him in the middle, where he can pretend to carry. He's all of eight stone, and short with it. Doesn't he look ridiculous?"

"We're lucky he's not wimbly-wambling all over the aisle," said Barnett. "That's what I saw him doing, back and forth across Boar Lane, last Friday night."

"He can't have had a drink yet. It's only half-past eleven."

"What a sweet, innocent creature you are," said Barnett, who knew better than most that she was neither.

The coffin seemed to take forever. The organ march went on and on, obviously something that could be stretched to the crack of doom if circumstances demanded it. The bearers shuffled slowly forward, their expression either dour or bored. Cousin Malachi was the only one who let his sharp little eyes stray indiscriminately around the congregation.

"Oh, get a move on," said Rosalind, turning round. "*Oh!*"

She swivelled her head back to the frontward-looking position.

"What?" whispered Barnett.

"Nothing ... I must have got it wrong ... It can't be."

Her husband always said that her whispers were more powerful than a public-address system, and behind her people reacted: some looked round unashamedly, while others continued looking straight ahead for a second or two, then attempted a slow, casual twist of the head.

"What can't be?" asked Barnett.

Rosalind merely shook her head. The coffin began to pass slowly by her row, seventh from the front, but Rosalind hardly glanced to see how Malachi was faring, fearful of catching his bright little eyes. Her face was set, its expression thoughtful, miles away from the Church of St Paul the Evangelist in Headingley. At long last the little procession reached the altar, and the coffin was slowly set down just in front of it, to a general but suppressed sigh of relief. Barnett noticed a woman slipping into a pew, and nudged Rosalind.

"There's that Mrs — something-or-other, head of the Leeds Society of Spiritualists."

"Pity someone from the Other Side didn't tell her the right time," said Rosalind sourly. She was a woman of limited mental powers, and that sort of tired joke about spiritualists was just up her street. "Why couldn't she just slip into a place at the back? There's plenty of empty pews."

"You don't get anywhere in the spirit world by being backward in coming forward," said Barnett. He was conscious of his wife twisting her head round and taking a longer, more blatant look. "What *is* it, for Heaven's sake?" he asked.

"Nothing," she said again, a blatant untruth.

"Dear friends," began the vicar, who knew next to none of them, "we are gathered here today —"

"— to see the old charlatan well and truly buried," whispered Barnett.

The vicar steered away from brutal truths of any kind, and tried to keep to truth of a more generous sort. He stopped short of claiming Clarissa Cantelo as a Christian, even of the "essentially" or "in her heart" order, but he dwelt, as well he might, on her spiritual side.

"Clarissa Cantelo had, as many of you here today have cause to know, a sense of a deeper reality than most of us can conceive of. She felt God in nature, as many of us surely do, but she made little distinction between the world that we know so well and that other world that we may believe in, but would not claim to *know*. To Clarissa those who had died had not 'gone before', but were still present, around us, functioning as before, affecting daily life in ways beyond our understanding. It is easy to call such people cranks, charlatans, even to suggest that they profit from other people's misery and loss. No one could say that about Clarissa, however. Hers was a joyful, life-enhancing belief, generously shared."

"That didn't stop her pocketing a fee, though," whispered Rosalind. "She knew the going rate for news from the Other Side."

"Clarissa was from a well-known Leeds manufacturing family, and she had the family's sense of responsibility. In her it took the form of a real and burning desire to *help*, to lead people at times of stress, at times when they felt the urge to go on a spiritual quest, and she did this out of love for her fellow human-beings."

"With a strong streak of showbiz and ego-trip into the bargain," muttered Barnett.

There was a disturbance at the back of the church, then someone scurrying forward and climbing across to a place in the row two behind them.

"Terrible hold-up at the Armley gyratory," said a male voice.

"Cousin Francis," whispered Rosalind at her most piercing. "Really, it would have been better not to come into the church at all if he was going to be this late."

"The powers she believed she had she always used benignly, and the people she helped were her friends for life —"

And so it went on, ecumenical and non-sceptical to the point of meaninglessness. Rosalind whispered that it was going down well – you could just *feel* it was. Rosalind sometimes thought she had powers of perception that made her especially akin to her aunt. When, after some seven minutes, the vicar's tribute drew to a close there were two more hymns, divided by an impromptu prayer and the one the Lord had formulated. The hymns were well-known and middle-of-the-road, Isaac Watts and Charles Wesley. The congregation knew them, and sang up with a will – naturally so, since most of them were in very good spirits. Then the service drew to a close, the coffin was taken up on the shoulders of the undertaker's men (missing Cousin Malachi's by a good five inches) and the little procession made its way back down the aisle, out of the church, turning left to a distant east corner of the churchyard where there were still vacant sites to be filled.

Rosalind kept her eyes glued to the floor as she went out. She did not want to see what she thought she had seen. Barnett looked around him, but couldn't for the life of him spot what had been worrying her. Seeing things, he thought. Like Aunt Clarrie in her bloody séances.

Aunt Emily stood by the clergyman with Aunt Marigold, representatives of Clarissa Cantelo's own generation of the family. Emily had made most of the arrangements for the funeral, helped when she felt like it by Rosalind. Cousin Francis stood close by them, to make up for his lateness at church, but Cousin Malachi took his hundred and ten pounds off and collapsed on to a tomb-like grave some yards away. The vicar scattered earth, and associated cousins and nephews and nieces followed suit. Her eyes on the immediate present, Rosalind scattered and murmured a little prayer. Then, clutching Barnett's hand, she took a deep breath and looked around at the assembled mourners.

Family, close to the grave, and beyond them all the expected people, every one in an aspect of deep gloom that was not always convincing: the lady from the Society of Spiritualists, neighbours and old friends, a young man Rosalind suspected was a reporter from the *Yorkshire Post*, representatives of the Leeds clothing industry, of which the Cantelos had been a mainstay for many years. And there, at the back of the group, not far from Malachi on his gravestone, *him*.

Or not *him*, surely, but someone who looked like him.

Light brown hair, with a strong chin, piercing eyes that Rosalind felt sure would be blue, sober suit, black tie, about the right height – five-ten, perhaps – and with a quiet, interested air. More still, more *considered* than the boy she had once known, but then people would say he had matured. Thirty-eight he would be now.

"It's *not* him," Rosalind said.

"Not *who*?" her husband demanded.

"You never knew him. But I'd have thought you could guess."

Aunt Emily was talking to various relatives about the drinks and refreshments to be served back in Congreve Street. Rosalind broke away from the group, dropped her husband's hand, smiled her thanks at the vicar and walked over to the bystander, who watched her coming without any alteration in his expression.

"I'm afraid I don't know who you are," Rosalind said, "but all friends of Aunt Clarissa will be *very* welcome to drinks and refreshments at the Congreve Street house." The young man looked at her for a moment or two, then, a tiny smile at the corners of his mouth, spoke.

"You know me, Rosalind. I'd be delighted to come for refreshments. It will be good to see the old house again."

Rosalind turned and marched towards the gate of the graveyard and her husband waiting by the car.

"After all, I was closer to her than anyone," shouted the young man.

Chapter Two
Funeral Bakemeats

The big dining room at number 15 Congreve Street had been transformed by moving the long table to the window and spreading the twelve chairs around the wall. The table had been decked with cold bakemeats, pies and gateaux, and an elderly retainer, who some of them recognised as Clarissa's long-time home help, went backwards and forward to the kitchen with tea urns and coffee pots. Some of the older members of the family had memories of uneasy meals here in the days of their father, the guiding force behind Cantelo Shirts. The memories didn't make them any happier, so the atmosphere in the room had been edgy from the start. The representative of the Association of Leeds Clothiers had gulped down a cup of tea and disappeared into the afternoon pleading a prior engagement.

"One doesn't have a prior engagement at a funeral," pronounced Rosalind.

Getting the groups to mingle proved an impossible task. Even getting the relatives to talk to each other was less than easy. They were all hugging to themselves the thing they most wanted to talk about, for fear of saying something that Rosalind or Emily might pounce upon, or of being interrupted by the arrival of the thing itself. Emily, in welcoming the guests, kept shooting glances at the door in case he slipped in in the wake of more expected arrivals. Even Barnett was uneasy, having been enlightened about the identity of the surprise guest in the car from the church, and he kept throwing surreptitious looks through the window. This inattention to his job of dispensing drinks, in which he was already hindered by his wife trying to do the same things as he at the same time, meant that he had an accident with the bottle opener, making a gash across his thumb that ruined his usually airy de-corking technique.

"Why doesn't he *come*?" demanded Rosalind under her breath. "He said he was."

"Maybe he's trying to produce the effect he actually is producing," said her husband bad-temperedly, sucking vigorously at his thumb. "He'll come when he's good and ready."

"I'm looking forward to having a chat with him," said Emily, bad omens in her voice. "I shall be interested to hear his recent history."

Rosalind nodded with a wicked relish: Emily had always had something of the Inquisitor in her nature. Cousin Malachi, however, incurred a put-down when he turned from his conversation with his brother Francis to say:

"Interesting to hear what he's been doing all the time he's been away. Probably been round the world."

Rosalind was nervily putting out little sandwiches and sausage rolls on a plate for Aunt Marigold, but she managed to throw in her penn'orth.

"More likely cooling his heels in a Turkish jail," she said.

"Merlyn was never in trouble with the law," protested Malachi.

"All he needed was time," said Rosalind, whose face had twisted when the name had been spoken for the first time. "And now he seems to think —" she began, and then seemed to feel she had been wrong-footed. "But of course it's not him," she lamely concluded.

What she had been about to say, as everyone around her realised, was "to think that he can come back and take over all this."

What she intended by "all this" was no palace. It was a three-storey detached house from the late 1880s. It had a fine cellar, good-sized ground-floor rooms, and five large bedrooms. It was situated in one of the good, but not best, parts of Headingley, too expensive to be converted into student lodgings. It would fetch a tidy sum on the booming property market, but it did not represent riches.

"Here he is now," said her husband. The moment he said it, all conversation stopped. They all watched as the figure of the man in his thirties proceeded across the street and opened the front gate, walking confidently forward.

"The hide of him – walking straight in!" said Rosalind, as he did just that.

"Merlyn never knocked at his aunt's door in his life," said Malachi. "Why should he now?"

Already two distinct pictures of the young Merlyn were emerging, the differences perhaps not unconnected with the question of whether the speaker had his or her own expectations from the dead Aunt Clarissa. Or perhaps the differences sprang from an ambiguity in the young Merlyn himself, the young sixteen-year-old they remembered. At sixteen, no one's character is set in stone.

Merlyn had followed the murmur of voices and now came into the long, high dining room. He stood in the doorway for a moment, looking around him. He was very English-looking, brown hair and blue eyes, and the edges of his mouth were again turned up in the tiny smile that was attractive as well as quizzical. Aunt Emily swallowed, then advanced towards him as she had to all the guests.

"So glad you could join us," she said, though her face was grim. "Have you come a long way?"

There was a brief laugh, unconcealed.

"Not from a fetid Indian or Pakistani jail, anyway, Aunt Emily." How could he know what they had been saying, they all wondered. "Actually from Brussels."

"How fascinating!" said Emily. "Please have something to eat, and Barnett will get you a drink. Wine, or something stronger?"

Barnett was holding his bandaged hand ready, looking at the man whom he was seeing for the first time.

"Squash would be fine if you have some," said Merlyn, smiling at him. "I need to keep my wits about me, don't I?"

Barnett had turned to the unopened bottle of orange squash, his expression quizzical.

"And why would you need to keep your wits about you?"

Merlyn smiled, this time an ingenuous, young man's smile.

"All these relatives. Everyone's changed after twenty or so years away, as I have myself. But they'll feel insulted if I get their names wrong, won't they? How is Rosalind?"

Rosalind had slipped across the room, and was now talking to her cousin Caroline and her two small children. Barnett sloshed water from a jug into the glass and merely said: "Mostly she keeps well."

Then he turned to Cousin Francis to signify that this conversation was at an end and Merlyn – if it was he – was now at the mercy of the lions.

Merlyn turned to Cousin Malachi, geniality itself.

"Cousin Malachi! Good to see you again. You know when I was a child I accepted that Malachi was the most normal name in the world. Children do, don't they – accept whatever they find around them, I mean. Now I wonder how you got it."

"My father was going through a phase with the Peculiar People," said Malachi, delighted to be singled out. "He was a bit of an oddball, as Clarissa was in her way."

"Yes – she was something else I just accepted."

"So how are you, Merlyn?" asked Malachi genially and apparently unsuspiciously. "What have you been doing? We've just been saying you've probably been around the world. I think the last we heard you were in India. I should think that must be a wonderful place. Full of mystery, Eastern wisdom, that sort of thing."

"I expect you're right," said Merlyn. "I've never been

there." He patted Malachi on the shoulder. "Don't believe everything you hear. It's not only Peculiar People who swallow tall stories."

He turned around, his quick eyes taking in the collection of family and friends. He immediately discarded the odd reporter and the lady from the Leeds Society of Spiritualists and focused on the figures that mattered, the family. He made a surprising choice and went over to shake hands with Caroline, his cousin as well as Rosalind's, with her two children keeping close to her in the unfamiliar surroundings. As an introductory gesture he mussed the hair of the smallest of them.

"Well, it *has* been a long time, Caroline," he said. "And what lovely little girls! They remind me of you at the same age."

"I was a bit older than Angela when you ... went away," said Caroline, who was fair, with a face lacking in firm contours. She said the words with a faint trace of a simper, which reminded Merlyn of figures on chocolate boxes. "I regarded you with awe and longing. I cried for weeks when people said you must be dead."

"People say what they want to believe half the time, don't they?" said Merlyn.

"Oh, I'm sure they wouldn't want ..." mumbled Caroline, fading into silence. She attempted to retrieve the situation. "Did I hear you say you didn't go to India after all?"

"Never been near it. Never been to Asia, come to that, unless you count Istanbul. Was that one of my ambitions twenty years ago? Some kind of backwash of the Beatles, I suppose. Some nonsense of George Harrison's, probably."

"It's disappointing in a way," Caroline said, pouting. "I imagined you in an ashram, in a loincloth, with your feet tucked up under you, thinking holy thoughts for hours on end."

"Sorry! I've hardly had a single holy thought in my life ...

Did you ever marry, Caroline?"

"Yes – I mean —" she gestured at the children. "For three or four years ..."

"I expect that doused your overheated imagination," said Merlyn.

"He still sees the children," said Caroline inconsequentially.

"But we all go through it, don't we," said Merlyn, ignoring her. "Imagining we're in love. Imagining nobody's ever been *quite* as much in love before."

"I don't know that I —"

"Mine was in Verona."

"Verona? That was —"

"Appropriate. Yes, it was. Her name wasn't Juliet, but she did have a balcony. She lived in a modern block of flats on the Piazza Simoni, but each flat had a balcony, so I used to moon around the streets nearby, imagining her letting down a rope of knotted sheets, and me shinning up it and enjoying her in her little bedroom. I suppose it was more Errol Flynn than Shakespeare."

"I don't think I've ever heard of —"

"Errol Flynn? You should watch the old daytime movies. A hundred times more erotic than the sweaty late-night ones. They really knew about titillation in those days. Anyway Cecilia was the love of my life. It overwhelmed me for six months. Every hour of the day, including working hours, I was thinking of Cecilia Carteri. And she was thinking of me. I know she was. I was the love of her life, as she was of mine... Damned horrible thing, life, isn't it? If only those emotions could last ... At least you have these two to remind you ..." He bent down and looked into their faces. "Now, you're Angela I'm told. Lovely name, that ... And what are you called?"

"I'm Jacqueline," said the blonde five-year-old.

"We call her Jackie," said her mother.

"I suppose you would. But Jacqueline is a lovely name too." He straightened up. "Well, I hope we'll meet again soon. I'd really like to make these family get-togethers a regular thing. We could meet up here – don't you think so, Caroline?"

Caroline nodded dumbly. She was not one of those who had expectations from Aunt Clarissa's will. She had thought her a charlatan, or "an old fraud" as she put it to her friends, and she had taken Clarrie's kindness in return as condescension. But she knew perfectly well that many of the others in the room had been banking on a substantial remembrance coming to themselves, and she knew that Merlyn's proprietorial tone, as if he was already in a position to *invite* people to *his* house, would arouse fierce antagonism among the family. She cast a quiet glance at Rosalind, and saw fierce antagonism at its most naked.

Merlyn had wandered, as if at random, over to where Cousin Francis was standing on his own, perhaps having been cast into the wilderness even by his brother for his late and conspicuous arrival at the service. His appearance was shambolic, as if he had dressed with boxing gloves on – his shirt buttoned only half way down, revealing a neat little paunch, his tie failing to conceal the top button. But there was about his manner a latent prissiness which seemed to proclaim that his inability to cope with traffic, the workings of cars, or even buttons, were the outward signs of an inner closeness to some tremendous spiritual truths.

"So glad you managed to be there for the service," said Merlyn, holding out his hand. "The situation on the roads around Leeds seems a hundred times worse than when I left."

"It *is*," said Francis. "Utterly unpredictable. Who would have thought there'd be a jam like that on a Tuesday afternoon? It got me one of Rosalind's fiercest looks, but it wasn't my *fault* —"

"I expect you'll survive. She's not quite the dominatrix she thinks she is. Are you still at St Clarence's, Francis?"

"St Cuthbert's. Yes. Another ten years before retirement. And every day a battle." He sighed. "Boys – what horrible little creatures they are. Every one a Jack Russell. What I would do without my Faith to hold me together I don't know."

Merlyn looked at him quizzically, as if he thought Francis was held together more by bits of string than by Faith. His cousin, however, seldom noticed anyone's reactions.

"I can understand why your Faith is so important to you," said Merlyn, who seemed to be leading everyone on in order to savour their peculiarities. "I once had the idea of entering the Catholic priesthood."

"*Really*? *Did* you? I considered going over myself when they let in ... *women*. I never thought the Anglicans would be so perverse, not to say heretical. But in the end I didn't, I don't really know why."

"Couldn't bear to lose all those C. of E. hymns probably. It would have been a wrench for me. I suppose it was the attraction of the *certainty* of the Roman Catholics that made me want to cross the divide."

"I know! Such a wonderful comfort! And yet that very certainty could be a snare and a delusion, couldn't it?"

Merlyn seemed to feel his feet getting itchy as Cousin Francis showed his usual inability to hold fast to any consistent line of belief. Turning slightly, he hailed in her chair his Aunt Marigold, now over seventy, but not apparently relaxing any part of her grip on life.

"Wonderful to see you again, Auntie. It's been much too long. And how have you been keeping?"

He squatted down beside her chair, and the old lady, eyes gleaming maliciously at the sight of a captive audience, began to itemise her medical history of the last twenty years. She seemed to be enjoying, in a heartless way, his inevitable boredom. Over by the wine and the sausage rolls and the prawn sandwiches Rosalind regarded Merlyn. She had watched his every move around the room and had overheard a large part of his conversations.

"Look at him! It's disgraceful!" Getting no response from her husband, she became specific. "He's worming his way in here!"

"Looks to me as if he's already wormed," said Barnett.

Merlyn certainly was the centre of everyone's attention – indeed the only focus for it. Even the elderly maid looked at him rather than at the better-known family members. When he had listened to Aunt Marigold for twenty minutes – paying her account, to his credit, the sort of attention a medical specialist might have given to an exceptionally interesting case history – he stretched, kissed her, and with a wave of his hand wandered off.

"Well, this has been interesting," he said, coming to rest beside his Aunt Emily. "Clarissa will have been watching us all, and been delighted. In fact, I'm not sure she isn't actually with us at this moment – in spirit, of course."

"I never greatly liked that aspect of Clarissa's life," said Emily, with pursed lips, her sourness gaining the upper hand over her more feeble desire to appear welcoming. "After all, she was in many ways a very worldly woman."

"Not worldly, just interested in life," said a spruce man, not much older than Merlyn himself, in a smart suit and a bow-tie more suitable for a wedding. "By the way, I'm your cousin —"

"Eddie. Of course I remember you," said Merlyn, holding out his hand. Another bull's-eye. Eddie looked gratified. "I think you're right about Aunt Clarissa. All life was interesting for her. Probably that's what made her such a good clairvoyant."

"Do you remember when I got hold of the *Karma Sutra*?" asked Eddie, sliding back effortlessly into his schoolboy persona. "Clarissa shrieked with laughter at all the pictures of the various positions. She thought the couples would need a pair of mechanics to disentangle them."

Merlyn laughed loudly.

"Yes, she'd have loved the job of prising them apart herself, wouldn't she? She never had much personal interest in sex, but plenty in other people's sexual habits ... Poor old Clarissa. And now she's taken up the only position left to her, the graveyard one."

Aunt Emily, whose expression had been darkening with every exchange, turned away and stalked off. Merlyn and Eddie refrained from laughing at her back, but only just.

"Don't mind Mother," said Eddie. "She has vinegar instead of blood. So what are you doing now?"

"Doing?" said Merlyn carelessly. "Oh, you mean work. Paid employment. Well, my paid employment at the moment, and for the last few years, has been in Brussels, so you can guess who shells out my monthly bonanza."

Eddie was impressed.

"The Common Market? Good Lord, you *must* be on to a good thing. The gravy train to end all gravy trains."

"People have an exaggerated idea of how much EU employees rake in," claimed Merlyn. "Not *much* exaggerated, but slightly exaggerated. We do very nicely. It's important work."

There seemed to be a suggestion of a wink in Merlyn's eye, and Cousin Eddie felt empowered to ask:

"So what do you do? Legislate about straight bananas or how to define chocolate?"

"I presume you read the *Sunday Telegraph*," Merlyn said, with a suddenly-assumed lordly air. "Actually I'm one of the First Secretaries in the Department of Economic Standardisation, with special responsibility for Eastern Europe."

"Good Lord! What do you actually do?"

Merlyn's hauteur was shed instantly.

"We're still trying to define the Department's remit."

They laughed together, as in the old days.

"And you'll be going back there now?"

"Oh dear me no. I've got three months' leave on three-quarters of my pay. Jolly nice of them, but they decided that the last three years have been exceptionally gruelling for me, with all the old Communist bloc countries having their applications vetted. And of course I pleaded special circumstances."

Cousin Eddie looked at him.

"Clarissa's death? I shouldn't have thought that the death of an aunt warranted three months' leave."

"You don't know the EU. And of course I emphasized that Clarissa practically brought me up."

Eddie raised his eyebrows.

"You stayed here with her for about eighteen months, so far as I remember."

"But several times earlier too. And she was always ringing up to see that I was all right before, in the end, I came up here to live for good."

"So what are you going to be doing?"

"Establishing my identity, I suppose. I wasn't expecting to have to, but —"

He gestured toward Rosalind and Eddie's mother.

"So, another long-drawn-out claimant saga, then?"

"I don't think so. Most of those were fraudulent, I seem to remember. Perkin Warbeck wasn't one of the Princes in the Tower, and the Tichbourne claimant wasn't who he said he was. Nowadays it can all be done scientifically, so there is no doubt."

"So you'll be staying on here?"

"Yes, I'll be around for a bit," said Merlyn. "Taking an interest and settling up my affairs."

"But what—? " Again Cousin Eddie rethought, then decided

to remain silent.

"Which really means Aunt Clarissa's affairs," resumed Merlyn. "We must all decide about the inscription on the gravestone, mustn't we?" he suggested, looking round at the assembled relatives, who were standing in an uneasy circle. "That shouldn't be too controversial, I don't imagine."

"I thought 'After a long illness'," suggested Malachi. "Vague but dignified."

"You mean not specifying whether the illness was physical or mental?" asked Merlyn.

"Well, yes. They say she went a bit bonkers."

"I couldn't understand why Clarissa specified she wanted to be buried," said Caroline in her plaintive voice. "She was such a *modern* person for her age, and burial is so old-fashioned."

"Oh, that was her wish, was it?" said Merlyn. "There could be all sorts of reasons why she insisted on being buried."

The whole room fell silent at this, but Merlyn showed no sign of embarrassment. He looked at Rosalind, as if expecting her to make the next move. Tight-lipped she obliged.

"I think all this discussion about Aunt Clarissa is absolutely disgusting. I mean, at her funeral! Is there no shame? And what's all this about her being mentally ill? Of course we all know she was flighty, had bees in her bonnet. But she's not the first person who's had a thing about 'the other side' and communicating with the dead. It doesn't prove she was mentally ill by a long chalk. And she was no different when she died. She wasn't senile or anything. Just a bit vague as time went by."

There was a little murmur of support, from Emily and others, but Barnett, who knew his wife's real views about Clarissa, slipped out into the hall.

"Well spoken," said Merlyn. "Since I hadn't seen Clarissa for some time it's good to know that she hadn't essentially changed. Still, I'm not sure you'll stick to that line, Rosalind ... Oh look," he broke off, looking out of the large window. "There's Mr Robinson from number twenty. Doesn't he look old? Those healthy people always age fast after fifty, don't they? ... No, Rosalind. I'm betting you'll be quite anxious to claim Clarissa was mentally ill after you've seen the will."

Again, there was a moment or two of utter silence.

"The will? What do you know about the will?" demanded Rosalind.

"Oh, just what she told me on the phone two or three weeks ago," said Merlyn. "And now I really must be going. Lots, absolutely lots to do. So kind of you to invite me, Cousin Rosalind. Goodbye, for now!"

He slipped out through the door. In the hall Barnett Frere was having a quick and welcome cigarette. Merlyn raised his hand in farewell.

"Thanks so much for inviting me," he said.

"Don't take too much notice of Rosalind," said her husband. "She was so fond of her father. Still is."

Merlyn paused for a moment, as if uncertain what relevance that had. Then he fled through the front door.

The relatives, now the only ones left at the wake, looked at him bleakly as he escaped from the room, and followed him with their eyes as he left by the front door. He waved to them as he passed the bay window, and crossed the road to his car.

"What a lot of nonsense he talked!" said Rosalind, attempting to rally the troops.

"I don't see why you call it nonsense," said Cousin Francis. "He talked a lot of good sense, I thought."

"He just sucked up to you all," insisted Rosalind. "Told you all what you wanted to hear. All that stuff about his beloved Cecilia and her balcony. Just the sort of romantic stuff that Caroline loves."

"How would he know what Caroline loves if he isn't really

Merlyn?" asked Eddie.

"He looked in her face," said Rosalind. "Just like Aunt Clarissa. Many of her best prophecies and character analyses were got by looking at people's faces."

"I don't think that I —" began Caroline, then stopped. Some of the family said her marriage had failed because her husband was aggravated beyond measure by her inability to finish a sentence. Others thought that was the only thing about her that left anything to the imagination.

"And all that stuff about considering going over to the Catholic Church," resumed Rosalind. "Just the sort of thing to go to Francis's heart."

"He didn't seem very up in Catholicism," said Marigold. "They sing all sorts of hymns at Catholic services, including C. of E. ones."

"He was living in Italy," Eddie pointed out. "I bet they don't sing 'Onward Christian Soldiers' or 'Glorious things of thee are spoken' in St Peter's."

"Does anyone *really* think he's spent the twenty years mooning over another teenager in Verona and then working in a plum job with the Common Market bureaucracy in Brussels?"

Rosalind's question pulled them all up, and they sat seriously considering whether they found the visitor's *curriculum vitae* convincing.

"There's an awful lot of 'Jobs for the boys' going on in the Common Market," said Eddie, rather half-heartedly.

"How did he become one of 'the boys'?" asked Rosalind. "A boy from a comprehensive in Leeds, practically an orphan, no smart connections?"

"I think you're missing the point."

The speaker was Barnett, who had come back into the room, bringing with him the delicious smell of nicotine. He was someone who had married into the family, and one who had never known the young Merlyn. That somehow seemed to give him a special authority. All heads turned in his direction. He collected his thoughts before speaking.

"I don't think he was trying to butter you all up."

"He certainly didn't try very hard with me," said Emily. "All that disgusting stuff about the *Karma Sutra*. Typical Clarissa, but *not* the sort of thing to bring up at a funeral."

"Actually it was your son Eddie who brought it up. The man we'll call Merlyn Docherty just played along. But Eddie accepted that it was Merlyn he was talking to. And all of us — even Rosalind when she wasn't thinking — spoke to him and about him as if he was Merlyn. And that's what he wanted. That's what he was aiming for. I bet he's smiling now."

All of them, even those who had liked Merlyn and had no interest in Aunt Clarissa's will, were quiet at the thought of having been fooled. Rosalind was both thoughtful and angry, and her anger was directed as much at herself as at her husband.

*   *   *

On the way back to the Crowne Plaza Hotel where he was staying, Merlyn's car, which was hired, got stuck in a traffic hold-up around the Headingley cricket ground. He sat, relaxed, waiting for things to unsnarl themselves. Looking at the cars around him he saw faces twisted with anger and impatience. His own face was very different: in popular parlance, he was smiling from ear to ear.

When he got back to the hotel he checked his watch and realised Danielle would be back from rehearsal and preparing for a performance at the Monnaie, whose chorus she belonged to. He rang her at the Brussels flat that was almost, but not quite, as much his as hers.

"It was weird," he said, when she asked him how things had gone. "Like being sixteen again, when everyone around you then had suddenly aged by twenty years, and had all sorts of experiences only they knew about."

"But they welcomed you back?"

"Not so you'd notice."

"But why not?"

"They had their reasons, or thought they did."

There was a pause.

"Why are you being so secretive about this?"

"Because I don't know the truth myself. When I know the whole truth, when I've got to the heart of the mystery, then you'll know too."

"It would be good to know what the mystery *is*, even if you couldn't come up with a solution."

"Believe me, you wouldn't understand the mystery unless you knew the Cantelo family ... Love me?"

"Not when you're in this mood. I'd much rather have the old, open Merlyn back."

"You will, you will," he said, more confident-sounding than he felt.

Chapter Three
Legal and General

"I am delighted to see you, Mr Docherty," said Mr Featherstone, as he ushered him into his spruce modern office in the would-be-Queen-Anne building in East Parade. "How did you know we were your aunt's solicitors?"

"I remembered," said Merlyn. Mr Featherstone's stone wall of a face did not reflect the fact that he had been checkmated.

"Of course, of course. You must forgive me if I am still somewhat surprised."

A tiny sliver of distaste managed to get into his tones. Harvill, Masters and Featherstone was clearly a firm not used to sudden reappearances from the dead.

"I'm getting used to the surprise," said Merlyn, sinking into a chair. "Any delight has been well-disguised."

"You can't expect —" began Mr Featherstone, in response to the implied criticism, then reined himself in: no point in antagonising a potentially lucrative client. "But I don't know the circumstances, so I'll say no more. I should tell you that I very often advised Miss Cantelo to change her will. This was not to damage your interests, of course. The fact is, the terms as they stood – stand – were bound to cause legal complications."

"Not 'bound', as it's turned out," said Merlyn quietly.

Mr Featherstone permitted himself a fractional raising of the eyebrows.

"Well, perhaps not – it remains to be seen. Hmmm. Now, do you know the terms of Miss Cantelo's will?"

"Yes, I do. I talked the terms over with her on the telephone ten days before she died."

This time Mr Featherstone's eyebrows shot up, and were hauled down with difficulty. He left several seconds' pause.

"I see," he said, but in a far from confident voice. "Was this a call in which you announced your ... continued existence?"

"No, it wasn't," said Merlyn coolly. "We had been in regular communication since I left Great Britain in 1982. We first discussed the will soon after that."

This news clearly aggravated Mr Featherstone enormously. Out-of-the-ordinary events usually did.

"So when she talked to me as if she did not know your whereabouts or your fate she was ... being less than honest?"

"Yes," said Merlyn, still conspicuously cool. "You should not hold me responsible for that. I don't have to tell you that, if my aunt decided on a course of action, no power on earth was going to argue her out of it."

"No-o-o." The lawyer sighed. "No indeed. That I quite understand. So you were in regular communication with Miss Cantelo ever since you left the country?"

"Yes."

"And you know the terms of her will?"

"I know what she told me. Perhaps it would be sensible if you could run through them with me now."

That Mr Featherstone could not dispute. He riffled through a file of papers on his desk and came up with a browning double-sheet of paper.

"There are a number of small charitable bequests, then some bequests to other members of Miss Cantelo's family —"

"Which ones?"

"Rosalind Frere, Emily Fowldes, Edward Fowldes, Roderick Massey."

"Right. Go on."

"And the remainder – a considerable sum, is left to you – if indeed you are Merlyn Docherty." Merlyn bent his head, a small smile on his face. "Pardon me, but I have to say that. It is many years since you have been in Leeds, many years since I or any members of your family have seen you, so —"

"I'm not sure that you have ever seen me, Mr

Featherstone."

"No. Frankly I'm not sure myself."

"Aunt Clarissa being dead, none of the other members has seen me or heard from me in these twenty-odd years. I should add that, apart from Rosalind and perhaps Aunt Emily, no one seems to have any doubts that I am Merlyn Docherty."

"That is far from conclusive."

"Oh, certainly. But we're not living in the age of the Tichbourne claimant, are we, Mr Featherstone? It should be a simple matter for everyone to be absolutely sure."

Mr Featherstone did a little old-fashioned drop of the head in acknowledgement, then continued, fingering the musty fawn paper of the dead woman's will.

"If you had died, the four recipients already named would have shared fifty per cent of the estate. Nominal amounts of two thousand each would have gone to other family members —"

"Which ones?"

"Caroline Chaunteley, Malachi Cantelo, Francis Cantelo."

"That seems fair and straightforward."

"And the remainder to go to the National Society for the Prevention of Cruelty to Children."

"I see ... I suppose that's a nod towards my neglected state during my childhood."

"I couldn't say ... You realise that if you were to, er —"

"Drop dead on the floor this minute?"

"Well, yes. If that were to happen, and if you were subsequently proved by the scientific methods you have hinted at to be Merlyn Docherty, then the money would go to your legal heir or heirs."

"Yes, of course."

Mr Featherstone paused impressively.

"What at the moment is your marital status? Have you any —"

"Let's not go into all that. The sensible thing, surely, is for me to make a holding will, leaving everything to the charity Aunt Clarissa named – heaven knows I have reason to think children can need help – with no legacies for the moment to family members."

"Ye-e-es."

"No point in providing hostages to fortune, is there? That could of course be changed when or if relations between us all get back to normal."

"Or, of course, if you acquire a wife and children."

"Of course. I have a partner in Brussels. But I suggest that the important thing is for the holding will to be signed and sealed now, *and made known*."

These last words were said with a new seriousness. Mr Featherstone nodded again.

"The making known will be up to you rather than me," he said.

"It will. I shall derive pleasure and profit from making it as widely known as possible. Perhaps, now, we could get down to writing this will, and making it legally binding."

Mr Featherstone clearly was not used to working at this speed, and not happy to find himself doing it, but his reluctance fought a battle with common-sense and prudence, and lost. He murmured "That should present no problems", and drafted a will a few sentences long, sent it for typing, went over it with Merlyn (who had been nonchalantly doing the crossword in the office copy of *The Times*) and then called in two of the partnership's staff to witness the document. When it was signed, sealed, and a copy filed away, with the original for Merlyn, Mr Featherstone unbent sufficiently to seek confirmation of his suspicions.

"I have deliberately asked no questions about this procedure," he began.

"But now you're going to. And quite right too," said Merlyn.

"It just occurred to me to wonder if you had any suspicions, any reason to think that anyone in the family...?"

"I think, Mr Featherstone, that you like to be careful, don't you?" asked Merlyn. The lawyer did his accustomed bob of the head. "I'm being careful with the thing I hold most dear. That is my life."

"I see." It was said dryly, but he seemed satisfied.

"So the first thing now is to get on to the DNA testing business. That's uncharted waters for me."

"It's not something that we in this firm have had much to do with," said Mr Featherstone, struggling to suppress any suggestion of distaste. Too much scientific certainty could put lawyers out of business. "However we do, quite naturally, come a lot into contact with the police, and sometimes have what today might be called a relationship with some of the senior people. Perhaps that DNA test is something you would prefer to be responsible for yourself, rather than let us do it?"

"Yes, I think it is," said Merlyn. "With you in the background to ensure that all the safeguards are in place."

"Yes, that we could see to. Now, there *is* someone, a totally reliable man. I must find his mobile number." He slipped out of the room, and when he returned (Merlyn having finished the crossword, all but a nasty little googlie obviously intended to separate the sheep from the goats) he had made all the arrangements, presumably preferring to give his contact some idea of the oddity of the case out of the principal actor's earshot.

"I spoke to Superintendent Oddie, our contact, and he thought the best person for you to talk to would be Sergeant Peace. They often work together and he has a high opinion of him. He's very bright, apparently, and probably will be an inspector before too long. He's more up in these newish developments. Not that the Superintendent isn't – he has to be – but he says it all will come more naturally from one who is younger."

"Of course."

"He's tentatively made an arrangement for you to talk to Sergeant Peace in the White Horse pub in Temple Street, about five-thirty tomorrow. Is that convenient?"

"Any time is convenient. I'm totally free."

"Ah – you have leave from your employment – whatever it is?"

"The European Union. Yes – three months' leave."

"Ah, I see." Mr Featherstone was sceptical of what he called the Common Market – Merlyn could always tell. "So I can tell the Superintendent that you would be glad to talk to Peace in the White Horse? Oddie felt it better not to involve Police Headquarters in something that is not a criminal matter."

"Quite right. Please tell him I'm grateful."

"Oh, and Sergeant Peace is black."

"Right, then I'm sure we'll manage to meet up."

* * *

The White Horse was totally deserted at five-thirty, so when five minutes later Sergeant Peace arrived meeting up would have presented no problems whatever his colour.

"Ah – Sergeant Peace?"

Peace smiled his "I know I stand out" smile, murmured "Charlie", and let Merlyn Docherty buy him a pint of bitter. Then the pair of them settled happily on to benches in a far corner.

"I knew it would be empty here after work," said the sergeant. "I thought there might be delicate matters at issue."

"I suppose there are," said Merlyn. "Family matters usually are." Charlie smiled agreement. He knew all about family ructions and odd modern permutations. "It's a question of whether I am Merlyn Docherty the long-lost cousin, nephew, whatever, of various members of the Cantelo family. It's a big family, and there are plenty of different viewpoints."

"I see," said Charlie. "Long-lost cousin, you say. How long and how lost?"

"Twenty-two years," said Merlyn, then hesitated before going on: "How lost is more difficult. These people will have heard nothing of me in that time except the rumour of my death. According to family report I went back-packing in India in 1982 – as plenty did at that time – and was not heard of after I told my aunt that I was heading for the Kashmir province, state, whatever it is. Troubled then, as now."

"So you were presumed dead, either in some local dispute, or in a kidnap that went wrong, or whatever? This was the story put out by Clarissa Cantelo, was it?"

Merlyn shot him a glance that showed he was impressed.

"You've been reading up, have you?"

"I usually have a look at the 'Deaths' column in the *Yorkshire Post*. Dispatches are much more useful to us than hatches or matches. Clarissa Cantelo, so far as I recall, was a part-time spiritualist or clairvoyant who died a couple of weeks ago."

"That's right. Yes, it was Aunt Clarissa who put the story around."

"And did you in fact go to India?"

"No. Nothing against India, but I never intended to go there. At the time in question I was in Italy, having my first real love affair, and I stayed there for six years, learning the language and getting a degree in economics."

"I see ... Or I see partially I suppose. Clarissa Cantelo wanted it thought by the family that you were dead. But in fact you and she were in contact?"

"Oh yes, regularly."

"And now you've come back, and the family would like to believe that you're not really Merlyn Docherty, is that right?"

"Some of the family. One in particular."

"Question of a will, is it?"

"Yes. Not riches beyond the dreams of avarice, but a tidy little sum. My view is that Aunt Clarissa intended it for me, never changed her will because she knew I was alive, so I should have it. I've made a temporary will leaving everything to a charity that was also named in her will, by the way."

Charlie's glance at him was shrewd.

"I see. And this is known in the family, I take it?"

"I rang Cousin Malachi and told him last night. It should be all round the family by now."

Charlie stretched his considerable length.

"Before we get on to DNA, humour me a little. Tell me about your Aunt Clarissa. I've never met a professional clairvoyant."

Merlyn smiled, apparently in genuinely affectionate remembrance.

"You should. If they're anything like my aunt they're a fine body of professional persons. They're in the *Yellow Pages*, you know."

"That's no guarantee of respectability."

"Well, Aunt Clarrie was a hoot sometimes, but I don't think that anyone would deny her respectability. Let me tell you about her as she would tell you herself if she could be here. She would say that when she discovered her ... her *gift* she would call it, she first used it for family, then for friends, then, as she began to be well-known, for customers. She would stress the word *for*: she was giving them character analyses, forecasts, warnings and so on *for their benefit* – for example so that they could build on their strengths and circumvent their weaknesses."

"Bully for her. When you say customers, you mean she was paid, I take it?"

"Oh yes. Aunt Clarissa was a typical Northerner: she

thought the customers wouldn't value anything they hadn't paid for. I imagine she charged the going rate – I was never interested enough at the time to go into things like that. She was comfortably off herself, and her earnings were in the nature of icing on the cake."

"What did she actually *do*?" Charlie's expression as he asked this was almost comical, as if he felt himself totally out of his own depth.

"Mostly what the client or customer wanted: crystal balls, palms, Tarot cards, whatever. She was really a sort of Agony Aunt with supernatural appendages. If the client was happy to do without those appendages she would just sit him down, talk with him, offer him a character analysis, a forecast, advice, and that would be that."

Charlie thought.

"So that's your Aunt Clarissa as seen by herself. What about as seen by you?"

"Not so very different ... Remember, I never saw her in action when I was an adult, with adult experience, only when I was an adolescent, living with her on and off. But looking back I'd put the emphasis on the common-sense side. For example, if a new customer rang her up out of the blue she always tried to keep him talking, rather than simply making an appointment. That way she had an idea about him, and some concrete information about his past and what he was looking for before he ever came to the house. Similarly when he did come there would be tea and biscuits as a preliminary, before any of the serious business began. She would say that she learned as much in those apparently casual chats as she did when the more probing sessions began."

"So the 'prediction' would be based on a straight character assessment such as a teacher might make of a pupil?"

"I think that formed the basis. Clarrie would say there was much more, that her occult 'gift' gave her special insight into the future, but then she would, wouldn't she? She saw things in palms, in star conjunctions, in cards – I don't think she ever stooped to tea-leaves. But if she got a reputation – and she did have a very good local one, among people who went in for that sort of thing – I'd say it was based first and foremost on common sense, and an insight into character. Though I might add that she only half realised this herself, and really did imagine she 'saw' things in palms and cards."

Charlie took a hefty swig of his beer, and thought for a while.

"That's a real piece of de-mystification that you've gone in for. But I've got to say that I still think of clairvoyants as frauds and charlatans."

"So are used car salesmen and peddlers of insurance policies. Some of them probably believe their own patter. Aunt Clarissa made no claims for what she was doing, and she was always careful how she put things: 'there could be'; 'you may be approaching'; 'there is a danger of' – that sort of thing. She was as honest as most, no more self-deceived than many."

"You may be right. She was your aunt, so I won't run her down. Almost a stand-in mother – am I right?"

"On and off, after my mother died. That was her sister Thora. She died when I was eight. Life was always better when I was with Clarissa rather than my father. More orderly, everything in place, clean clothes when I needed them and meals at set times. Children appreciate that sort of thing. So you can see auntie wasn't a madcap in everyday life."

"She sounds quite a character. My mum is one too, so I appreciate the sort of interest that gives to a child's life – though it can be an embarrassment too."

"You're telling me!"

"Now – you need a DNA test," said Charlie, becoming businesslike, having filed all Merlyn's information and impressions away in his police brain. "The people to go to are the

Forensic Science Service. Here's their address and telephone number. You can ring and arrange a preliminary meeting in advance, and then leave it all up to them. They won't be cheap. They're about to be privatised."

"What difference will that make?"

"If you go by the railways they'll be slower and more expensive."

"I'll slip in before that happens then."

"Well, the truth is that they've never been cheap. If we use them it has to be a last resort. That's partly because of the number of samples that have to be analysed in important cases, to cover every possibility. Your business should be a lot simpler than that, but it will still cost you. And if you want the job done quickly you could offer them a bit more than the basic charge."

Merlyn thought about that.

"I don't know that I will. One quite enjoys stringing the family along, leaving them in uncertainty."

"That could be dangerous," said Charlie seriously.

"Could it? When all the estate is willed to the NSPCC? I don't think so."

"What if the hostility displayed to you by some members of the family has nothing to do with money?"

"I hadn't thought of that ... But the hostility comes from a reluctance to believe I am me. They – well, Rosalind mainly – are hostile to me as an impostor, not as Merlyn Docherty. Surely that *must* spring from money, from Aunt Clarissa's will."

"I don't know ..." Charlie paused for thought. "You could be in danger as an impostor, you know."

"Not once my DNA sample has been taken. Then it's in all of our interests to await the results. They could kill me and then find that all the money still went to the NSPCC because I am who I claim to be."

"Well, it's your business, not police business at this point. Are there any questions?"

"I don't think so, though some may occur to me later."

"Here's my card if any do."

Merlyn took it and slipped it in his wallet.

"I'm at the Crowne Plaza if you need to get in touch."

"I don't imagine I'll need to." The pair of them got up and made for the door. As they left their glasses at the bar, Charlie said:

"There's one thing you haven't told me."

"There's a lot I haven't told you," said Merlyn. "The details of the Cantelo family for a start. A very odd bunch. I haven't told you because you'd get all the different oddities muddled in your mind."

"I don't think I need to know about them. But I am curious as to why you 'disappeared' in the first place. Was it your idea to put your family behind you, be rid of them, all except your aunt?"

"Oh no, it was my aunt's idea, not mine. She more or less sent me away." Merlyn hesitated a moment, obviously wondering whether to confide in this sympathetic young man, or to keep it hidden, as he had with the solicitor. Then he made a decision.

"You see, Clarissa sent me away because she was afraid that someone would try to murder me."

He raised his hand, went through the door, and walked quickly in the direction of the Crowne Plaza Hotel.

Merlyn drove away from his interview with the Forensic Science Service with an expression of satisfaction, shading off into one of unmixed pleasure, written on his features. He had not only been interviewed about the nature of his problem, he had had blood and saliva samples taken, and the interviewer had made a promise that if necessary they would seek access to number 15 Congreve Street. Then he had been asked the name of his father.

"John Jacob Docherty, known as Jake."

"And where was his last place of residence?"

"The last that I know of was in Sheffield. Twenty-one, Cutlers Avenue."

"When was this?"

"1981."

"And is he still alive, so far as you know?"

Merlyn shrugged.

"For all I know. Or dead for all I know. He just went out of my life, or rather, as I've told you, I went out of his."

"And did – does – your father have a criminal record?"

"I have no idea. I should think it's quite possible."

"And your mother? You've told us she died when you were quite young. When and where did she die?"

"1974, I think it was. In the big hospital in Sheffield – I forget its name."

"That should be useful. Hospitals keep samples for a very long time."

Now, driving back to Leeds, he thought seriously about John Jacob Docherty for the first time for many years. He wondered whether his father had gone to pieces, in the common phrase, when his mother died, or whether even before that he had been unsatisfactory, erratic, inclined to go off the rails. He thought that perhaps mingling with his wife's family could have inclined him to indulge in manic periods, but at that date Sheffield was far enough away from Leeds, and was served by a sufficiently slow and unreliable train service, to ensure that contact with the in-laws was occasional, and at times of his father's choosing. Merlyn certainly never remembered being visited by any of the relatives at home, only visiting them here in Leeds. He did remember that Clarissa was rather fond of his father, and he had registered that it was as a sort of covering-up for the vagaries of her dead sister's husband that she had first started taking in her sister's son, himself.

Merlyn, having thought it through for some time, concluded that the serious break-up had started when his elder sister died of leukemia, two years after her mother's death. She had been the apple of Jake Docherty's eye, and the loss of her had left him ravaged by grief. Merlyn himself came nowhere near Deborah in his affections, and it soon became a matter of course, as soon as one of his father's drinking bouts started, that Merlyn would raid the little cache of money that Clarissa had provided for him and take the train to Leeds, to clean clothes and a warm bed, and in particular to a regular supply of nourishing and rather delicious food.

Was Jake still alive? Leaving aside the DNA investigation, Merlyn neither knew nor cared. It did occur to him that when he came into his Aunt Clarissa's house, its contents and her money, his father might come shambling back into his life. Only to shamble straight back out of it, he thought grimly. Still, it might be as well to be prepared. He wondered who, among the rich array of family members he had already re-met, would know what had happened to poor old Jake. He had always liked his children to call him Jake. Perhaps he didn't like being reminded that he wasn't much of a father.

As he showered and changed in his hotel room he went through the family members in his mind. All in all he thought it likely that the one who would know most about all of them would be Rosalind. But she would be the last person to give out information to him, since she believed – or affected to – that he was an impostor. Finally he decided on Cousin Malachi: he was, or seemed, well-disposed towards him, he was the oldest of his cousins, and he had sometimes been his father's drinking companion on his occasional visits to Leeds. Malachi would, for all he knew, have kept in touch with Jake.

It was by now early evening. Dinner in a hotel restaurant did not appeal. He rang Directory Enquiries, got Malachi's number, and rang it.

"Leeds 2658 421," the high, precise, rather epicene voice answered.

"Malachi, it's Merlyn Docherty here."

"Oh – er –Merlyn." After a hesitation there was a chuckle. "Rosalind has issued strict directives that we are not to call you Merlyn Docherty."

"Oh really?" said Merlyn. "Do people in the family take notice of Rosalind's directives?"

"Hardly any notice at all. In my case none. You look like Merlyn. You walk like him, which tells even more in your favour in my eyes."

"I think you're probably right. I once saw Prunella Scales on television trying to do the Queen. Everything was right except the walk, which was a hundred miles off. But anyway, I've just set in motion a full DNA test, so when that's completed you will know."

"Oh, don't blind me with science, dear boy. I've heard of these things, and I know that long-ago murderers keep being arrested because of them, but I really have very little idea what they are. I'll stick with your walk."

Merlyn laughed.

"In that case why don't we walk to a pub and have a drink together? Or what about a restaurant?"

A little silence for thought ensued.

"Ah well, normally I'd say let's go to a pub. But funds have been very low recently, and meals rather basic. I've never been much of a cook, and I get rather tired of bangers and hamburgers and fish fingers and that kind of thing. And oven chips are quite horrible, aren't they?"

"I don't think they have oven chips in Belgium," said Merlyn. "Is there a recommendable restaurant near you?"

"There's the *Belle Provence*, but it's rather pricey."

"That sounds just the place. What about your brother Francis?"

"What about him?"

"Would he like to come too, do you think?"

"I have no idea. I shouldn't think he's been in a real restaurant since he took Mother to the Mitre in Oxford and they had poached eggs on toast. Francis can be an awful bore. He'll probably want to talk about proposed liturgical changes in the Anglican Communion service."

"He'll talk about what I want him to talk about," said Merlyn grimly.

"Oh, masterful!"

"Being one of the European Union paymasters makes me feel masterful, when it's necessary. What's his telephone number?"

Francis sounded surprised to be invited, but without Malachi's enthusiasm he agreed to meet his cousin and brother at the *Belle Provence*.

"You'll have to forgive me if I do things wrong," he said, rather touchingly. "I'm only really used to school dinners."

Malachi lived in his old home, a small stone cottage still blackened by industrial smoke, on the borders of Kirkstall and Horsforth, in a very narrow side street with ten or twelve similar dingy houses. Malachi, clearly, had not prospered in Merlyn's absence. When he knocked on the door Malachi sidled out, obviously not wanting the mess in his front room to be visible to his visitor. He clearly didn't have the courage of his Bohemian convictions, Merlyn thought. They got into the car and Malachi directed him back to the main road, talking in his nonchalant way the while. Francis was already at the restaurant, put in an obscure corner very near the kitchen, but Merlyn managed to get them all seated at a table by the window, well away from any of the other diners. The restaurant proved to be French in its menu but Spanish or Portuguese in its waiting staff. Malachi ordered lavishly and enthusiastically, but Merlyn had to order for Francis, choosing soup and fish, afraid that over-bloody meat would lead to a disquisition on vegetarianism and the spiritual dangers of complacency or pride on the part of its practitioners.

"This is a treat, this," said Malachi, looking around him appreciatively. "Times are hard, dear boy. Sometimes I don't know where the price of my next pint is to come from."

"I should have thought that with a stable economy, low inflation, low interest rates and so on, things would be booming at the bookmaker's," Merlyn said.

"There speaks the EU mind," said Malachi bitterly. "I must admit business isn't too bad at the bookie's. But the money doesn't seep down to the mere hirelings ... And I've had one or two bad investments in the communications market."

"You and thousands like you," said Merlyn. "But I am sorry times are hard for you. And of course you and Aunt Clarissa weren't the best of friends, were you?"

"Oh, I wouldn't say ... No, we weren't. I never could stand that sort of fakery. Clarissa was no better than a quack doctor, and anyone who paid her for her so-called predictions was getting nothing better than a quack's coloured water."

"You always were anti-religious, I remember," said Merlyn.

"I suppose this is part of the same thing."

"Probably, dear boy. You'd have been anti-religious if your father had been a Peculiar Person."

"He was, but not in the religious sense," Merlyn replied with feeling.

"And I had the same father," said Francis. "No one could call me anti-religious."

"You should be fair to Clarissa," Merlyn insisted. "She always made it clear to her clients that she wasn't making predictions, merely estimating probabilities based on the positions of the planets —"

"And the fall of the Tarot cards or the lines on the palm. You're not a boy any longer, Merlyn. I don't have to mince my words. Your Aunt Clarissa was a charlatan, and you don't have to shut your eyes to that out of gratitude. She was very good to you, that we all know, but you're much too old to pretend there could be anything in that sort of nonsense."

"Well, maybe," admitted Merlyn. Food seemed to be stimulating Malachi to his remembered liveliness. He was tucking into his paté, waving his knife, and taking copious draughts from his glass of Burgundy.

Francis, on the other hand, though apparently enjoying his soup, was losing much of it down his tie.

"You mentioned my father —" began Merlyn.

"Just in passing, dear boy," said Malachi. "Just to show you that you had nothing to complain of, compared to mine. What's a mild addiction to alcohol evidenced by the occasional binge, compared to my father's madnesses: a slavish addiction to the Authorised Version as the word of God and a belief in faith healing comparable to the beliefs of Clarissa at their barmiest? Your father and I used to go on the occasional pub crawl —"

"I remember."

" — and you can say what you like about him, but he

wasn't barmy."

Merlyn nodded.

"Oh no. Not barmy. In fact, quite on the ball when he was sober. I'd just quarrel with the word 'binge' to describe his drinking. At what point does a binge become a bender? Three weeks? Four weeks? Five? He had drinking sprees as long as a teacher's summer holiday from when I was eight onwards. In the end it was easier to stay with Aunt Clarissa and save on the train fares back and forth. We said it was so I could keep going to just one school, but really Clarissa was afraid I would come to serious harm."

"Ah – well, I never knew that, old chap."

"He came up occasionally on token visits, but really he wasn't interested."

"I suppose it was on those visits that he and I —"

" — went on your sprees. Yes, it was. Have you had much to do with him since I ... left?"

"Why would I, dear boy? He would hardly come back to visit Clarissa, would he? To her he was her sister's widower and your father, and I think she quite liked him too, but beyond that? Nothing. As for the rest of us, he didn't give a fig for any of us. No, my drinking days with him ended when you went to India. He never came here after that, that I knew of."

"I went to Italy."

"Wherever. India sounds much more adventurous."

"Have you ever heard that he's died?"

Francis perked up at the fascinating topic of death.

"Died? He wouldn't be more than sixty-five now, would he? No age. Anyway, you'd be the one to know that, surely?"

"No, I wouldn't. Everyone thought I was dead, remember. If Clarissa hadn't heard of it, there was nobody else who could tell me."

Malachi digested this, along with a piece of red beef which

he chewed appreciatively. Francis, even, was attacking his sea bass with something like relish, and getting most of it into his mouth.

"Wonderful chicken!" he said appreciatively. Malachi smirked at Merlyn.

"The French really know about food," he said.

Merlyn refused to be sidetracked on to French cooking.

"Have you ever heard anything about him since I left? Has he got into any scrapes, for example? Got arrested, maybe?"

Malachi looked shifty.

"Ah, well, I wasn't going to mention it. No point in upsetting you."

"You wouldn't. Tell me."

"Well, a while ago – maybe ten years, at a guess – there was a report in the *Yorkshire Post* about a really horrendous piece of driving which resulted in a second car turning over on the hard shoulder and someone being quite severely injured."

"And the driver turned out to be Jake?"

"Yes. I can't remember who spread this around. It must have been one of the *Yorkshire Post* readers – Rosalind, maybe, or Emily."

"When you think about it, the Cantelos are a pretty *Yorkshire Post* sort of family."

"I suppose so. So it could be almost anyone. Anyway the tale was that the driver had been found, it was your father, he had been drunk at the time, and eventually he was tried and sentenced – I think to a short jail sentence."

"Good."

"I say, that's a bit hard, dear boy, isn't it?" said Francis.

"Not really. It means there might be something in police records that would help the DNA people."

"I see," said Francis, who clearly didn't. "Why are we talking about your father, old chap? You can't have expectations from him, can you?"

"None whatsoever. But he's one way of proving who I am."

Malachi and Francis thought about this, then went on forking in the last of their main courses. Later in the meal, after Cousin Malachi had drooled his way through the dessert menu and chosen the most monstrous and calorific of the confections and was eating it avidly as if it would make him grow to the height of the other men who had carried Clarissa Cantelo's coffin, Merlyn asked him:

"So what are the rest of the family up to now?"

Malachi did not pause in his stuffing himself, but he did look up.

"I presume you don't mean what do they do for a living?"

"No. I mean how are they reacting to my reappearance?"

"In their own ways," said Malachi, bored with the interruption to his eating. "Most of them are doing nothing at all."

"That's sensible."

"You're right. It is. 'Why should we bother?' – that's the view we take. We had no expectations of Clarissa, and it's nothing to us if everything goes to you rather than to Rosalind. We'd prefer it, in a way. Rosalind is nobody's favourite person – not even her husband's, if the truth be known. And of course we all know that Clarissa loved you, but didn't care greatly for Rosalind."

Francis, who had refused a sweet on the grounds that he was not used to eating full meals, said meditatively:

"You know, one does try to be charitable, and it's not always easy, but when someone is universally unpopular, one does feel there must be some reason. I mean, when I was late for the funeral, there was no need —"

Merlyn interrupted hastily.

"You know, it's not occurred to me before, but why was Rosalind one of the favoured three heirs in the event of my death? Was it because her father was Clarissa's eldest brother? And if so, why didn't he inherit the house in the first place?"

"Because he was on the way to becoming a financial big fish even in the Seventies, when Grandfather Cantelo made his will," said Malachi. "Grandfather thought there was no point in leaving him something he didn't need and would never use. He despised Leeds, and always said he was aiming to make London his power base, which is what happened. But he died at fifty-three, all burnt out, and his wealth was all personal, and most of it went to his second – wife, was it, Francis?"

"I can't remember. His London woman. She got most of it, and used it to acquire a replacement. I think it meant that Clarissa felt some kind of obligation to his eldest child – all honour to her."

"That sounds like her," said Merlyn "For all you call her a charlatan there was always a strong strain of duty, doing what was right, about Clarissa. Benefiting the weaker ones, the ones who'd had a raw deal, would appeal to her ... So Rosalind is, or was, one of the next heirs. That leaves the interesting question: what is Rosalind doing at the moment? How is she reacting to my turning up like a bad penny?"

Malachi began digging around in the lower recesses of the glass for any remains of cream, meringue or sorbet, and not looking at Merlyn.

"Well, you saw her at the funeral," he said.

"Spitting fire and rage and denying that I'm Merlyn Docherty."

"Yes."

"And she's still doing that?"

"Well yes, to anyone who will listen. Now and then she does say that this test thing will settle matters, but she doesn't say that often, or with any conviction."

"She knows the test will find in my favour. Otherwise why would I call in the DNA people at all?"

"There is that, I suppose. I hadn't thought of that ..."

Francis put his oar in, obviously feeling strongly about

Rosalind.

"She's not a very well-balanced person, you know, Merlyn. She keeps going on about you, and things that you've done, and it's just spite and not relevant. If you're Merlyn Docherty you're the heir, no matter what you've done."

"Of course I am. What does she know about me anyway, apart from the things I told people at the funeral? Nothing."

"Ah ... Well, the things she is talking about are things that happened before you went away."

"*Before*?" Merlyn gulped down some coffee, then scratched his head. "I can't remember doing anything very dreadful in my youth."

"Oh – this is her talking, rather than me, remember – she goes on about how you sucked up to Aunt Clarissa to get made the heir, says you got money out of her, thieved it if she didn't cough up, and then took off when you got that girl pregnant."

"Got which girl pregnant?"

"Oh – what was the name? – Jenny something-or-other."

"I did not get Jenny Watson pregnant, and I can be quite confident on that point because we never slept together. In any case I felt tender towards unwanted children. Jenny was pregnant when I left Leeds, but we hadn't even been seeing each other for several months, and so far as I know the father was someone called Lee Hunter."

"I think Rosalind's just picking up on all sorts of rumours that went around in the family at the time," mumbled Malachi. "There were a lot of rumours."

"I bet there were. Most of them didn't get as far as me. The one about stealing money is new to me. My friends were all at school, not family members apart from Eddie, and so I didn't get to hear much of what was said. Clarissa heard the rumours though, and now and again we laughed about them. Rosalind must be hard-pressed for material if she's relying on that old stuff."

Malachi looked cunning.

"Ah, but we don't know anything about your later life, do we? You said as much yourself. We only know what you've chosen to tell us yourself."

"Point made," said Merlyn. "But when I'm confirmed as the heir all that will be totally irrelevant. Whether my life is something I should apologise for, boast about, keep schtum about or whatever – it has no bearing whatever on the fact that most of what Clarissa owned will then be mine. End of story."

But after he had said goodbye to Francis outside the *Belle Provence* and dropped Malachi off at the front door of his pokey house (where he stood in the doorway waving primly his thanks for the evening and not opening his door until Merlyn was well out of sight of the bomb-making equipment – or whatever it was he was bothered about – in his front room), Merlyn drove back to Leeds, past Kirkstall Abbey, past Yorkshire Television, and then to his hotel, thinking of what Malachi had told him, and what he had said to Malachi. He regretted asking which girl got pregnant. It was no more than an ambiguity in the English, but Malachi was just the sort of person to soak up delightedly a wrong impression. Girls, for Merlyn, really started in Verona.

He wondered whether he was being unfair on his father, was still nurturing exaggerated adolescent grievances, and whether he'd been the victim of nothing worse than a perfectly routine case of parental neglect. But when he reviewed his actions since he came back to Leeds, he felt on the whole that he had acted rationally and carefully, and done no more than he ought to have done, in accordance with Clarissa's warnings all those years ago, and the occasional repetition of them during their regular phone calls. She was convinced that there was danger, emanating from someone in or around the family. And though clairvoyancy might not normally impress him as a reason for taking care, the fact that his Aunt Clarissa's normally had some rational basis surely justified some degree of caution.

Chapter Five
Nocturne

Merlyn was used to hotel rooms: overnight and short-stay hotel rooms, long-term hotel rooms when negotiations were tricky or impossibly detailed. Being used to them made them feel better; in fact a characterless room in Plovdiv or Brasow could be a comfort in its international ordinariness. You could convince yourself you were in Le Touquet or Manchester.

That sort of fantasy was not working in Leeds, the reason probably being that he was not on international business but on personal business. He could go to the bar for a drink, or to one of the nearby restaurants or wine bars for a meal, but his situation went with him, his personal worries and fears remained there, sitting on his shoulder, prodding him now and then to remind him: if Aunt Clarissa was right, someone just might be trying to murder you.

That even made his phone calls to Danielle difficult.

"How are things going?" she would ask (in French).

"Not too bad. I'm still pretty much in the dark," he would reply.

He had never been able to tell his girlfriend just what it was that he was worried about, what he was trying to sort out. He had had no difficulty conveying to her the idea that this was not simply the death of an old aunt: she understood that Clarissa had been a surrogate mother to him for his last years in England, that he had expectations from her, even that the family as a whole would be less than enchanted by his return.

But he had never got beyond that, never been able to convey to her the real reason for his uneasiness, the real difficulties of his mission to his one-time home. He realised now that those years on his own from the age of sixteen (albeit a matured and independent sixteen) had made him secretive, unable to confide or to share. All his girlfriends had felt it. None of them had lasted. He did not keep Danielle at arm's length because he wanted to. He did it because he couldn't help it.

The evening, even though dusk was approaching, seemed to stretch endlessly ahead of him. The early evening soaps were over and the rest of the evening was crap on all five channels. The porn channel and the rest of the extra-terrestrials presented crap of a different kind. He could have a drink that he didn't want from the minibar, or call room service for a sandwich or a meal he didn't want either. He decided that if he was going to be forced to look in on himself and his past, he was going to do it while walking the streets. But when he got outside and into the centre of town he found there were too many people around, even at that hour, for brooding, and certainly too many for an analytical thinking-through. He took a bus up to the university, then made his way along Headingley Lane and down towards the house where he had spent his adolescence. As he walked he thought of that time, twenty-two years ago, when he had taken his leave of Headingley and Leeds.

He found he could no longer remember precisely what Clarissa had said. He had known for some time that she was disturbed, worried about something. Then at last, when he had come home after his last GCE exam, she had spoken. She had not used the word "vibrations", because she knew it amused him. What had she said?

"I'm getting some very bad signals."

It was something like that. He had not laughed, and had been quite serious as she explained that the signals had suggested violent death: death in the past and death in the future – perhaps his own. He wondered now why he didn't scoff at the suggestions, whether it wouldn't have been much better if he had. But he thought that being virtually adopted by one who was intimate with the spirit world, at least in her own estimation, meant that he had grown to accept the unlikely or the outrageous as part of his life too. So he had not reacted with hostility to the suggestion that he should disappear for a time.

"Where do you think you'd like to go?" Clarissa had asked.

"France, maybe?" Merlyn had said, knowing the language. Clarissa had frowned.

"Too close. Too many English tourists."

"Maybe Italy?"

Clarissa, probably feeling she could not insist on some non-touristy place like Finland or Albania, had had to agree. She had arranged for him to live with an English art historian and his family in Mantua for six months. Merlyn would have preferred to be with an Italian family, but he stuck it for six months and then branched out on his own. Merlyn aged sixteen had suggested Italy with no feeling for its art, its music, its fine buildings. But his casual expression of what was hardly even a preference had led to twelve wonderful years in a country whose problems of corruption, inefficiency, fissiparousness and worship of phoney messiahs was by now known to him better than to most, but made no difference. Those times when his loves had lasted more than a few weeks meant he had been embraced into that warmest and most idiosyncratic of bodies, the Italian family, and he could sample for the first time its joys, its embarrassments, its high-temperature emotional life. He loved it. He loved above all being part of it.

He had left Headingley Lane now, and was nearing Congreve Street and Aunt Clarissa's house. He slowed down. Here be ghosts, he thought: himself going to school, himself and the (mostly suspicious) Cantelo family, making rare visits to Clarissa's to see what was going on, himself and the neighbours... He had sometimes felt like an outsider, but – to

Clarissa's credit – he had never felt unwanted.

"I think you should disappear," said Clarissa to him on the phone, after he had been in Italy about three months.

"I thought I already had," he replied.

"A bit more. You wouldn't need to be definitely dead, but you could be reported missing and never heard of again till I die."

Merlyn thought.

"There's a lot of kidnapping here, but it's either politicians or rich people, not people like me."

"I've said you've gone to India anyway. A much better place for you to disappear in. And the only people who go there are young ones or people generally considered weirdos. I think you could vanish in Kashmir and no one would think it odd."

And so, apparently, it had happened. She had told him later that the ruse had been entirely successful – that was when she agreed to pay the fees for a crammer in Pescara who would make sure he was able to get into an Italian university and profit by the experience. Clarissa was not very pleased when he chose to go to university in Verona, but she approved of his doing an ordinary job first to accumulate money, and she encouraged him to change his appearance, in case among the tens of thousands trouping to see the supposed balcony of Juliet or *Aida* in the Arena there might be someone from Leeds who would recognise him. He had dyed his hair blonde, coming to resemble an Australian surfie, and he'd become very popular with Veronese girls.

It would have seemed odd, had he come to think about it: to have a new existence under his old name. Presumably if he had ever landed a high-profile job – actor, opera-singer, politi-cian – he would have changed his name. As it was, being a civil servant in the vast Common Market apparatus in Brussels was as anonymous as it was possible to get, and even there he saw to it that in published lists he always appeared as M. Docherty. The Merlyn had been a freak of the imagination perpetrated, he presumed, by his father. It did what Clarissa didn't want to happen: it marked him off.

So he believed Clarissa's rather melodramatic scenario, that someone was trying, or might try, to murder him?

Not all the time. Days and weeks went by without his even thinking of it, and he certainly did not live in fear. But yes: respect for his aunt's judgment as well as his liking for her did make him take seriously the precautions she advised.

He turned into Congreve Street and took his first leisurely look at number 15 since he returned. How it all came back! Particularly his departure from the house, in Aunt Clarissa's battered old Hillman Minx, in the middle of the night. She had deliberately booked him on to an early morning flight to Rome from Manchester Airport, so they could leave when the neighbours were asleep.

"That's better," she said as they got beyond the Leeds suburbs and got on to the M62. "No more nasty signals for you. You can breathe freely now."

"What about you, though, aunt?"

"Oh, I never felt they were directed at *me*." The old car wheezed its slow, erratic way along the motorway. "Are you excited?"

"Oh yes!" said the young Merlyn, truthfully. "But I keep thinking of silly things, like what I've forgotten to pack. It's not as though you can't send anything important to me."

"No-o-o. Though I'll probably do it from Bradford or Halifax."

This was the first time Merlyn registered her obsession with postman-spies. It remained with her, and they had very little written communication.

"I hope I'll be able to get English books in Italy," he said.

"Of course you will," said Clarissa, who had never been

there. "And if there are any old favourites you can't find, I'll get them to you somehow."

"All my old favourites are things I've grown out of," said Merlyn. "I don't suppose they will have the same variety of books in the Italian bookshops."

"I don't suppose so. But you'll soon be reading Italian."

"Maybe ... What I'll miss is not being able to come back here on a visit."

"Yes, I suppose you will. But if the situation changes, then of course I'll tell you. You can suddenly reappear like a pantomime prince."

But she never had, and he never had.

He walked from the corner and stood on the pavement opposite number 15 looking at the house. It held for him many happy memories – not deliriously or ecstatically happy, but the happiness that sprang from solid, worthwhile contentment, nourished by Clarissa and welcomed gratefully by him. She had always been interesting, and had always fed his interest in any other subject, so that he regarded her as one of his educators, and more important than any single teacher he'd had at school.

He tried to sum up his feelings about the place in his mind: he had been ripe for flight, for new worlds and new adventures when he left, but it was in this house that he had been matured to a stage when he could take responsibility for himself and benefit from the exciting changes.

"Well, it's young Merlyn, isn't it? Merlyn Docherty?"

Merlin turned round. It was Mr Robinson from number twenty, followed as usual by his dog.

"Mr Robinson! Nice to see you again. And what's this fellow called?"

"This one's Duke. Small but perky. You probably remember Sam."

"I do. It must be ten o'clock. You always walked Sam at ten."

"That's right. Has the added advantage now that I miss the ten o'clock news. By 'eck, you look well, Merlyn. I'd heard you were back, but I hadn't caught a glimpse of you."

"I've caught one of you. I was at the funeral, then at the wake afterwards."

"So I heard. *That* would have caused flutterings in the Cantelo dovecote!"

"It did rather. Though the ones who knew they wouldn't benefit from Aunt Clarissa's death took it in their stride."

"They would, I suppose. It usually comes down to money, doesn't it? It's a pity really. This was a pleasant house in your auntie's time – when she was in her prime. With you, and little Rosalind, and some of the other younger ones around. It was a lot pleasanter than when it was your grandfather's, God rest his soul, though he doesn't deserve rest. She wasn't money-mad, wasn't Clarissa. Mind you, we all thought she was a bit mad in other ways – spirit-mad, you might say. But she was well-intentioned, and she always lived up to her responsibilities – *you'd* know that, lad, better than most."

"I do. I loved her. I hope she realised that. It wasn't always easy to get it across."

"But why did you cut yourself off from her? We thought you were dead."

Mr Robinson looked at him, wide-eyed as he explained.

"Well, I've never heard anything like it. Mind you, when I think about it, things fall into place."

"Things? What things? Things she said?"

"That's it, lad. One night we were talking here in the street, just like you and me now. It was after one of those terrorist outrages, and she shivered and said: 'Sometimes I feel terrified at the violence in my own family.' I was a bit surprised, though the family as a whole wasn't *liked* around here, and I asked what they'd done, and she said 'Done, and might do. I can't talk about it.'"

"I see. Anything else?"

"Well, similar things. Mention of 'hatred', 'jealousy', 'grudges', all in the family context."

"Any particular family member?"

"Oh no, it was all general talk. You knew your aunt. It was as if she sensed there was evil somewhere around, but didn't know the source."

But Merlyn, after he had said goodnight and walked on towards the cricket ground, wondered if Mr Robinson was right. He thought that if his aunt had sensed evil she would probably have had a very good idea of what the source of it was. But like any good medium she would have couched her ideas in generalities, not made accusations against a specific figure. It was a sort of hedging of her psychical bets.

The next day he rang Danielle, always seeing her, as they talked, against the background of the Grand Place, where they had first met.

"Things are marching," he said, after loving preliminaries.

"Really? Are you finding out who you are?"

"Well, maybe. Though I've always thought I've known who I am."

"You've certainly given that impression. Now I'm not so sure."

"I'm on my way to getting DNA confirmation as to who I am, which is rather different. But that will mean general, if reluctant, acceptance of me as my aunt's legitimate heir."

"I suppose I should congratulate you."

"You better had! We could be looking at the cost of our first flat together."

"If I agree to moving in with you."

"You will. Anyway, who I am isn't really the point at the moment. I'm learning about my family, some of whom I can't remember ever having met. It provides a sort of context for me."

"Belgians always know their families. Perhaps all too well."

"Italians too. But I think the Cantelos are unusual even by English standards. Most people seem to have liked my mother, but beyond that suspicions and antagonisms seem to reign."

"Why are you so pleased about getting to know a family like that? I certainly hope you don't find you share the family traits."

"Oh no, I'm sure I don't. Getting to know them doesn't help me to understand who I am. But I'm hoping it will help me to understand what happened to me."

"What happened to you when?"

"When I was suddenly bundled out of England."

"Didn't English families once ship their problem children off to the Colonies? I suppose bundling them off to Europe is the modern equivalent."

"That sounds plausible enough. But get it into your head, darling: I was not a problem child. I've yet to discover what the problem was, and in what way I was part of it."

"*Bonne chance!*"

Chapter Six
Fairest Rosalind

Merlyn saw Rosalind as he drove along the Headrow. He had gone wrong as he drove along West Street, and it had proved impossible to get back into the right lane. So now he was going to have to snake through the non-pedestrianised streets of Leeds to arrive eventually at his hotel car park. He was turning up between the Town Hall and the library when he saw Rosalind Frere emerging from the Headrow entrance to the library and start towards Briggate. Merlyn immediately rethought his morning. By a miracle he found a vacant place in the Temple Street car park, paid a two-hour fee, then started rapidly but carefully towards Briggate and the Headrow. Standing casually by the corner of Allders store he looked towards the pedestrianised section of Briggate and saw, starting down it, Rosalind's hat.

Rosalind's hat was not large or ostentatious: it was in fact a head-hugging dark green number, with tactful decoration. But he had noticed it on the brief sight he had of her at the library, and he noticed it now. As he proceeded after her, still casually, he noticed that she was almost the only woman he could see who was wearing a hat, and all of the others were pensioners, most of whom looked as if they were on a visit to Leeds centre as a special treat to themselves or from the institution they now lived in. Most fortyish women no longer wore hats except (Merlyn was guessing here) to weddings, christenings and funerals. Rosalind, apparently, was the last of the hat-wearers. She had been wearing a black number with a veil at Clarissa Cantelo's funeral, probably bought joyfully when the occasion offered her the excuse.

He watched her go into Borders and come out with what looked like a paperback in a plastic bag. He saw her look intently at the windows of Harvey Nichols, then decide against going in. Then he saw her march determinedly into House of Fraser, as if this was currently Her Shop. His first instinct was not to go after her but to wait for her to come out. Then he remembered that the shop, when it had been part of another chain in his earlier days in Leeds, had had a back door to it. He went cautiously in, lingered about half-way along the ground floor, and established that the back door was still operative. He pored over a display of women's tights and, fifteen minutes and a lot of suspicious looks later, he saw Rosalind sailing down the escalator and making for the back door. He followed her out towards the market, then past the Corn Exchange, and then down towards the Calls. She ended up by Leeds Parish Church, sitting on a public seat, her bags around her, her eyes fixed on the back of a Bingo Hall. She was, Merlyn concluded, deep in thought.

He casually strolled up to her.

"Hello, Rosalind."

She looked up sharply, then glared.

"What are you doing here?"

"On my way to the Armouries to be fitted for a back plate."

She didn't deign to reply. He sat down beside her. This made her give voice.

"I'm not aware that I asked you to sit with me – *or* gave you permission to use my Christian name."

"Oh, I think you did, at least by implication. It would have been back around 1980, when I was just a snotty-nosed teenager, and you were the female equivalent. We were really quite close at one time."

"I've no recollection of that. And it remains to be seen whether —"

"I am who I claim to be. I think your impatience should be satisfied in a few weeks' time, Mrs Frere. You've probably heard that I've put matters in the hands of the Forensic Science Service."

"Oh, I've heard *that*." Her glare was unremitting. She seemed to be refraining only with difficulty from uttering the Thurber line about "Mere proof won't convince me."

"Meanwhile here you are shopping in town, and here is a man who is claiming to be your long-lost cousin, and the world is our oyster. It would simply beggar belief if we didn't have something to discuss. In fact we both know we do. What about a cup of coffee?"

Rosalind looked at him for a moment, as if tempted, then shook her head. Clearly it was a dismissal, but he refused to be dismissed.

"Are you waiting for someone, or just taking in the view?" he asked pleasantly.

"I'm waiting for Barnett."

"Going somewhere nice?"

"We're going to inspect a school."

"A school? Then you have children. I didn't know. I expect Aunt Clarissa told me, but I've forgotten. How many?"

"One son."

"I see. Of school age, then?"

She nodded.

"Yes. He's about to go to boarding school."

"Oh, I see. About twelve or thirteen then?"

"Eight. It's a prep school." Merlyn deliberately kept his eyebrows lowered, but continued to look at her, and she seemed to feel the need to supply him with an explanation. "Robin's sport mad, and it's a very good school for sport. And he's been neglecting other things for running and cricket, so they'll give him remedial classes to get him up to scratch for public school."

"Public school! I say, that's quite a leg-up for one of the Cantelos. We sometimes went to private schools – you did –

but Eton or Harrow is something else!"

"He'll be going to Burnside. Barnett's old school."

Merlyn suppressed the query whether Burnside was good for sport. Rosalind might think he was implying it was probably good for nothing else.

"How will you fill your time when he's gone, Ros — Mrs Frere?"

"The fact that I don't call you Merlyn doesn't make me any the less Rosalind," snapped his cousin.

"I'm sorry," murmured Merlyn. "I thought I needed permission."

"And I shall have no difficulty filling up my time. I do a great deal of charity work as it is. And I expect to have a lot to do going through Aunt Clarissa's possessions and disposing of them. If the house hadn't been sealed off ..."

"It seemed necessary to Mr Featherstone, my solicitor," said Merlyn, "and I must say I agreed. We couldn't have all sorts of people who thought they would inherit scrabbling around in there. Nothing should be done until the will is granted probate. If I were found to be not Merlyn Docherty you would probably have problems with the possessions, since half of the estate has to be shared among three of you."

"Things can be valued if necessary," said Rosalind, who had clearly talked the matter over with her husband. "I'm sure it will be simple enough with a little goodwill."

"Perhaps," said Merlyn. He didn't need to underline the unlikelihood of general goodwill in the Cantelo family. "But this is all quite academic at the moment. Everything is in the hands of the Forensic Science Service. They'll be trying to get specimens from both my parents, but it's all just a question of time before they pronounce on who I am."

A tiny light seemed to come into Rosalind's eye at the mention of Merlyn's parents, and her voice was firm and dismissive when she said:

"They're hardly likely to get a sample from your mother, after all these years."

"They said it shouldn't be a problem. She died in hospital, and they keep medical samples there for years." Rosalind's shoulders sagged. "But you say nothing of my father."

"Should I? Silence is best, I would have thought."

"I mean, you mention my mother as dead, but not my father."

"Your mother *is* long dead, before you started worming your way in with Aunt Clarissa. Your father I know nothing about."

"Except that he's been in trouble with the law. The family knows all about that, don't they? Was it you who spread it around? Anyway, the trouble may help the forensic people, because the police will have kept his samples. I'm getting interested in my father, oddly enough. I don't remember thinking about him more than occasionally after I took off for Italy. Now I do. I wonder what he's been doing all these years. And why the Cantelo family should be interested in him at all."

"Why shouldn't we? He was married to Aunt Thora. And people are generally interested when someone's in trouble with the police. We're a proud family —"

"But not at all a close-knit one."

" — so we were bound to talk when he was sent to jail."

"Ah – he did go to jail, did he?"

"So it said in the paper. I've never heard of him since."

"Well, he can't still be in jail. He didn't cause a death or anything from what I've heard. I expect he's either gone straight, or he's dead."

"I don't know how you can talk about your father in that cold way. I loved my own father! He meant everything to me!"

"Really? I don't remember much about him. When I was

living with Aunt Clarrie he was already on the way to being a high-flier in London in something or other. British Petroleum, wasn't it? I don't think I saw much of him."

"He was a very busy man. Enormously successful. And of course I was the apple of his eye. I don't know how you can talk of your father as you do. It's not natural."

Merlyn shrugged.

"I think that depends more on the parent than the child, don't you? I certainly was never the apple of Jake's eye. More the discarded pip."

"You're so bitter ... I'd be worried if I really thought you were Merlyn Docherty. But everyone's told me about Thora. She was a beautiful person. Everybody loved her. You can't be her son."

"I expect it skipped a generation, this lovability. Maybe I take more after Grandfather Cantelo —"

"Well, he —" Rosalind pulled herself up. "Anyway, I'm quite sure you just took Merlyn's name when you heard of Clarrie's death."

"You could soon find out that's not true. I've been working at the EU for more than ten years. I had English, French and Italian when I joined them, and they put me on to learning Romanian and handling their bid to join the Union. That rather fizzled out, but I've been saddled with Eastward expansion, investigating human rights in the applicant countries – that kind of thing. Interesting and frustrating in about equal measure."

Rosalind looked as if she was struggling to understand what he was talking about.

"And you're working there under the name of Merlyn Docherty?"

Merlyn smiled, and nodded.

"Utterly under my own name, yes. Any one can ring up EU headquarters and check." He looked her straight in the eyes. "You can do it if you like."

Rosalind's mouth dropped in outrage. Any passer-by, seeing them, might have thought that Merlyn was quoting something. Might even have guessed that he was quoting from Rosalind herself. But they were just two people, roughly of an age, sitting unhappily together on a public seat.

"Where is Barnett?" Rosalind said, looking at her watch. "We've got an appointment at the school."

"Oh? Where does he work?"

"Just over there." She pointed back to the little streets between the Parish Church and the city centre. "A *very* good firm. They specialise in property, but he keeps in touch with *all* aspects of the law, and knows the best people to consult on *any*thing."

"Bully for Barnett. By the way, you talked about my 'worming my way' into Aunt Clarrie's affections."

"Well, what else could you call it?"

"Something more generous, perhaps? I'd been without a mother for four years when I first started coming to stay with her, and effectively without a father for long periods. And Clarissa herself was a spinster, and childless of course. Affection seems a very natural emotion between the two of us."

"That's just self-pity. I was without a father practically the whole time of my childhood. He loved me so much, but he needed to earn so as to leave us financially secure."

Merlyn was puzzled about that. Did he know he was going to die young?

"You never told me that. But you had a mother. Clarissa was mother and father to me – and entertainer to boot. Staying with her was an end-of-the-pier show, as well as an education."

"She was a charlatan. You knew that as well as I did."

"Yes – we talked about it once, didn't we? But I think you

can only be a charlatan if you yourself don't believe in what you're peddling. I'm quite sure Aunt Clarissa did believe it."

"Well, I'm quite sure she didn't, and had a good laugh at all the people she was fooling and robbing."

"No. No!" Merlyn was becoming heated. He knew Rosalind had fixed unerringly on his aunt's weakest spot. "Clarissa wasn't like that. Yes, she would laugh about clients from time to time, but she never had any doubts she could help them, if they let her."

Rosalind shrugged. She looked, as she had throughout their talk, to the right, at the cars coming.

"I think that's Barnett ... Yes, it is."

She gathered up her packages and handbag, and put on her gloves. Gloves? In May? Merlyn thought. She really was, at thirty-seven, a sort of anachronism. Barnett's Mercedes pulled up in front of them. He got out of the car, ushered Rosalind into the passenger seat, then shut the door and looked straight at Merlyn.

"Tough being both husband and father," he said. "And footman too." He winked, got into the car, and pulled away.

Merlyn sat for a few moments, then began to walk thoughtfully towards the Temple Street car park. Barnett, obviously, was brighter than his wife. He must have realised from the moment he heard about the Forensic Science Service being brought into the matter that calling them was not the act of an impostor. Any hope he had that Rosalind might inherit a good share of the spoils must have been given up then. The news that Merlyn had made a will leaving the whole lot to charity must also have made him think. The implication that the family, or one of them, had Merlyn in their sights must have made Barnett want to distance himself, as far as that was possible, from the Cantelos. This was becoming the sort of family story that any man whose livelihood depended on his respectability would want to steer well clear of. Hence his access of friendliness.

Rosalind was more difficult to fathom. She still clung, or pretended to, to the idea that he was an impostor. Was this greed, clinging to the last shred of hope? She was obviously comfortably off, and money never seemed to bring any particular glint to her eye. Was it fear that made her still hope that he was not who he claimed to be? Fear that Clarissa had told him something? Fear that his establishing his claim would lead to all sorts of other family skeletons tumbling out of the cupboard?

He arrived back at his car, and drove off around the circle of streets to get back to his hotel, his mind still working. Rosalind had been fairly often to Congreve Street, she had even been interested in him in an early-adolescent way – though whether her teenaged offer of herself to him was serious who could now decide? She had known that Clarissa had treated him as an adult, talked to him as if he were one, made him for the first time part of the Cantelo family. Was Rosalind afraid he had been told something? And that now he was back he would want to use it?

He parked his car carefully, then walked round to the front of the hotel and up the steps. He went straight to Reception.

"Room 417, please," he said.

Clutching his room key he turned towards the lifts.

"Merlyn Docherty?"

He turned again. Coming up behind him there was a grey-haired man, untidily dressed, but far from down-at-heel, with an enquiring expression on his face.

"Jake," said Merlyn. "What do you want?"

"What do you want?" Merlyn asked.

The man was unfazed.

"Well, nothing really. Nothing specific. It's just that, hearing you were home, I thought we should make contact."

"Why?"

"Because – well – I thought I had a lot of making up to do."

"Ah really? Now would that be making up in the sense of reconciliation? Or would it be making up in the sense of compensating? Or would it, even, be making up in the sense of inventing, fabricating, concocting, making a fiction out of —"

"You talk like a fucking lawyer," said Jake.

"I am a fucking lawyer. I suppose what you want is a bit of a talk, is it?"

"Yes. That's it exactly."

Merlyn paused, then turned on his heels and went towards the bar. He could not have rationalised it, lawyer though he was, but he did not want to invite Jake up to his room. Even though they were in a hotel, it would have seemed like letting him into his space. And that would have meant having a pow-wow, working towards peace, acknowledging a relationship Merlyn did not feel existed. Jake had once had charge of him, and had neglected his trust. That was all.

Meanwhile Jake was beside him, puppyish, looking up at him, one half pathetic, one half disreputable, full of uncertainties and unsureness, but also full of hope and sheer cheek.

At the bar Merlyn turned to his father and raised his eyebrows.

"Pint of bitter, Webster's if they've got it," said Jake. "I haven't changed my tastes."

"I was never with you in a pub, remember?" The barman,

grateful for something to do at that time of day, pulled a pint of Webster's and got Merlyn his Scotch and soda. For some reason Merlyn didn't feel he had to keep a clear head with his father, as he had done with the Cantelos. The disorder of Jake's personality seemed to lull him into a sense of security, true or false.

"So you're not in jail, then?" said Merlyn as they sat down.

"In jail? No, of course I'm not in jail."

"The Cantelos seemed to think that you might be."

"Oh that. Did they see that report in the *Yorkshire Post*? That would have had them rubbing their hands. Anyway, that was years ago."

"But you did get put inside?"

"One year," said Jake, as if a sentence so short hardly counted. "I was out after eight months. I don't have any quarrel with the judge – I earned it."

"Big of you."

"It was the making of me. Made me understand all those things I'd been messed up about in my mind."

"That would take eight months."

"You've become right sarky, Merlyn. It doesn't suit you."

"It wasn't inborn, it was induced by experience. So how did prison help you? Did it make a man of you?"

"It was there I met my wife."

"Really?" Merlyn raised his eyebrows. "Prisons are so up-to-date these days, aren't they? Positively Scandinavian."

"She wasn't a prisoner. She was in the education office. Still is. We hit it off right from the word go."

"I'm so glad. Was it footsie over Virgil's *Aeneid*, Book I? Or simultaneous swoons over the 'Ode to Autumn'?"

"We just looked, and that was it. You know – 'across a crowded room'. I knew then that it was a new beginning. I was going to go straight, get a job, stop drinking."

"Cheers."

"Cheers. And that's how it's turned out."

"So what sort of job did you get?"

"Well actually, I became a house husband. Roxanne has two kids by her former partner, and she was pregnant when I came out."

"Oh? Some kind of in vincular fertilisation? A quick naughty behind the *Dictionary of National Biography*?"

"Never you mind. Anyway, we've got this lovely little girl. She's the light of my life." Merlyn felt a sudden stab of jealousy. It was absurd! To feel jealous of a child of an elderly father whom he despised – a father who had never been one, a father who, if he had offered love, Merlyn would have kicked aside with contempt. What strange emotional gymnastics the brain performed, Merlyn thought. How humiliating to be at the mercy of them.

"And you've got stepchildren too, you say?"

"That's right. Sandra's nineteen. She'll be moving out before long, I wouldn't mind betting. There've been plenty of boyfriends I can tell you. Jason is fifteen. He'll be around for a while yet. He's a very bright boy. We won't let him go easily."

"Lucky Jason."

Jake shot him a glance.

"I'm not going to make the same mistake again. It wouldn't make my treatment of you any better if I was to repeat it with Jason, now would it? You've got to realise I wasn't my normal self when you were growing up. Losing your mother, then Deborah – both my womenfolk. It knocked me over – I was just a shell of my old self. I needed help."

Merlyn's face twisted with contempt.

"Oh, and how do you think I felt, a young lad who had just lost his mother and elder sister. Didn't *I* need help?"

"Yes, of course. I realise that now."

"My mother was intensely lovable, even during her long illness. Deborah was the sister who had done everything for me, comforted me when I was lonely or afraid, mothered me when I needed someone just to hug me. Did you expect me to take my loss of both of them in my stride?"

"No, no – of course not. I just didn't think."

"That's right. That's exactly right. It was yourself from beginning to end. You didn't think of me at all. Obviously your new family is luckier."

"But it didn't turn out so badly for you, did it?" said Jake in a wheedling tone that Merlyn found nauseating. "I mean, Clarissa was a mother to you. Of course I didn't plan it like that, but that's how it worked out."

"And like a good mother she left me everything she had – is that what you're counting on? A share in the spoils?"

"No," said Jake, suddenly forceful. "That's totally unfair, Merlyn. We may not have been close, but you should know me better than that. I've never been a grasper or a grabber, never had much interest in money."

"No-o-o," admitted Merlyn, grudgingly. "But it's surprising how many of the hippy generation turned out to be good at amassing a very large pile of dosh in later years. Half the people who went to sit at the feet of the maharashis are now sitting in penthouses on the East River or Canary Wharf. Right little doctrinaire capitalists most of them turned out to be."

"Not me," protested Jake. "Roxanne and me and the family, we live in a semi-detached house in Carlyn Street in Sheffield, and we're happy as birds. I'm *not* after your money, Merlyn. Good luck to you, enjoy it. But don't let it spoil you, boy."

"I won't. I won't."

"And come and see us. You have another family now remember. Not just the Cantelos."

"Hmm, maybe. As a matter of interest, when did you last

speak to Clarissa?"

Jake shrugged, apparently uninterested.

"Lord only knows. We lost touch while I was in jail, I suppose."

"So before that you spoke occasionally?"

"I think so. I don't remember. I was a bit ... well, it was a crisis in my life, and it got worse and worse. The drinking, I mean."

"And do you remember if Clarissa ever told you whether I was alive or dead?"

"She told me you were missing ... I remember that. I'd seen you ... not long before, and it was a surprise when you went to India, and then soon after to hear that you were missing."

"But did she tell you I was *alive*?"

"I ... don't think so. I don't remember. I tell you, son, those were bad times for me ... But I shouldn't think she did tell me."

"Why? Because you were always drunk, and couldn't be relied upon to keep the secret?"

Jake thought about this.

"Well, yes. But why was it a secret? If I've got it right, Clarissa let everybody think you'd gone missing in the Hindu Kush or some such goddamn place. And she never let on she knew that you were alive. Now, why would she do that? You're asking *me* things, now I'm asking you. *Why*? Was it one of Clarissa's strange fancies?"

"You could probably call it that. But Clarissa usually had perfectly sound reasons for what seemed to be odd notions."

"Did she? If she did they passed me by. She once told me – just out of the blue, like she did, to catch you off guard I always thought – that I'd never settle down in life. If I didn't settle with Thora then I'd never settle with anyone. She was wrong about that."

"Oh, I didn't say she was never wrong. She could be just as

off-beam about character as people who use more orthodox methods of assessment."

"Still, she was a good mother to you, wasn't she? If I'd chosen her as surrogate mother I couldn't have picked a better."

"If anyone chose I suspect it was me," said Merlyn, sour at his father's hints of making decisions, when as far as he could remember Jake's whole life twenty years before had been geared to the avoidance of making decisions, especially ones for the welfare of his son. "She chose me too, though, I suppose. We looked at each other and saw we were suited."

"You did. And that was nice. Good for both of you. But you haven't told me why Clarissa wanted you dead, or wanted it generally thought you were dead."

"No, I haven't, have I? I must say I took to non-existence like a duck to water. In one stroke all the Cantelos were out of my life, and all the Dochertys too."

Jake looked astonished.

"I never involved you with any of my family. If you saw the Docherty grandparents once it was as much as you ever did."

"Well, *one* Docherty. There I was free of the lot of them and of you, except of course for Clarissa. Heaven! I went to Italy, did a lot of menial jobs, educated myself, got a degree, got to understand the system, so that by the time I was twenty-five I had used the degree in law, with economics as a second subject, to get a highly respectable job. And by the time I was thirty, I was working in Brussels."

"All your own work, eh?"

"All the essential part. Clarissa sent me a sub now and then, if I asked her for one."

"And plenty of girlfriends too, I should think. Knowing Italy ..."

"I don't think Britain can cast the first stone, as far as available teenage girls are concerned."

"Maybe not. I wouldn't know."

"You seem to have a teenage daughter with plenty of ... admirers from what you say. Anyway, yes, I had the love of my life in Verona, and after that plenty of girlfriends when I studied in Naples and Turin. Oddly enough, it seemed to help that I'm British. We don't think of ourselves as romantic catches."

"Maybe they just wanted you for conversation practice. Or to learn the secrets of English cuisine."

"Maybe. You can be sarky yourself if you try, can't you Jake? Now, I'm a bit busy —"

"Oh, I thought —"

"We've made contact. I think that's enough after twenty-two years and eleven months. If you'll give me your phone number —"

"Here's my card."

"Oh right. Well, maybe I'll be in touch. Goodbye."

Merlyn held out his hand, briefly took his father's, then strode to the lifts without a backward glance. He could see his father in the mirrors of the foyer, and in the stainless steel of the lifts. He pressed the button for the fourth floor, then, when he got there, pressed the ground floor button. When he got back to the foyer the glass door giving on to Wellington Street was just closing, and he saw his father disappearing down the steps. He went to the door and saw him turn right, going towards the centre of Leeds and the railway station. He waited a few seconds and then slowly followed him.

As he began the stalking he asked himself why he hadn't found out how his father had known he was back in Britain, and where he was staying. The more he thought about it, he had missed chances. The fact that his father had reappeared when he was about to inherit money did genuinely make him wonder: had he in the past only seemed to be unworldly, above money? Could he not in fact have engineered his son's whole connection with Clarissa Cantelo, knowing she had in her sole control a large part of the family fortune?

He kept his distance. Jake went past the demolished central Royal Mail sorting office, past the old Wellesley Hotel, now flats, past little businesses – the inevitable sandwich shop, a duplicating shop – concerns too marginal for a central position, then towards the Queens Hotel and the station. He did not turn right into the station however, but continued on, then crossed the road, past the British Home Stores, then on, finally stopping at the Square on the Lane, turning into it without a moment's hesitation.

Merlyn kept going, and glanced through the window as he passed. His father had merged into the vastness of the largest pub bar in the land, invisible, undistinguishable from the punters dotted here and there throughout the drinking hall. Merlyn turned, crossed the road, then went back towards the Crowne Plaza. It was illogical to conclude from the fact that his father went from a drink in a bar with his son to another drink in a bar on his own that he was not quite the reformed and blissfully contented and changed person he claimed. But illogical or not, that is what Merlyn did conclude.

Chapter Eight
The Old Folks at Home

It was two days after Merlyn's confrontation with his past in the form of his father that he made another, less direct, confrontation with the force that had made him what he was. This second encounter came from an unexpected source. When he got back to the Crowne Plaza after lunch for his usual siesta, relic of his years in Italy, his key had a note on it: "Ring 2415676. Peace." His first thought was that he was being solicited by an evangelical Christian group. Then he remembered Charlie.

"Detective Sergeant Peace."

"Merlyn Docherty here. Are those the sounds of the Leeds CID solving the city's crimes?"

"They are."

"With Sergeant Peace at the forefront of the struggle?"

"Absolutely so. And it may be Inspector Peace soon, so let's have a bit of respect as a preliminary gesture."

"Well, congratulations first, and then increased respect."

"I said 'may be'. My wife calls me Pollyanna. I go around saying 'Be glad' without having anything to be glad about. But the signs do seem to be encouraging ... It's something my wife has come up with that I'm calling about."

"Your wife?"

"Yes. Felicity's in the fiction business – like most of the people I deal with here, now I come to think of it. She's got nothing on them for sheer invention. She's at the stage of getting a nicer sort of rejection letter. She thinks she's going to make it to publication and I think she's going to make it to publication, but then some people might say we're biased and she's as much a Pollyanna as I am."

"The idea would never have crossed my mind."

"Good. Meanwhile she's doing a bit of teaching and supervising for Leeds University English Department. Recently she's been doing a lot of reading in minor Victorian novelists in the Leeds Library – that's a private library dating back to seventeen-something-or-other, and older than the London Library, or so they keep telling people. All the books from the cellar come up with a quarter of a pound of inbuilt dust."

"Sounds inviting."

"It *is* for some people, including Felicity, particularly when they tell her that what she wants to read was last borrowed in 1852. But while she's there she does work on her own behalf, especially in local history. Her next book – next manuscript I should say – is set in Headingley in the 1920s, among the comfortably-off classes."

"I begin to get your drift."

"Don't get your hopes up too high. The local Leeds historians are not primarily into the middle-classes. It's the mill-workers and the tanners and the forge men they like. All very interesting, but Felicity isn't aiming to be the next Catherine Cookson. So when I told her about the Cantelo family she did her best in all the background books on Leeds, and came up with nothing – not even a mention. She wasn't surprised. But just as a last resort she looked up Cantelo in the general card-index (they're not computerised in the Leeds Library, and probably won't be until the twenty-second century). And there was a card for a book by an X. Cantelo. It was a novel called *Family Business*.

"Sounds a possible title for a novel by a Cantelo. What is its date?"

"No date on the card. Felicity took it to the librarian. It was a typed card, typed on a very dirty manual in fact, and the librarian thought it would be some time in the Seventies. He compared it with cards for other books – early Martin Amis, late Greene, Spark and Olivia Manning – and they seemed to confirm that sort of date."

"Seventies. Old Man Cantelo, Clarissa's father, would still be alive then."

"Yes, it's — But I shouldn't be talking about this. I'm the world's greatest ignoramus about such things, and anything I throw at you is the sort of thing I've picked up from Felicity since we've been together. Any chance of your coming round to see us, so you can talk to her? She thinks it could be of some relevance, or at least of background interest."

"I'd like that. It would be getting things from the horse's mouth. If your wife knows anything about Leeds in the just-after-the-war years, she knows more than I do. I was born in the 1960s, but I didn't come visiting Clarissa, and then come to live with her, until the late Seventies and early Eighties. I'd like to talk to her."

So it was that, that evening around seven, Merlyn parked outside the nineteenth-century house in Cumberland Road and went up to the first floor flat that was spacious and suitable for a small family, though the square patch of garden at the front and the small wilderness at the back made it less than ideal for older children.

"We'll get more garden when I get the inspectorship," said Charlie. "Though goodness knows, inspectors aren't paid a fortune any more."

"Better put your faith in fiction then," said Merlyn.

At that point Felicity came in with Carola, already dressed for bed but raring to put on a performance for a twenty-minute charm session before going quietly. A born pop-star couldn't have done more to woo her audience. Merlyn reserved judgment on Charlie's confident pronouncements on her intelligence and her intuitive good taste, but her determination was evident on the slightest acquaintanceship, and so was her calculated charm. On the evidence of that session, she would go far.

When Felicity had put her to bed they all drank coffee, and soon Felicity went to the desk in her study and brought out for Merlyn the copy of *Family Business*.

"Not very impressive, as you can see," she said.

Even on a first flicking through he could see that the pages were browned – the cheap paper used, though, had later become standard for English books: some of the typeface was askew on the page, and the binding was the cheapest imaginable, with only the author's surname and the title on the spine. On the title page the publisher's name at the bottom was simply given as Hurstmonceaux. On the verso title page no date was given, and no publisher's address.

"Looks a shoddy job," he commented.

"In every respect," agreed Felicity. "This was when vanity publishing was just that. No half-way houses, as there are now. You paid to have something in print that you could hand to your friends. This firm clearly made no pretence at all that it was anything other than a commercial bargain between writer and printer."

"They took the money and ran?"

"Probably. Or a kinder interpretation might be that they were honest, and made no pretence of being a mainline publisher."

"Hmmm. So one of the Cantelos vanity-published a book in the late Sixties. Do I take it that the Cantelos themselves are the family whose business – that's an ambiguous word, isn't it? – is dealt with in the book?"

"That's for you to decide," said Felicity firmly. "I've only flicked through it. I have the collected masterpieces of Mrs Trollope, Caroline Norton and G. P. R. James to gorge myself with, to supervise eager-beaver Ph.D. students. All I can say off the cuff is that the plot seems to follow the fortunes of two younger members of the family, one male and one female. And that an early chapter – the second, I think – has a family scene, with the members all assembled at breakfast, the whole thing presided over by the formidable figure of the paterfamilias – a Victorian father well out of his time."

"The usual tyrant?"

"No, not really. But someone with firm opinions and a sententious manner – someone who apparently always gets his own way. It's really a sort of comic caricature – something out of Dickens or Waugh."

"But the novel is set in what was then the present day?"

"Seems to be. I've seen references to the cinema and the radio, but not so far television. It existed then, of course, but maybe Dad thought it beneath the family."

"Maybe. Clarissa had an old black-and-white set she almost never watched."

Merlyn sat thinking, flicking through the already fragile pages. There seemed nothing in the book that brought back the past, but of course it was not his past.

"I'm trying to calculate my dates," he said. "The member of my family – my mother's family, that is – that I can most readily imagine writing a novel, maybe as a species of revenge, would be Malachi. Now, I think we can take it that the X is a sign of an unknown quantity. There is no Xavier in the family, and I can't think of any other normal Christian name beginning with that letter."

"Xenia," said Felicity. "But it's not common."

"Why do words that start with X get pronounced as if they started with a Z?" asked Charlie.

"I'll give you a short lecture on that," said Felicity, "when I've found out why myself."

Merlyn cut them short.

"However, I do rather doubt whether Malachi has the staying power to write a whole novel as an act of revenge or anything else, let alone to get it published. He'd flake after chapter three."

"A lot of people do that," said Felicity.

"Not you," said Charlie. "We're piling up rejection slips and putting a star on the ones where the manuscript seems to have been read."

"Not many of those," said Felicity. "Now, if we're thinking seventies we're talking about almost forty years ago. I'd say an age of twenty to twenty-five is the lowest we could imagine for writing a novel and getting it vanity published. So we are looking for someone who is now at least in their early Sixties, and probably older. And at a guess I would say a woman."

"Why?" asked Charlie.

"Because if it's a young person who wrote it I feel the men would be active getting qualifications and starting in a job, making a place in the world for themselves. Even at that late date in Leeds middle-class women were expected to have a mildly good time when they were young, while fitting themselves to become virtuous wives and mothers, which was their destiny. This seems to be the world view of the father of the family, if we can believe the picture to be based on the Cantelos. So the women had more leisure time, more unexpended emotional energy, more sheer frustration."

"That sounds convincing," said Merlyn. "Except that Hugh seems to have been the only Cantelo boy who was interested in money and a career. Gerald got religious mania quite young, if my memory serves, and Paul took off to America, leaving a wife and child, and becoming a sort of intellectual hobo, if the family gossip when I was living with Clarissa is to be believed. Which admittedly is a big if."

"Then perhaps we should leave open the sex of the writer. Is it terribly important anyway?"

"I suppose I'll have to read the book to decide."

"I wanted you to see the book mainly to get an idea of the sort of atmosphere in the family when the children were all younger."

Charlie had been thinking.

"Why would you use the misleading initial X when you were willing to put the name Cantelo to the book?"

"Maybe because he or she wanted to have the family identified, as part of some kind of revenge or scheme to bring ridicule down on them, but he didn't want his own identity to be identified. There were enough Cantelos to spread the suspicion," said Merlyn.

"Fair enough," said Felicity. She turned to Merlyn. "Well, it's up to you now. You're about to have an encounter with your family in earlier days – if I'm right, of course."

They all three (because Felicity was as interested as Charlie) chewed over the case, had a drink, went into the DNA test, and the implications of Jake's coming back into the picture. Merlyn reported on his talks with Malachi and Rosalind, they had another drink, and then started to talk about Carola. Normally Merlyn was perfectly willing to talk about other people's infants and toddlers, and rather looked forward to the day when he would have one or two of his own, but that was when he felt the copy of *Family Business* burning a hole in his briefcase.

It was the first thing that he extracted from it when he got back to his hotel room. He put on his pyjamas, brewed himself a little pot of tea, then sat down in the easy chair with the book. In the bright light of the standard lamp it looked an even less impressive production than it had seemed in Charlie and Felicity's flat – like many much more recent British books it seemed to be made to fall to pieces at the first excuse. Luckily it had probably had few readers, if it had had any. Then he thought about that. Who had read it? Members of the Cantelo family? Perhaps. Especially if copies were not distributed gratis among them. He seemed to remember that several of them had shares in the privately-owned library – perhaps shares were the sort of thing that the Cantelos were given on their twenty-first birthdays. And the book could have been a creator of disunity and grudges and have been intended as such.

He flicked through the later chapters, as Felicity obviously had done. A story of two young people making their ways in the world, against the combined opposition of parents and siblings. It was hardly riveting stuff, Merlyn thought, and the pall of adolescence hung over it – grievances nursed, naiveties nourished as if they were blinding insights. It was saved, if at all, by the humour of the pictures not only of the parents, but also of some of the siblings: as they grew up in the story the ambitious Hugh, the tiresomely conventional Emily, the bible-bashing Gerald, all took on a sort of fictional life.

When he went back to the beginning of the book to find the breakfast chapter he made a discovery that Felicity apparently had not noticed. The family were introduced in a rather amateur way in the opening pages, and by each fictitious name there was in pencil in the margin a faint initial. Were these the author's identifications, before giving the book (they would hardly have bought it) to the Leeds Library?

He went through in his own mind what he knew about his aunt's generation of Cantelos. Rosalind's father was Hugh, Caroline's mother was Marigold. Malachi and Francis's father was Gerald, Edward's mother was Emily. Here, as the children of the family appeared, were an H, an M, a G and an E, as well as a Th for his own mother and a Cl for Clarissa. A P identified the man who had flown the nest before Merlyn had ever gone to live with Clarissa, and was never mentioned except with a sharp intake of breath by Aunt Emily.

The identification had one big advantage: when he came to the chapter of the family at breakfast he could substitute in his own mind the real name of the person mentioned, in place of the fictitious one. Taking it up, the second chapter had something of the broad humour one would hope for from a picture of a disunited family seen from inside.

"Kidneys!" said Mr Cantelo, waving one on the end of a fork, and taking care none of the rich sauce dripped down on to his blue and silver tie. "The prince of breakfast meats. You children don't know what you're missing."

"Ugh!" said Marigold. Her mother blinked reproof at her.

"Your father always says a good breakfast sets you up for the day," she said.

"Yes, he always does," said Paul.

The irony passed Mr Cantelo by. His substantial stomach swelled, as it always did when he was about to make a pronouncement, which was frequently.

"And bacon!" he pronounced, his voice throbbing with passion. "The essence of Englishness, that's what bacon is. It's what marks us off from 'lesser breeds without the law'."

His wide lips, sensual and self-regarding, opened to receive a forkful of streaky, after the napkin had been adjusted over his tie.

"Perhaps Kipling should have said 'lesser breeds without the bacon'," said Paul.

"Perhaps he couldn't find a rhyme for 'bacon'," said Clarissa.

Mr Cantelo treated his children's lightest remarks as if they were possible specimens of childish wisdom.

"Perhaps he couldn't," he said. "The ways of poets are beyond the understanding of a practical man of affairs like myself. If you can't find a rhyme for a word like 'bacon', why on earth put it at the end of a line?"

His tummy swelled, and his children were reduced to silence, with some twisting at the corners of their mouths. Their father was king of the breakfast and dinner tables, but the first rumblings of revolutionary republicanism trembled beneath the surface calm.

"And how," asked Mr Cantelo in the apparently cowed silence, and turning to Hugh, "did your essay on Disraeli's foreign policy go?"

"All right," said Hugh. Then, fearing he might have given a hostage to fortune, the boy amended that to: "not too bad."

"Disraeli was a great charlatan," asserted his father.

"Well, perhaps," said Hugh. "But that doesn't get one far on the subject of his foreign policy."

"He had not a principled bone in his body. And *that* could probably be discerned in his foreign policy."

Hugh was one of those who pursued the useless strategy of battling with his father on his own terms.

"The trouble is that I thought 'foreign policy' was something big, something highflown and difficult to grasp —"

"Do you mean 'abstract'?" his father asked, showering condescension.

"Yes," gulped Hugh, grasping at the straw. "Abstract. But all it is is bits and pieces – things he did when something or other turned up. Not a principle at all."

"Exactly what one would expect of an unprincipled person. Reacting to events, taking chances. Like making the poor old Queen Empress of India, a piece of foolish vanity on both their parts which burdened the British crown for seventy years."

"Well, yes, I said that ... Something like that ... I think I did all right. At least I hope so."

Having reduced his confident son to a nervous jelly, Mr Cantelo pressed home his advantage, smiling around the table with teeth that flashed warning signals.

"I hope so. I really hope so. Or you will suffer where it hurts you most, Hugh: in your pocket." He put his knife and fork across his plate, and the maid immediately whipped his plate away and put the tea-plate and knife on to his placemat. "And what you lose, someone else will gain. If I find that good work has been done, the worker will be rewarded." He smiled his civilised-crocodile smile. "But mind: betas and beta minuses are not regarded as good work in the Cantelo family!"

Most assuredly they were not! Mr Cantelo's master-stroke in child-rearing had been to devise a series of rewards and penalties, and a week's pocket money could be seriously eroded by two or three poor performances. The fact that the money docked was then awarded to a child whose performances at school had rated beta plus or higher did not improve relations in the large brood.

"I'm not going to do History in GCE," said Gerald. "I'm going to take Religious Knowledge."

There was silence. No one except Gerald would have lobbed a bomb like that across the breakfast table. All eyes were on Mr Cantelo. His cheeks became larger and rounder, as if a volcano was casting foul air up from the depths of his oesophagus. He glared at his son, taking in his uncombed hair and his tie congenitally askew and showing his top shirt-button.

"Religious Knowledge? Religious *Know*ledge! A subject for plain girls in pinafores in love with the curate! Over my dead body are you going to do Religious Knowledge."

Gerald looked as if he was ready, nay anxious, to take that risk. However he merely muttered: "I'm going to do it, though."

"And what does Religious Knowledge do for you in the great wide world? Who is impressed by it? Who would care to employ a *boy* who had a grade – whatever grade – in Religious Knowledge?"

Mr Cantelo faded to a silence, and seemed to be engaged in a fight to calm himself down.

"I don't care who's impressed. I'm never going to impress anyone whatever subject I take. That's the one I want to do."

Mr Cantelo leaned forward, sorrow-not-anger suffusing

his face.

"Gerald, Gerald. You know how we do things in this house. We discuss things. We sit down and go through the pros and cons. What the decision could lead to, what the advantages and disadvantages might be. Certainly we must discuss this, because religion has never had great importance in our family. What can you have against rational discussion?"

"Perhaps he's noticed that the discussion always ends with us doing what you want, not what we want," said Hugh, his nerve restored now he was no longer in the firing line. The puffed up red cheeks, the scimitar eyes, were turned on him at once.

"If that happens it is because a sensible child acknowledges that its parents have the experience, and the knowledge of the way of the world, that makes *his* judgment safest to follow."

"His or her, I suppose you mean," said Paul. "You and mother, whose two votes somehow outweigh the seven of ours. I must say it seems unfair for you to decide on a matter like this when you have no religion yourself."

His remark gave Gerald courage.

"I can't think of any subject more important than religious faith. It's being brought up in a godless family that's made me see that."

His father stood up. He thinks he's prime minister, thought Paul. Facing a motion of No Confidence. He even put his hands on the lapels of his jacket. He was Gladstone, preparing to outface the sceptics.

"If this family has been sceptical in the matter of religion," he intoned, "it is because it believes in the supreme value of personal endeavour. It is through your own efforts and endeavours that you will make your way in the world, not by clutching the imagined hand of some supernatural figure in the skies. Have confidence in yourselves children, and you will need no comforting fictions about a God in an after-life."

And he stalked, exuding self-satisfaction, out into the hall and began rummaging in the cupboard for hat and overcoat.

"Listen to what your father says," murmured Elspeth Cantelo. "He only wants what is best for you."

"I think we all want what is best for ourselves," said Hugh.

His mother shook her head. She was imbued with the family philosophy as interpreted by its undoubted head. She knew that the Cantelo method of child-rearing had been developed over several generations of the family. The Cantelos gloried in their reputation as pillars of the community, models of a responsible and thoughtful response to moral and social questions. The idea of physically punishing children had been abhorrent in the family for many decades – indeed this idea had resulted in the family being considered eccentric. But Mr Cantelo's system of rewards and penalties mainly of a financial kind was (he believed, and thus so did his wife) proving brilliantly successful in directing his children towards the goal of self-sufficiency and financial probity. They would be model businessmen (and businessmen's wives), and in their turn, model parents. Such a view of future generations was a much more concrete hope, Cantelo believed, than any trust in so dubious a concept as eternal bliss.

As the maid cleared away the Cantelo girls talked with their mother, overheard by their father in the hallway.

"Do you really think father's way of docking our pocket money if we do poor work is the right one, mother?"

It was Clarissa speaking.

"But of course it is, dear. And augmenting it when you do good work. Your father has vast experience, and he does know what works best."

"Sometimes it seems as if all it does is produce arguments and bad feeling," said Thora.

"What it produces is a spirit of competition between you," said Elspeth. "And that can't be unhealthy."

Mr Cantelo threw back his head, placed on it the trilby which had been his headgear for two decades, and sailed through the door on a billowing cloud of self-satisfaction which conveyed him down to the street and to the company car whose door was being held open by the company chauffeur.

God was not in his heaven, but all was right with the world.

Merlyn shut the book and turned off the light. It was early for bed, but he had had enough of Mr Cantelo, and Mrs, too, for that matter. He was glad that it was his mother who had made that point, the one that exposed the fatal flaw in the Cantelo method of upbringing. What the self-satisfied Mr Cantelo's method produced was not healthy competition but enmity, grudges and bitterness – that he felt quite sure about.

And he thought that it was this spirit that Clarissa had always been conscious of in those she should have been closest to, those she should have been able to call on for support and love. It was her consciousness of the spirit her father had unleashed that had made her perceive the jealousy that her virtual adoption of him had aroused, and to sense, too, that jealousy was getting out of hand.

And, if what the neighbour Mr Robinson had reported was accurate, she was disturbed not just by the prospect of violence in the future, but by a knowledge of violence in the past.

The phone rang at ten o'clock in the morning.

"Merlyn Docherty."

"Er – hello – is that Merlyn Docherty?"

Merlyn sighed. He knew the voice and he felt he knew the dimness behind it.

"Hello Caroline. Good to hear from you."

"Oh, did you recognise ..." The brightness in the tone faded as she realised she was not being too sharp. "But of course, you said my n ..." The voice contracted into silence, then cranked up again like a train after a long stop. "Er – I hope you don't think this is a silly idea ... it's just ..."

"Tell me, Caroline."

"What? ... oh, you want to hear the idea ... of course ... silly of me ... it's just — Well, it's Jackie's birthday tomorrow, and I'm having a party for all her little friends —"

"How nice."

"Yes ... if they don't quarrel ... They often *do* quarrel, but I suppose that's just children, isn't it? Anyway, I've asked some of the family round —"

"The family? You mean the Cantelos?"

"Oh yes, the Cantelos. I don't have any contacts with their father's family."

"I see. So you've asked the Cantelos round at the same time as the party?"

"Well yes, sort of ... I mean some of them don't have any ..."

"I don't have any children myself, Caroline."

"I know that, but you don't ... I mean ... you don't dis*like* —"

"Oh no. Quite the contrary, actually. I don't know about Malachi or Francis."

"Oh I think they ... I haven't asked Rosalind. She really is quite ... well ... you know ... I mean almost unpleasant. And she's always difficult."

"Yes, I had noticed. I talked to her recently, and it wasn't exactly a meeting of minds. Is her marriage happy?"

This question, demanding an answer on an intimate matter, seemed to throw Caroline entirely.

"Well, I mean, so far as I ... I mean, how can one *know*, unless one asked, and I wouldn't ... but *some*thing is ... I don't know ..."

"Bugging her?"

"Well yes. I suppose so. She is very ..."

"Isn't what's bugging her the fact that I've reappeared, and am going to inherit?"

"I suppose so. But I'm not sure ... anyway," she finished up triumphantly, "we'd all, the rest of us, be awfully pleased if you could come."

"I'd be delighted. Should I bring a bottle?"

"Well, it would help, if you don't — It's from five o'clock-ish."

"I'll be there. Look forward to seeing you all."

Merlyn pondered as he went about the various routine tasks for the rest of the day. It couldn't be said that Caroline intrigued him, but puzzle him she certainly did. He could imagine a mother throwing a side-party for the parents of the children invited to a birthday party, though the noise might be off-putting and he imagined most parents would prefer to dump their children for a few hours and then decamp to enjoy peace and freedom. But he did not see the point of Caroline's inviting her own relatives, and he wondered what she was up to. It seemed likely that one of her motives might be influencing him in favour of her own little girls. Or – more daunting – influencing him to consider herself and her maleless predicament. If that was her idea, her plans were doomed to failure. He had always preferred women of spirit and grit, and Danielle certainly had both. Guile, however, he could do without.

Next day in Oddbins he selected a middling-to-good bottle of white wine, the current national drink, and then hesitated between a bottle of whisky and one of brandy. He himself preferred the latter, but to take it might be deemed unpatriotic, particularly in a servant of the European Union, so he went along with the national preference for whisky. He decided that he would try to introduce the bottle as unobtrusively as possible, and brandy would have stood out as an unlikely offering.

He realised the next morning that, typically, Caroline had not given him her address or telephone number, and that he couldn't remember her married name, though Mr Featherstone had mentioned it. He rang Directory Enquiries, but the only C. Cantelo in the Leeds area was his aunt Clarissa. So Caroline had retained her married name, no doubt so as not to confuse the girls. In the end Merlyn rang Malachi at his bookmaker's job and got the information from him.

"Her married name is Caroline Chaunteley. Doesn't it just sound Olde Worlde? Her husband's father was a bricklayer, but never mind. She lives somewhere in Pudsey. It's in the phone book."

"Right."

"Do I take it you're invited to the kiddies' party?"

"That's right. Or to a family affair in the next room."

"So am I. What *fun*!"

"Well a bit more fun than the funeral bakemeats anyway."

"Maybe. I'm sure everyone will be glad that you're coming. But what is Caroline up to?"

"Probably nothing very startling," said Merlyn easily. Malachi sniggered nastily.

"No, she wouldn't be able to carry it through, would she? Any more than she can carry through a sentence to its full stop. She probably doesn't know herself what she's up to."

Caroline Chaunteley, Merlyn found, lived in Mountgrave Rise, and when he got there on the appointed day, earlyish, he found it was a gently ascending street of houses ten minutes walk from the centre of Pudsey. The houses were post-war semi-detached, well-cared-for, and even spacious beside the scrimped houses of the recent developments, including a group of stone houses apparently designed for midgets at the bottom of the hill. Merlyn could have found the house inhabited by Caroline by the noise alone: the party was already in progress. He got out of his car and stood for a moment in the warm May sunshine. Then he got his bag of bottles from the back seat and went up to the front door.

"Oh hello Merlyn, I'm so gl —"

Caroline's eyes had lit up, bright centres in a care-worn face.

"It sounds as if everyone is having a good time."

"Oh yes. I'll just get them all out into the garden round the barbecue, and then we can ..."

"It's good you can trust them not to start a fire."

"Oh, their father's here. I always invite him to birthdays. It shows him what he's missing."

Merlyn caught a brief flash of malice pass over her face at this rare finished sentence. Then she gestured to a door on one side of the hall and herself turned and went through one on the other side. Briefly the noise was deafening – over a dozen children there, Merlyn guessed from his swift glimpse of them – then the door shut on the sound of french windows being opened and children rushing out into the garden. Merlyn turned and went through to the drawing room.

Edward was there already, and Aunt Marigold was ensconced in a wheelchair in a corner, ministered to by a stern-faced Emily. There was also a young man, looking early-twenties, though with something of a Peter Pan or Cliff

Richard air about him that suggested to Merlyn that he was older than that. He was wearing a rather old-fashioned sports jacket and grey trousers, and was standing a bit apart from the rest by the window.

"I'll just get rid of my bottle," murmured Merlyn, and unloaded both on to the sideboard. Though Edward was the most congenial person in the room, and Aunt Marigold the one he most wanted to talk to, he felt he ought to get a handle on the young man – too young to be Caroline's husband, he decided, but too old to be the result of an early indiscretion of hers. He went over, holding out his hand.

"Hello, I'm Merlyn Docherty."

"Yes, I sort of guessed that. I'm Roderick Massey. You probably won't remember me."

"Not really. But I know you're Paul's son."

"That's right, or at least ... I don't quite know why I'm here."

"It's good to meet you, anyway."

"That's what Caroline said, that we ought to be on speaking terms, all of us. The idea seems to have got around that I'm mentioned in the will."

"You are. If I had died you would do quite nicely: twenty-five percent of half the estate. But I'm afraid I'm alive, so you shouldn't get your hopes up. I've made a will, just a temporary one, leaving everything to the NSPCC. I'll make another one when the fact that I'm Merlyn Docherty is recognised, and I'll try to respect what I can gather of Aunt Clarissa's intentions. But nobody's going to get riches. Lottery winners are luckier. I hope you weren't depending on hundreds of thousands?"

"Not at all. I wasn't depending on anything. I hardly knew Aunt Clarissa, and I can't think why she mentioned me, unless it was for completeness. All the rellies, as Australians say."

"I can assure you all the rellies were not in the will. Just a select few."

"So I ...? Oh well, never mind. I imagine things are in train for you to be declared the heir. It's a case of winner takes all, isn't it?"

"Well, nearly all."

Roderick Massey swallowed any disappointment he might feel.

"It must be very confusing for you, meeting all these Cantelo relatives again."

"It is, rather. It's as if a film had suddenly skipped forward twenty years and the make-up artists had had to get busy putting lines on faces, grey powder on the temples, and so on. Luckily I haven't made any mistakes so far, never taken one person for another, which would have been seized on. And it would have been easy to do, because there is a sort of family likeness that several of them have, and others not."

"I suppose so," said Roderick, looking round the room. "I don't really know most of the people here. My mother wasn't a Cantelo, of course, and my father took off soon after I was born."

"And your mother married someone called Massey?"

"That's right, and changed my name then. Quite right too. I've had practically nothing to do with my birth father, and I'm very fond of my adoptive father, so it *feels* right to call him father. What else? It would feel very odd to call Paul Cantelo father if he reappeared."

"I suppose it would ... Actually *my* father has just reappeared."

"Oh? Had you lost touch?"

"Totally."

"How did it feel?"

"Odd, as you've just said. But in this case there's no rival or alternative father. It was not much more than re-establishing contact with a not-particularly-close friend. I felt all the time

I was checking for resemblances to and differences from the person I had once known."

Roderick nodded.

"I see. Interesting."

"Complicated by the fact that he claimed to be a new and changed personality – caring, responsible, possessor of all the cardinal virtues."

"But you're sceptical?"

"By nature."

"Merlyn!" It was Edward and Francis, the latter newly arrived, who came over carrying glasses of whisky and barged into the tête-à-tête, breaking it up, whether intentionally or otherwise. As Roderick slipped away Merlyn turned reluctantly to his cousins. He felt moderately close to Edward – the tie of being schoolfellows as well as of the same family oddly surviving all the years of separation.

"Back in the lions' den?" giggled Francis.

"That's right. Caroline dangled a children's party before me, and I couldn't refuse."

"Ha!" said Edward ironically. "But at least you did come. Does that mean that when you come into your inheritance you're not going to cast us all off? Not going to wash your hands of us, like Pip did with the Gargeries?"

"No, why should I? It's only Rosalind who's making a fuss. With some help from her husband and from Aunt Emily perhaps. I don't think there was ever a chance of my getting close to Rosalind, though Barnett may be having a change of heart."

"Barnett is generally seen in the family as long-suffering. But we may have got it all wrong." Francis tittered as he spoke. "You've got to remember, Merlyn, that we're not a close family. We never have been."

"Haven't we?" said Merlyn, creasing his brow. "I know all of you, or nearly all."

"That's because your mother was generally loved, and the

one member of the family all the rest got on with. When she died, and when your father went to pieces, everyone felt protective of you, asked you round, slipped you five shillings."

"That's true. I remember the five shillingses."

"But how many of them visited Clarissa, how many of them asked her, or any of the other Cantelos, to their homes? The truth is, many of them loathe each other, and the others are suspicious of each other. It's that sort of family."

"It's true," said Edward, in genial corroboration. "They're always in competition with each other." He turned towards the window. Out in the garden Caroline's husband was engaged with about a dozen children, cooking them hamburgers and sausages, and generally making sure they had a good time. If he was being forced into being a good father for the day, he was disguising it well. "And marrying a Cantelo is not much fun either," added Edward.

"Like buying into a high-powered business?" suggested Merlyn.

"Something like that. Though none of the husbands of Cantelo girls was ever invited into the actual family clothing business in Grandfather Cantelo's time," said Edward. "I'm sure poor old Barnett would have jumped at any offer, but by the time he married Rosalind the family business was nothing more than a tidy little sum in the bank balances of the family survivors. I'm sorry for all the male mates – the female ones too, for different reasons."

"I got the impression Barnett is built on the same lines as Rosalind herself. True soul mates, but I may be wrong ... Do any of you know of a book, a novel, based on the Cantelos?"

The looks he got back were both blank.

"Who'd base a book on us?" asked Francis. "We don't know any novelists, or any local historians either."

"I didn't suggest it was by anyone well-known, or even professional. But I've dipped into the book – there's a copy in the Leeds Library – and it gave the sort of impression you've just been giving me as well: that the family was brought up on the sort of system that set each of them against the others. Quite possibly with the best of motives."

"Sounds a wow of a novel," said Edward. "But it also sounds as if someone had been observing Grandfather Cantelo and his brood."

"Possibly someone from the inside," said Merlyn, "someone who had experienced the system."

"One of the brood, you mean?"

"Quite possibly. The book is called *Family Business*, and it was published privately —"

"You mean vanity publishing?" asked Edward.

" Almost certainly – under the name of X. Cantelo."

The faces of Edward and Francis lingered around the other faces in the room. There were, though, only two faces there who were part of Grandfather Cantelo's extensive brood. The face of Emily was dismissed almost at once, but Marigold's was not. Merlyn noticed that Roderick Massey was observing them, hand clutched tight around a glass of whisky. He was more interested than Merlyn would have expected. Merlyn nodded towards his Aunt Marigold.

"She's enjoying herself," said Merlyn, looking at the brown liquid in her glass. He raised his voice and went over to her. "I say it's good to see you enjoying yourself, Auntie Marigold."

"Oh, I am," said the old woman, her face amused but cunning. "Someone rich must have brought along this whisky. Poor Carrie could never have afforded it. I wonder who it was."

She looked at him roguishly.

"You like a drop of Scotch, do you, Auntie?"

"Oh, I do. My husband – God rest his soul, if there is one and if he had one – used to have a dozen favourite malts, and taught me to distinguish among them, sight unseen ... Oh, those were the days. We had a bit of money then ... Pity this is blended, but better that than all this white wine piss."

"I'm afraid I don't remember much about Uncle Stanley," said Merlyn.

"Lovely man. Funny too. He'd have been a semi-invalid by the time you came to live in Leeds. We married late, and Caroline was a very late first baby. But I got through it, thanks to plenty of malt whisky and the smoke from Stanley's cigars, which I always loved. Oh, those ante-natal people these days don't know they're born!"

"It must be a great joy to you to have Caroline and the children around you."

Marigold puckered up her mouth.

"So so. But they're not around, thank the Lord. I live on my own, fend for myself, with a little help from the Social Services. Carrie's a poor thing — no spirit, and a bit sly to boot. But the girls are fine. They'll come good."

"I was reading a book about the Cantelos the other day."

There was a pause, and Merlyn noticed Aunt Emily position herself where she could be seen by her sister. There was a sour expression on her face, and it was clear she was taking control of the situation.

"A book about the Cantelos?" said Aunt Marigold at last. "There's no such thing. We're not important enough."

"This is a book by a Cantelo. It's in the form of a novel."

"Well I never! Who's been publishing stuff about us?"

"This was published twenty-five or thirty years ago. When you were a young woman."

"And the world was young and gay." She cackled. "I don't remember a world like that. It never was for us. I only started living when I got married and moved out of Congreve Street. Stanley Sowden – Dr. Stan, people called him – was the making of me. I had never had my independence before, more fool me for not standing up for it."

"The author of this book was 'X. Cantelo', Auntie Marigold. So naturally I wondered ..."

The cackle came again.

"The X was meant to make you think, I imagine. Well, you needn't think of me. I couldn't write a book to save my life. I should think it's ten years since I wrote a letter."

"This was a long time ago."

"So you say. I never made much of a fist with a pen. I was the dunce of the school and the shame of my family. My father could have written a book. One of my brothers could have too. But the only one of the girls who could have was —"

"Clarissa."

"Yes, your fairy-auntie Clarissa."

"Come along, Marigold," said Aunt Emily, her interruption brutal and final. "You wanted to go into the garden with the children, didn't you? Let's get you out there."

She had stationed herself behind the wheelchair, and now directed it straight at Merlyn. He had to jump aside to let them pass, a fact that seemed to give Emily pleasure.

"Mowed down by a wheelchair," said the inane voice of Malachi in his ear. "Not a heroic way to go."

"I'm not looking for a heroic way to go," said Merlyn firmly. "I'm much too young to be thinking of 'going' at all."

"Of course you are. And remember I'm of the same generation, even if a somewhat older branch. Sorry I'm late. I had to get two buses after work." Malachi's bird-like glance shot around the room, then back to Merlyn, beaming with satisfaction. "Well, aren't we one big happy family? And there's even one I don't know." Merlyn was aware that Emily had paused on her way out to the garden beside the door to the hallway, and was watching the pair of them closely. He was beginning to get very uneasy vibrations from Emily. "I think he must be Roderick Massey," Malachi went on. "A nice-looking young fellow he is too! One has heard so much, so many things, about him."

"Malachi!"

"I really don't need bossing about, Emily," he said, turning to face her. "I've had a hard day with the punters, and I came here for a bit of relaxation. Golly — whisky!" He poured himself a good-sized slug and then took a swig from it. "Luxury! Bliss! You may consider yourself guardian of the family name, Emily, but nobody appointed you that or asked you to be it."

"Malachi, you are a loose-tongued fool of a man, and I —"

"You want to protect the family from me and my wayward fancies. How right! How dutiful! How completely you show yourself your father's child!"

"Shut it, Malachi!" The command came this time from Edward. "You can't be drunk on half an inch of whisky."

"And a stiffener on the way here. Everyone needs a stiffener before facing his nearest and dearest. But you're quite right. I'm not drunk. I am a soothsayer possessed. And the sight of a newcomer to the family circle —"

"What *is* all this?" demanded Roderick Massey, pushing himself forward into the family group. "I can't understand why everyone seems to be talking about *me*. Especially as, apart from Merlyn, no one has swapped a word with me so far."

"Embarrassment, dear boy," said Malachi, waving an airy hand. "They don't quite know how to approach you. Or who to approach you *as*."

"*As*? But I —"

"It's a wise child — But perhaps you don't know the quotation. Best say no more. But —"

"No buts, Malachi!" boomed Emily. "Just zip up your mouth."

"But I just wanted to say to Merlyn that he left Leeds too young to understand all this, and he was never told by Clarissa because she lived in the future not the past. It was the past she was afraid of."

"Afraid of?" boomed Emily again. "What nonsense! She was just a crank, a silly, credulous crank."

"She was a lot sharper than anyone here," put in Merlyn. "And a whole lot nicer, kinder, more generous."

"You've got us taped, haven't you," said Malachi spitefully, replenishing his glass. "Or so you think. But the point is that you won't understand the Cantelos by studying Clarissa, or Rosalind, or Emily, or any of us here."

Several of the family took steps forward, as if they were going to fall on Malachi and suffocate him to prevent him talking. His voice rose to counter-tenor pitch.

"You'll only find out about the Cantelos if you find out the truth about Grandfather Cantelo – clothier, town councillor, shirt-maker to the nation, and —"

"Malachi!"

"And — But I think I'll let you find that out for yourself, Merlyn."

He downed his glass, looking around him and preening himself with self-love. The expected explosion seemed to have been averted, but family members remained around him, and their intent was clearly not benign. Merlyn cast a glance of sympathy at Roderick Massey, then went over to the window. Out in the garden the contented eating of junk food had given way to shrill voices. The children were quarrelling. Anyone would think they were all Cantelos, Merlyn thought. Jackie and Angela's father was trying to stop the ill-feeling, but his inexperience showed. Caroline was watching from the back door with a tiny, satisfied smile on her lips.

As he watched, Merlyn was conscious of a shadow at his shoulder. Looking around he saw it was Roderick Massey, his face red, but imbued with sympathy. When he spoke it was with a louder voice, one fused with indignation or grievance.

"You really were well out of it, Merlyn, all those years you were away. They're a terrible lot, aren't they?" His voice rose still louder. "I didn't tell you earlier, because it didn't seem to be the time or place. I've never met my father, but I have spoken to him on the phone. Paul Cantelo, that's how I think of him now. He's a professor of creative writing in a university in Arkansas. I wanted to know why he had taken off from Leeds and never been heard of since. He said he took off because he wasn't my father and was sickened by family life. He said I wasn't to have any doubt at all: I'm not his child. So you see," he said, turning round, "I'm not a Cantelo, and my God I'm glad I'm not! What a crew! I've seen football crowds that have been better behaved. I'm only glad I'm seeing the last of you."

And he turned and barged out through the door, then out the front door to the street. Merlyn looked all around. There was no sympathy on any of the faces, merely curiosity and, on Malachi's, a definite expression of self-satisfaction.

He banged down his glass and followed Roderick through the family group and out through the front door. Enough was enough, and with his family the saturation point was reached earlier than with most families. In fact, he would be glad when his mission was accomplished. He said as much to Danielle, on the phone to her later that night.

"Well, things seem to be about to hot up. I'm getting to know more about my aunts and cousins, and I've just met a Cantelo who has apparently discovered that he's not a Cantelo, and is quite delighted."

"Sounds like a sensible person. You should cast off your Cantelo inheritance."

"That may sound good, but you forget it would leave me with just the Docherty inheritance. Probably not much of an improvement, if any."

"Forget all about them, and just come home."

"Tempting. You know, England should feel like home, but somehow it doesn't. I've been gone too long."

"Have you tried to make contact with your father?"

"No, but he's made contact with me. I found him waiting for me here in the hotel when I got back a few days ago."

"What did you feel?"

"Nothing very much. He's the same shambling, unsatisfactory piece of humanity that he always was."

"Popping up because he's heard about the money?"

"Maybe, but I don't think so. Money was never one of his major weaknesses. Maybe he's reappeared because he feels guilty about his neglect of me. Maybe he himself doesn't know why he sought me out, so I've got no chance of getting to the bottom of it."

There was a pause at the other end.

"Merlyn, what is all this about? What are you getting out of it, or hoping to get?"

"It's difficult to describe, but I think it's a sort of clearance. A clean sweep. Something that had to be done before I could move on."

"Is that ever possible? You are what you are because of what you've done and who and where you've come from."

"It doesn't feel like that. Everything I'm meeting up with here seems like a pile of dust in a forgotten corner of my life."

"And what are you going to move on *to*?"

"To marriage with you, and a completely fresh start."

"Really? Well, I look forward to being asked properly. Then I can think how I will reply properly."

And she put down the phone, but Merlyn could imagine the teasing expression on her face.

Chapter Ten
Déja Vu

The acrimonious little party at Caroline's gave Merlyn a lot to think over, or, more accurately, to speculate about. It seemed as though he was being pointed – by Malachi, if by no one else – in the direction of Grandfather Cantelo. Why had Malachi not done this during their meal together, as payment for his treat? But Merlyn dismissed this thought as soon as it came into his mind. Malachi was a disorganised mess of impulses, and to try and detect a clear and logical path through his behaviour would be a futile struggle: Malachi had acted as he did at Caroline's to annoy his fellow Cantelos, nothing more sinister than that. He could have instinctively held back on his insinuations about Grandfather Cantelo to Merlyn from the natural cunning that would tell him that they could form the basis for another free meal.

The thought even struck Merlyn that the Cantelos' obvious opposition to any revelations about old Cantelo could have been staged. Any fool could have guessed that Malachi's broad hints would only spur Merlyn on to further investigations in that direction, and this could have been exactly what they all wanted: to keep him away from ... from what, exactly? And from whom?

That possibility had to be taken into consideration, but it still seemed to Merlyn impossible to ignore the old man. He seemed to have sown in his time several fieldsful of troubles – or to have had them attributed to him. Merlyn had been struck, while Roderick Massey spoke, about a non-sequitur in his harangue: Paul Cantelo's claim not to be Roderick's father rang true, and so did Roderick's relief: he rather suspected that he had accepted Caroline's invitation precisely with the idea of wiping the Cantelo dust from his shoes, which, stoked

up by whisky, he had duly done. But there was a leap from saying that Paul was not his father to saying that he was not a
Cantelo. Merlyn's feeling on the morning after the party was
that the last people he ought to go to for information were his
Cantelo relations, and on impulse he slipped, later in the day,
into the offices of the *West Yorkshire Chronicle* and various sister papers and asked to consult back files in their library. Once
settled in he saw they had serried shelves of the *Dictionary of
National Biography*, and quickly ascertained that Grandfather
had not made it into those pages. He knew that Clarissa had
not owned the house in Congreve Street very long before he
started going there, so he put her father's death as in the late
1970s. Luckily there was an index year by year to the paper,
and he discovered an obituary for him in the issue of October
5th, 1978.

It was not very revealing. It began: "Merlyn Cantelo was
born in 1905 ..." He guessed that the older Merlyn's mother
had had a dated and Pre-Raphaelitish nostalgia for Arthurian
legends, extending even to its wizard. The fairly brief notice
went on:

"He inherited the family clothing concern in 1938, when it
was a modest but thriving business. It survived triumphantly
the wartime difficulties, and in the 1950s the Cantelo shirt –
usually checks or large squared patterns and a wool-mix material – was a national success and a basic must-have clothing
item for the well-dressed middle-class male. This success bol-
stered the firm, and enabled it to survive the switch in popular taste symbolised by the name of Carnaby Street. Cantelo
was helped in his long career in the clothing industry by his
loyal wife Elspeth and a large and talented family. His wife's
death in 1971 hit Cantelo hard, and the firm suffered, being
sold in 1975. His last years were sad, and his mental decline,
more notable by reason of the vigour and originality of his
mind in earlier days, meant that his death yesterday was in the

nature of a relief to the man himself and his family."

It was brief, less than hagiographic, but suggestive. As Merlyn sat back in his chair considering the account several things struck him. Though the firm had "suffered" from his mental decline, there was no suggestion that it was anything other than a going concern when it was sold. Where had the money gone? So far as he knew, and in spite of what the obituary said about help from his family, none of the children (sons, it would have to be, Merlyn guessed) had gone into business with his father, and might have hoped to take over. This may have been because they realised he would never loosen the reins of his control, and would be an impossible partner.

He got a strong sense from the obituary that the earlier Merlyn had been a first-rate businessman by the standards of the time, and that his years of decline had not only been sad, but had been in some way embarrassing. That would certainly bear further investigation.

But further investigation *where*? *Of whom*? Malachi, of all the Cantelos, seemed the only possibility, but he mistrusted the man's butterfly mind, powered by malice and some real or imagined grievances. People who had married into the family might be a possibility, but Caroline's husband and Rosalind's had both entered the family well after Grandfather Cantelo's death. There was no evidence that Gerald's wife or Emily's husband were still of this world, or that they would co-operate if they were. Of outsiders the family lawyer Mr Featherstone might well know most, but he was by nature a close man who would say as little as possible. A good lawyer keeps his mouth buttoned.

Then Merlyn suddenly remembered his father.

He had married into the family in the years of its prosperity, and had been in communication with it, at the least, during Grandfather Cantelo's years of increasing senility. Merlyn's father and his mother had been, so far as he knew, a close pair, so he would have been in on all the family secrets. Ideal.

Doubts immediately invaded him. Because Merlyn himself had only the vaguest memories of his grandfather – memories, he rather thought, based on no more than one or two actual meetings. What picture he had of him in his mind was of an unruly grey beard and fearsome eyebrows – a physiognomy somewhere between God and the present Archbishop of Canterbury. The vagueness of his memories did not suggest that there had been much traffic between the Dochertys and his mother's father.

Still, the more he thought about it, the more he became convinced that Jake was the best bet, or at least the best of a bad bunch. He would be inhibited by no vestigial loyalty to the Cantelos, he would be impartial, and he would be bribable. The moment this last thought came into Merlyn's head he drove it out. He had once talked to a woman whose father had collected British folk songs. At the sight of a half-crown in the palm of his hand, aged crones in remote Scottish glens had obliged in cracked tones with an apology for a tune that the man's daughter was convinced they had thought up that very moment. And these songs had entered instantly the Folk Song Society's treasury of our musical heritage. Mention money and you're given what it is thought you are after. He was not conscious of knowing what he wanted as far as information about Grandfather Cantelo was concerned. He just wanted to know the truth.

He dropped into Waterstone's bookshop when he left the newspaper offices and bought a road map of the Sheffield area. Then he went along to the Leeds Public Library and looked up in the telephone directories J. Docherty of Carlyn Street. He knew his father would never go ex-directory. There he was at number 35.

"Daddy, I hardly know you," sang Merlyn to himself. But it was time to get to know him. And through him to get to know his grandfather a whole lot better.

The next day, Wednesday, Merlyn took off for Sheffield in mid-morning, taking it easy, going off the motorway for a leisurely half pint, trying to think through his tactics before he arrived. He neared Sheffield, ignored exit roads to the dreadful Meadowhall shopping centre, and got to Carlyn Street about half-past one. He drove slowly up it, and identified number 35 before he arrived outside it. It was a few doors away from an intersection with a major road, and had a Chinese takeaway on the corner. It was a warm day, and windows were open in the solidly built Victorian house, and voices but not words could be heard. Merlyn parked outside the house next door and opened his car window. Rap music was coming from upstairs, but now voices and words could be heard.

"If you'd gone to fucking school today I wouldn't be yelling at you now," yelled Jake's voice. "There's nothing wrong with you."

"I didn't say there was. I'm supposed to be studying for GCSEs but there's no classes today worth wasting time or bus-fare on," came back a younger voice – that, surely of the brilliant young Jason.

"If you think you're brighter than your teachers you're heading for a fall, young man."

"Everyone's brighter than our French teacher. They should have brought over a French village idiot – at least the pronunciation would have been better. I get far more out of just reading the set texts."

"Well go and read them in the public fucking library, and turn off that awful CD on the way out."

A minute or two later the music stopped. Merlyn sat looking in his driving mirror. The front door opened and a pleasant-looking schoolboy came out, banging the door behind him. He wondered if arguments such as he had just heard were commonplace, part of a regular routine.

The house was quiet. Merlyn decided to let his father have a bit of peace, to put him in a better mood. He slipped out of the car and went to the Chinese takeaway, emerging ten minutes later with prawns and cashew nuts, fried rice and a plastic fork. He settled himself in the car and began eating. He was half-way through his meal when a young woman breezed down the street and through the gate to number thirty-five. She was about eighteen, blonde, nubile, and dressed in jeans and a t-shirt. She let herself through the front door. Merlyn waited for shouting, but beyond a call of "Hi, Jake – I'm just passing through" there was nothing. He was just finishing his meal when the door opened again and the girl came out, a well-stuffed rucksack on her back, and a small case in her hand.

"She's leaving home," he thought, his mind reverting to the music of his childhood.

He licked the fork, got out of the car and stuffed the cartons and plastic bag into a bin. Then he went through the gate and up to the front door. There was a pause after he had rung the bell, then shuffling feet along the hall.

"Merlyn!"

Jake's face seemed to be torn between interest (rather than pleasure) and regret at the interruption to his nap. His hair was ruffled, one of his feet was shoved into a slipper, and he looked, apart from a gleam of roguishness in his eyes, all of his sixty-odd years. He obviously decided that he was, on the whole, pleased and a touch flattered that his visit to Leeds had elicited from Merlyn such a prompt response. He stood aside and ushered him into the living room.

"You'll have a can, won't you?" he asked, with appeal in his voice. Cans obviously figured big and enticingly in his day-to-day routine.

"Just wet the bottom of the glass," said Merlyn. "I'm sure you can drink the rest."

"I expect so," said Jake, his smile conspiratorial. Merlyn's taking the trouble to seek him out had obviously given him the confidence to be himself, and that was preferable to the rather bogus figure he had presented at their last encounter. "Roxanne should be home soon. It's her half-day at Sheffield Jail. Jason's studying in the public library, and Sandra's half living at home, half with her boyfriend, depending on whether she wants a meal cooked for her or whether she's willing to do it herself. Children!"

"And your own little girl?"

"Win? She's at school. I'll have to fetch her at three-thirty if I can't get Roxanne to do it. Here — is that enough for you?"

"Plenty," said Merlyn, taking the glass. He looked around the living room. Newspapers, *Private Eye*, school books, compact discs, beer cans and half-empty wine bottles covered most of the available table and chair places, and littered the floor. Merlyn had a strong sense of déja vu. "Ah, Wilderness!" he muttered to himself.

"Clear yourself a place," said Jake, doing just that. "Some things don't change, you notice."

"It's fine," said Merlyn insincerely, clearing and sitting.

"So to what do we owe this honour?" asked Jake. "It's not a fortnight since we talked."

"It's information I want," said Merlyn. "I'd like to talk about the Cantelo family."

"I thought we had," said Jake.

"No, we haven't. We just talked about Clarissa. I'm getting interested in other figures."

"Why? Why don't you just take the money and run?"

"Because — oh, never mind. But you must have had a fair bit to do with the family, before Mum died."

Jake screwed up his face.

"Not that much. While we were engaged, I suppose, because most of the courtship took place in Leeds. Quarrelsome lot, I thought them. Oodles of bad feeling flying around. After we were married and came here to Sheffield to live, I did my best to avoid them. Your mother went home to see them from time to time, but not that often. She was rather fond of Clarissa and Paul, but beyond that —" Jake shrugged. Beyond that, very little, he implied.

"And what about Grandfather Cantelo?"

Jake shifted very obviously in his chair.

"Never saw much of him."

"What sort of person was he, in your view?"

"Just what you'd expect from someone heading a fairly important company. A bit pompous. A bit full of himself. No – totally full of himself. Saw himself as the fount of all wisdom ... I forgot to tell you they've been in touch from this DNA testing place, by the way."

Merlyn was puzzled. Why the uneasiness? Was this an attempt to change the subject?

"Oh yes, the Forensic Science Service."

"That's them. That's how I knew you were in the country, and still alive. I told them to get stuffed."

"Oh? Why?"

"They said they didn't really need any fresh samples, because they could access police ones I gave ... years ago. You know when. We discussed it. So I didn't see any point in wasting my time."

"I see ..." Merlyn thought hard, and then risked asking: "Why are you so uneasy?"

"I'm not uneasy," said Jake belligerently. "Just wondering where Roxanne's got to. I'd better be getting to school to fetch Win —"

"You're not uneasy about that. It's since I mentioned Grandfather Cantelo, isn't it? The man I was named after."

"Bloody silly name. Why name a boy after a wizard? Unless you're into Harry bloody Potter I suppose."

"You tell me."

"Well, it's really a question of why your grandfather was named that, isn't it? People always said it was because his mother was infatuated with Tennyson. Did he write about King Arthur and that lot?"

"He did, yes. Nobody reads it these days. Where did the 'y' come from?"

"Search me. I expect she thought it sounded more olde-worlde. Like the pubs that advertise 'pub fayre'."

"Maybe. But why call me after Grandfather Cantelo if you didn't like him?"

Again Jake shifted uneasily in his chair.

"Don't be so bloody naive, Merlyn. He was the one with the money. We thought you'd be put down for a hefty sum in his will if we did what he wanted."

"Oh, he wanted it, did he?"

"Thora was his favourite daughter. Anyway, he said that the original Merlin was named after *his* maternal grandfather. Ah! There's Roxanne. I've got to nip off and fetch Win. Hello, love. This is Merlyn, come to pay us a visit. Won't be a tick, then we can introduce him to his half-sister."

Roxanne was a matronly figure, perhaps in her early forties – much younger than her husband, but his rather childish insouciance and her air of greater responsibility made this less obvious. She had reddened hair and was wearing workaday, drab clothes. She turned to the door.

"I could go and fetch —" But the front door had slammed. Roxanne shrugged and sank down into a chair. Her smile was warm, tinged with satire. "Hello Merlyn. You're very welcome. I ought to set to and clear up this place a bit, but that's Jake's job, and I've had a hard day at work. Did he feed you beer? I expect you'd have preferred a coffee."

"I just had a mouthful. I'm driving. I think I made Jake a bit nervous."

"Maybe ... He's not a bad man, Merlyn, however bad a father he was to you. He's a bit feckless, definitely lazy, goes off at tangents the whole time, and he'll never really make anything of his life, not now. But he gets on all right with the kids — rows with them off and on —"

"I heard him and Jason, but it sounded all pretty normal."

"Getting him out of the house, I expect. He likes it to himself to have a snooze, watch the racing, whatever. He's just like their real father might have been — rows and threats, but underneath, *all right*. We're just a standard, normal family."

"When I said I thought he was uneasy, it wasn't so much that he feels guilty about me, I don't think. His uneasiness seemed to start when I asked him about Grandfather Cantelo."

Roxanne looked mystified.

"Thora's dad?" She shrugged again. "Don't know anything about that. Way before my time. I know about her, just as I *know* about you and Deborah. I think Win's taken Deborah's place now. What I'm saying is we don't *talk* about any of you. We're 'now' people, I suppose, not people who want to churn over things in the past."

"Fair enough."

"So you'll have to talk it over with him, I'm afraid."

"If he will, of course," said Merlyn. "I get the impression that's the last thing he wants to do."

"You have to force him into a corner. Make it so that it's easier for him to talk than to run away. I have to do that all the time, even on quite trivial matters. It's become a sort of game. I quite like it."

"You know the rules and the match-play techniques. I don't think I have the skills."

"It's your best chance. Here he is now."

Jake came through from the hallway with a small girl clutching his hand and looking at their visitor shyly. Jake was now smiling the blissful smile of one who thinks he has just circumvented a difficulty and with one bound is free. He led Win over to Merlyn.

"This is Merlyn, darling. He's just dropped in on a visit. We used to know each other very well, but we haven't met up for a long, long time." He gave Merlyn a meaningful look that meant that he considered it a bit too early to tell Win that he was her brother, or a sort-of brother. With perhaps a subsidiary meaning that with a bit of luck Merlyn might disappear from their lives once again, and explanations would not need to be given. But Merlyn reminded himself that it was Jake who had introduced himself back into his son's life, not vice versa, so perhaps he was interpreting the expression wrongly.

"Go upstairs and put your school things away, Win," said Roxanne obligingly. As the little girl scampered away, Merlyn said:

"You were going to explain, Jake, why I was given the name Merlyn, after my grandfather."

Jake's face changed to one of obstinacy.

"I told you: we were hoping for something nice in the will. Now give it a rest, Merlyn. You're becoming a bore."

"I'm sure I am. But the fact is, Jake, I don't remember you as particularly greedy, or as a particularly calculating person, apart from wondering where the price of your next drink was coming from."

"I wasn't, Merlyn, but still —"

Merlyn came up close to him, with a strong sense of being younger and fitter than his father. Jake took two steps back and found himself in a corner, with his face showing surprise that he'd been trapped.

"So it was my mother who insisted that I be named after her father?" Merlyn persisted.

"Well, she wanted it, yes."

"And did you get the idea later, after she was dead, that Grandfather Cantelo might have been my father? And was that why you never gave a damn for me after Mum died?"

Jake looked at him with the terror of a trapped weasel. Then he raised his right leg and gave Merlyn's left kneecap a hefty kick. As Merlyn bent down in agony Jake scooted by him out of the room and then out of the house.

"I don't think I've got the hang of this game," said Merlyn.

Chapter Eleven
In Search of Times Past

It was six days later, the Tuesday of the next week, that Merlyn received notification from the Forensic Science Service that their investigation had concluded that he was the son of Thora Docherty, née Cantelo, by her husband John Jacob Docherty. The letter appended two pages of succinctly summarised scientific reports, and the reports noted that the full scientific records of the investigation would be retained at the offices of the FSS for twenty years, in case of any dispute arising from the conclusions that had been come to. The bill for the service was enclosed.

"Eureka!" said Merlyn.

His training as a lawyer and as an economist made him instinctively take thought before acting. Sometimes, indeed, in his job at the European Union, his department bosses had meditated for several years before taking action, or deciding not to take any, on reports laid before them, and experience told. However Merlyn made an appointment next day with Mr Featherstone, then drove to Stanbury and went walking on the Haworth moors to think the consequences of the letter through.

At some stage his father Jake had become convinced that he was not in fact his son's biological father, and, more importantly, that this son was the result of an incestuous relationship between Merlyn Cantelo and his daughter Thora. This conclusion, typical of Jake's random thinking and undisciplined powers of reasoning, was conceived after his wife's death, so it seemed likely that it came into his mind as a result of Merlyn Cantelo's behaviour in the last years of his life.

Merlyn decided that his grandfather had gone off the rails sexually after, and as a consequence of, his wife's death. She, as *Family Business* had made clear, was his prop, his centre, his butterer-up-in-chief.

Had his grandfather's aberrant behaviour included incest with one or more of his other daughters, and was it this that had given Jake his idea? Had his grandfather in fact had a much earlier sexual relationship with Thora that had been without result? Or had he had eyes in those last years for any young woman in his vicinity, including the wives of his own sons? This idea appealed to Merlyn as more likely, as the sort of thing that would send Jake off on his hare-brained course of thinking. It also threw an interesting spotlight on Roderick Massey, and on his mother, the wife of Paul Cantelo.

He tried to get a picture in his mind of the Cantelo family and its dynamics. A strong, opinionated man, of considerable power in his smallish world, who has ruled his family by dividing them each from each other, loses his wife, the emotional, sexual and ego-boosting prop in his life, and starts behaving like a dictator in the last, demented years of his rule. That seemed to make sense, to cohere as a picture.

Other possibilities grew up around it: that Merlyn Cantelo's behaviour earlier had been similar, but more discreet; that his behaviour was aggravated by the fact that he was losing, or had already lost, the control he had once enjoyed over his family, particularly the male members, and hated his loss of power.

When Merlyn went to the Cantelos' lawyer in East Parade next morning he took the papers from the Forensic Science Service along with him. However the firm had been associated in the request for a DNA test, and already had a copy of the letter and the appended scientific material. Mr Featherstone's manner was notably warmer than it had been on the previous meeting.

"I think the whole unnecessary dispute can now be put to rest," he said, shaking Merlyn's hand. "You are Miss Cantelo's nephew Merlyn Docherty, therefore the provisions of her will based on the assumption that you are alive can be put into effect. Very satisfactory all round."

"Not to some of my relatives," Merlyn pointed out.

"Perhaps not. They will no doubt receive the news of the new development in different ways. I have already drafted a letter informing them of the Forensic Science Service's findings, and I shall send it today. Now, there's the question of the house in Congreve Street —"

"Yes, I've thought about that," said Merlyn, sinking again into the chair in Mr Featherstone's office. "I presume that the firm that boarded up the place can now undo their work?"

"Of course. I can phone them as soon as you like."

"I wonder if you could ask them to change the locks, both front and back, and deliver the keys to me at the Crowne Plaza Hotel?"

Mr Featherstone nodded thoughtfully.

"Ah yes. You think that necessary?"

"I think some members of the family had free access from the time of Aunt Clarissa's death to the time it was boarded up, so it's probable that I'm merely asking you to shut the stable door. Frankly, I don't think the contents were of great value, though the house is. But still ... I have to say I don't like the idea of anyone in the family having free access at any time I'm not there."

"Naturally. In any case, this is a perfectly normal procedure when a property changes hands."

"I suppose so ... I wonder if you could satisfy my curiosity about something – merely to save time, because it's a matter that's already in the public domain."

"I will try," said Featherstone, his caution returning in some measure.

"I should like to know the terms of Grandfather Cantelo's will."

"Hmmm," said Mr Featherstone, obviously not entirely pleased. "That is going some way back into the past."

"One often has to, to understand the present. There is a great gap in my knowledge of the family time-wise, remember."

"Quite, quite ... You have to remember that the old man's last years were ... shall we say sad?"

"Sad may cover it. And embarrassing I gather?"

"I believe so," said Mr Featherstone quietly to show his discretion. "I know no details, and don't wish to know any. There was talk in his last years of his affairs being taken out of his hands."

"*Really*? And was his will made in those years?"

"Yes, it was. In 1975. There was one great difficulty about that proposal to take control of his affairs."

"My grandfather himself?"

"Exactly. He would have fought it. And really the main evidence – apart from the usual, fairly trivial signs of old age – was in his ... irregular behaviour. It was not possible to argue that this made him incapable of managing his own affairs. He just —"

"Went off the rails?"

"Exactly. And the people arguing for affairs to be taken out of his hands would have been accused of the most obvious self-interest. He would certainly have fought it, and would have won. The will itself was perfectly sane, and in accordance with views he had held for much of his lifetime."

"And the terms of the will?"

"He left the house to Clarissa – his favourite daughter, and the one who looked after him in his last years. And the accumulated fortune, including the money from the sale of Cantelo and Co., the clothing firm, was to be divided among all his children including Clarissa."

"I see. Divided equally?"

"No," said Mr Featherstone decisively, as if he was taking on the character of the man he was talking about. "He had always brought up his family to believe that the men were for the hurly-burly of earning their own livings, making their own way in the world, while the women were to provide the graces of life – the beauty, the delicacy ... It's not a fashionable viewpoint."

"Practically actionable ... But some of the women were married."

"Yes, both Emily and Marigold, though Marigold's husband was much older than her. Your mother was dead, but her share was left to Clarissa in trust for you."

"Ah. She always said she had money that was really mine. It financed my stay with an English family in Italy and my years at university."

"And what's left will come to you now, with all of Clarissa's own money."

"So how was the money divided up?"

"The boys shared thirty per cent of it – ten per cent each. The women shared the remainder – seventeen and a half per cent each. So all of them got an appreciable, a *useful* sum."

"But the men very much less than the women. Was he annoyed none of the men went into the family business?" asked Merlyn, something that had bothered him.

"Maybe. Who knows? He could hardly say so. Or that Gerald was a dead loss, Paul unsatisfactory, and Hugh on his way to not needing any help. He'd always put a lot of emphasis on independence, initiative, carving your own way."

"If you were a man."

"Exactly. He was at least consistent, in tune with his own beliefs."

"Yes, indeed. But I don't think I'd have liked Grandfather Cantelo all the same." Merlyn got up. "I'll wait to hear that the house has been opened up, and the locks changed. Then I

might go to a car dealer and buy myself an old banger, something dispensable, for use during the rest of my time here."

"You don't anticipate settling in Leeds, then?"

Merlyn shook his head.

"I have a job in Brussels." Then he decided to be honest.
"Somehow the call of family seems just as faint now as it has
done for the last twenty years."

Mr Featherstone smiled bleakly. He liked dry humour. In
fact, it was the only type of humour he recognised.

So Merlyn fetched his car from the hotel car park and took
it back to the hire firm. Then he went to a used-car dealer's
ten minutes walk from Congreve Street, and looked over their
older stock, most of which he suspected of having had their
mileages gently massaged. Honest Sam of Sam's Wheels followed him around, a hulking presence, to see how high up the
price range he could be expected to go.

"What you want it for then?" he asked.

"Just to get me around for a few weeks, then to get me
home to Brussels," said Merlyn.

"Brussels? You one of these Common Market bureaucrats?
You could afford something better than an old banger."

"I could. But I've got a BMW at home."

And he picked up a ten-year-old Ford for £1500, went
through all the paperwork and drove it to the Crowne Plaza
Hotel, where a set of house keys was awaiting him at
Reception. He paid his bill, packed, and drove off to the house
he must temporarily consider his home.

The houses in Congreve Street were too old to have any
garages, and the streets of Leeds, he had found out during his
stay, were not the best place to leave cars of any pretensions.
Still, beggars can't be choosers, he thought, as he left the old
car outside the front gate.

So Merlyn went back to the house where he had spent
some fairly happy years of adolescence. He went back, how-

ever, without any expectations of sentimental reactions. He was aware that his sudden exile at the age of sixteen had left him cool, uninvolved, a man who stood on his own. If he felt strong emotion about anything in his current situation it was for Clarissa, not for her house, even though at the time when he had lived there she had been just beginning to make it her own. Warmth, fellow-feeling, sympathy, sheer fun, all these he had got – it seemed sometimes as if for the first time – from his aunt, but the house had been a mere setting, hardly more than a stage set, apart from the little room that was his bedroom. Love and security meant people, and for Merlyn houses could not offer more than a symbolic version of them.

Unboarded, the house looked like any other in the street. He got out of the car and raised his hand to Mr Robinson further down, who was cutting back shrubs in his front garden. Then he turned, took out the shining new keys, and in the declining evening sun went into his old home.

The hall, he noticed for the first time, had not been redecorated since his time in the house, in the early Eighties. Typical of Clarissa to take the view that a hall was a mere convenience, a transition, and not worth bothering about. Its neglect meant it exuded a feeling of desolation, non-occupation, though Clarissa had only been dead for three or four weeks. Merlyn turned into the dining room, where the wake had been held. Then a collection of tables, large and small, had been dotted around its length, but now it had reverted to its state, presumably, in Clarissa's later years: the large table had been shunted to beside the wall – no big family dinners in her time, then. In fact, the large table had been virtually unused even in his time in the house, and Clarissa and he had, as often as not, eaten in the kitchen, or off their laps. A couple of the other tables were still in the centre of the room, but in spite of the fact that some redecoration had taken place in it, it seemed a space that had not had a purpose since the big family gatherings of Grandfather Cantelo's time, only regaining it briefly for the family get-together at the funeral.

Crossing the dim and probably dirty hallway he went into the sitting room. This was the centre of life in the house, but also Clarissa's professional backdrop as well. The low table surrounded by sofa and easy chairs still had packs of cards on it – ordinary playing cards, Tarot cards, and others Merlyn could not put a name to. The curtains were heavy and dark green, which Clarissa found a comfortable colour, but they would only be drawn closed in daytime if his aunt thought her current subject would be happier in near-darkness. On the whole she tried to establish an atmosphere of normality and everydayness, and eschewed any suggestion of the bizarre.

"Let's sit down, dear, and you can tell me a bit about yourself," she would say, and this opening part of the session could last anything from half an hour to an hour, and was usually thoroughly enjoyed by the clients, who had a strong vein of egotism (as well as credulity) in their make-up. When it finished and Clarissa got down to the real business of the consultation she had learnt quite as much as any more conventional counsellor would have done. Often she would have guessed what the consultation was about, and was on her way to working out the most sensible solution to her client's problem.

She sometimes talked about these sessions with the young Merlyn.

"I had a right old fool today," she would say. "He just wanted me to advise him to do what he'd decided to do already. I told him it would end in disaster."

"Why did you do that?" Merlyn asked.

"Because what fools decide to do normally does end in disaster."

The memories of his aunt when she was a vigorous, capable 45-year-old woman came flooding over Merlyn. He saw her at her writing desk (she had a whole string of correspondence-clients), he saw her coming through from the kitchen with one of her sizzling casseroles in her gloved hands, he saw her standing at the window commenting on life going by in the street.

"Mr Robinson would hardly exist without his dog," she had once said. "That and the doings of the neighbours. He's lost now number 15 only contains me, not the whole Cantelo clan. We gave his life an interest."

Remembering that remark, Merlyn now realised, as he had not at the time, that until Grandfather Cantelo died there had been at least some family activity centred on the Congreve Street house. Family had come and gone, mainly to visit the old man himself, with motives pure or self-interested as the case might be. After the house became Clarissa's there had been little or no activity. Why was that? Resentment at her inheriting the family home?

When he went upstairs those early memories of his aunt merged into later ones. By her bed was an extension telephone – an obvious precaution for an elderly person living on her own. It was from bed that she had often conducted her side of the conversations with him in the last year or so of her life. Those were sad memories. The vital, funny aunt had given way to someone who had to struggle to keep her conversation on an even keel, someone who knew she was failing but did not know how to conceal it. There had been no question in his own mind that she was sliding gently towards senility, but all suggestions that he come over, make arrangements for her care, met with agitation and blank refusal. She didn't want to be cared for, and that was that. Equally clear was the fact that she didn't want him to come back home, though she dearly wanted to see him. Merlyn had been made aware that her old conviction that he would be in danger was still strong.

So in those last phone calls – regular and loving as always – the poor mind slid backwards and forwards from wandering to urgency, from homely advice to vague, apocalyptic warn-ings. What part of all that rambling discourse was to be taken seriously, acted upon? That, he had never known.

"I'm writing something," Clarissa would say, and his heart would sink. It surely would be nothing more than evidence of her ramblings, testimony to mental decay. "It will explain everything," she would say, not even sounding convinced her-self. It would explain nothing, Merlyn thought. She still alighted on reality now and then, but she was incapable of sus-tained thought.

As he shut the door of his aunt's bedroom, overwhelmed by sadness and a sense of waste, another remark of hers came back to him.

"I'll put it in the usual place," she had said.

There had been "usual places" for a lot of things, to be col-lected by a lot of people – a key for young Rosalind, for emer-gencies, money for the paper boy, even a place where one or two favoured clients could collect a weekly horoscope. However the "usual place" for Merlyn was underneath the bedclothes in the airing cupboard. Money was left there for emergencies, and for paying any tradesman who called. This gave rise to standing jokes, and often the milkman or the baker's roundsman would wink when they received the warm notes and say:

"Nothing nicer than a well-aired fiver."

They were nice men, who probably hadn't the faintest idea who he was – probably thought he was a by-blow of Clarissa's, or her very-much-younger brother. Only the older residents of Congreve Street, in all probability, could have said precise-ly that he was the son of Thora, and that just because she had been a general favourite.

Merlyn wondered whether the airing cupboard still existed: central heating had been put in since his time, with probably a new boiler elsewhere. But when he went over to the large

Edwardian bathroom there it still was in the corner – a tall, white-painted cupboard stretching to the ceiling: not warm now, perhaps never warm, but still containing piles of bed-linen and smaller piles of clean clothes, some of which Merlyn recognised. He thought for a moment, swallowed, then slid his hand under the bottom of the pile of sheets.

He brought out two pages of exercise-book lined paper.

His heart stopped. He recognised the spidery, all-over-the-place handwriting of Clarissa's later letters to him. He was under no illusions. His aunt had been in no state of mind to lay out a coherent argument. There would be no answers on these pages.

Nevertheless he felt a distinct excitement as he took the sheets down to the sitting room, poured himself a glass of his Aunt Clarissa's brandy, with soda from the drinks cabinet and ice from the fridge, and sat down in the easy chair by the empty grate.

The pages were very difficult to decipher. But then, he told himself, so were her later letters, and these had in some ways trained him for the task: the first read-through gave you no more than a vague sense of what was on her mind. Then you had to set to and read again, and then again. As more and more of the letters became legible you got a clearer sense of what she was trying to say, though her mind was always sadly way-ward.

There was one line in the middle of the first page that, to one well-acquainted with her writing, was legible at once. It had clearly had pains taken with it.

"They were all in it except me."

So far so good, but still puzzling. Who were "they"? The family? That was the most likely explanation, Merlyn decided. But what was "it"? He took a sip of his drink, then deciphered a scrawled phrase that slanted down from the legible sentence.

"They knew that I would be the first"

There was no full stop. The first what? To condemn? To argue? ... To be suspected, Merlyn wondered.

The spidery trailings of some of the rest of the random jottings made him very sad. Here was Clarissa, trying to send him a message from the grave, and many of the things she wanted to say degenerated into total illegibility. The grave, as usual, would keep at least some of its secrets. Perhaps she hadn't been clear in her head what she wanted to say, and hence the illegibility.

But as he read the sentences through more often, as with the letters, more words and phrases became legible, or at least capable of some speculative reading. But might they be misreadings, sending him off at a tangent – perhaps never to realise his mistake? There was something that looked like

"Ros too y___"

Might that be "Rosalind too young?" The letters were so ill-formed that there was no way of telling. Still, the idea played around in the back of his mind. Too young for what? *When* had she been too young?

But having once made the leap into guesswork one little collection of jottings going over the page in various directions but written with the same pen and seeming to form a group seemed to give a message to him.

"Silly family p___? Or money?"

"Together, but by *one.*" (Underlined shakily three times.)

"If p. Merlyn wd not underst. *Not* a C."

Taken together the first and last seemed to be toying with motives for a deed, and one of them – family pride? – Merlyn himself, not a Cantelo, would not understand. Merlyn was sure he was the one intended by this note, not his namesake. Clarissa would never have referred to her father as Merlyn.

He folded the two sheets of paper and went upstairs. He knew what he would find when he opened his bedroom door, and he had deliberately not done so before. "Nothing's been altered," Clarissa had often said to him. Did he want, so late at night, to revert to his childhood, or his adolescence at least? He switched on the light, and suddenly the past was with him: he was sixteen again. He decided he could not take it in with a clear brain.

He went across the landing. In the guest bedroom was a single bed, with pillows and an eiderdown, though not made up. He decided he didn't need sheets and blankets, his aunt's preferred bedclothes, nor for that matter pyjamas, because the night was warm. He would sleep there, like the guest he, in a sense, was. He went downstairs to get himself a glass of water.

It was when he switched on the light in the kitchen and was standing with a glass at the sink that he heard noises. First they seemed like little moans, and he had nightmare visions of a woman lying wounded on the back step, visions that did not go away when what sounded like scratchings at the door succeeded the moans.

Then suddenly Merlyn was back twenty-odd years, in that same kitchen, and Alex, his aunt's mongrel dog, who sometimes disappeared on his nightly tiddle-walk before bedtime, would come back when someone was making a late-night milk drink or fetching a snack from the fridge, and he was afraid he would not get back in the warm before morning. Often the last person in the kitchen had been Merlyn.

He went and unbolted the door – barks accompanied that – and then opened it. A small brown bundle of long hair hurtled in and ran around the kitchen and hallway, yelping and snuffling in an ecstasy, then running back to sniff Merlyn's feet and bare legs, then back out to explore the whole ground floor room by room, obviously in quest of something.

"You won't find her, my girl," Merlyn said.

This was clearly Dolly, his Aunt Clarissa's last dog, whom he had heard about often enough on the phone. He blamed himself for not asking what had been done with her.

Presumably one of the neighbours had taken her in, or one of the family who didn't live too far away. Though both dogs and cats, he knew, could trail enormous distances back to their former homes, Dolly did not look as if she was at the end of an exhausting trek. He switched off the kitchen light and began to make his way upstairs. The dog barked its pleasure and got between his feet as he made for the light in the spare bedroom. Once on the landing Dolly darted straight into Clarissa's room and on to the bed. Merlyn heard whimperings when she found the bed was empty.

In the spare bedroom Merlyn finished undressing, got under the eiderdown and switched off the light. A minute later, as he expected, he felt the little dog jump on to his bed. His face was licked, as a sign of acceptance, and then Dolly settled into the space at the back of his knees. She gave a long, contented, withdrawing sigh, and soon he heard something rather like a genteel snore. Then he himself, less contented, less at peace, nevertheless sank into a healthy sleep.

He did not hear, in the early hours of the morning, the sound of a crash of some kind, several streets away, or the sound of the activity it aroused. Dolly got up, pushed her nose under the curtain, but saw nothing in the early morning light. She jumped back on the bed, walked around to find a new place that suited her, then flopped down. The two of them slept soundly until the front doorbell rang at seven-thirty.

The young woman outside the front door was wearing a dark blue uniform and a peaked cap. Merlyn, in hastily thrown-on trousers and unbuttoned shirt, blinked and did a double-take. He had a vague impression this might be a parking warden or a member of one of the social services who hadn't been told his aunt was dead.

"Is there some mistake?" he asked ungraciously. Then he looked down at the young woman's ID. Her name was Shirley Dutton and she was a WPC. "Oh – I'm sorry," said Merlyn hurriedly. "Is there anything I can do?"

"Are you Merlyn Docherty?"

"That's right."

"Did you buy a car yesterday, registration number M563 TUM?"

"Yes, I did. How did you—?"

Merlyn blinked again. His eye had strayed from the young woman's face to the street outside. Where his newly-acquired car had been was an empty space.

"Yes, I'm afraid —"

"Well, this is bloody quick!" exploded Merlyn. "I knew there were a lot of joyriders these days in Leeds, but just one night —"

"I'm afraid it's not as simple as that, sir. Do you mind if I come in?"

Merlyn stood aside and led her through to the sitting room. The young police woman looked around her.

"Are you the owner of this house, sir?"

"I am. Just inherited it, as a matter of fact. I took control of it yesterday, as well as buying the car."

"I see. I thought this didn't look like a man's room – if I'm not being rude."

"It's my Aunt Clarissa's. A well-known spiritualist and clairvoyant."

"I see." The woman blinked. "Well, that's something I haven't come across before."

"They have entries in the *Yellow Pages*, believe it or not."

"So you took possession of the house yesterday, and bought a fairly old car at the same time?"

"Yes. I'm not interested in staying in the country long, and I didn't want to fork out any more money to the car hire firm. You got on to me quickly."

"The computers at the DVLA are very efficient. We rely on them a lot ... So your aunt died recently?"

"About a month ago."

"But you've only just returned to Britain?"

"No, I've been in a hotel. I was back for the funeral – I timed it deliberately. Most of the family thought I was dead."

The young woman was bewildered.

"Why would they think that, sir?"

"Because that's what they were told. Actually I've been through all this with Sergeant Peace, from Millgarth Police Headquarters."

"Dexter Peace? Charlie? It's quite likely he'll be here before long."

"Good ... But can you put me in the picture? Is there usually so much police interest in a car stolen by a joyrider?"

WPC Dutton shook her head.

"No, of course there's not. It's usually a matter for the fire brigade and maybe one of us. This one didn't end with a fire, perhaps luckily, but it did end with a death. The young man in the car died when he crashed at high speed into a Heavy Goods Vehicle down the hill towards the Kirkstall cross-roads."

"I see. I'm sorry."

"There were probably others in the car, or at least one, but they got out and we haven't yet found any trace of them. The boy was dead on arrival at Leeds General Infirmary."

Merlyn looked hard at her.

"But there's something else, isn't there?"

"Yes. The accident happened towards three – two fifty-five to be precise. The car was turned over just above the Kirkstall Lites pub. We've been able to examine it."

It was like a strong hand gripping Merlyn's throat.

"Go on."

"The brakes seem to have been interfered with."

Merlyn's trunk fell forward and his hands went to hold his head. He found the information hard to absorb. Eventually he straightened up and looked at WPC Dutton.

"I feel like I've killed that young man myself."

"That's nonsense. I'm sure you've no reason to feel that. The person who put a hole in the brake pipe is the one who needs to feel that. Had you any reason to think that there was someone trying to kill you?"

"Not really. Though the suggestion had arisen ... I've tried to guard against anything like this happening by making a will, leaving everything to the NSPCC."

"That is, nothing to anyone in your family."

"That's basically it." He shook his head sadly. "Doesn't seem to have worked, does it?"

"I'm afraid it doesn't. Money wasn't the motive if someone is after you."

"Sergeant Peace knows all about this. If he's coming ..."

"Just wait one moment while I get on to Millgarth. I'll see if he is going to be on this one ..." She went to the front door and down to the gate, taking out her mobile. When she got through she nodded a few times and then came back to Merlyn at the door. "They're taking this very seriously. You can see why, can't you? Either these joyriders did this themselves – for added kicks, for a really exciting ride before they jumped out of the car —"

"They'd need to be off their heads."

"Some of them are, helped by drink or drugs. Or the alternative is that it was aimed at you. In which case all sorts of questions arise about how they knew this was your car."

Merlyn grimaced.

"It's been parked outside this house since early yesterday evening."

"So someone has presumably been along and seen it. Anyway, these are not matters for me. I'm just the messenger. Charlie will be along soon, and Superintendent Oddie will be with him. He's the one in charge. Apparently they both know something about you and your position – Sergeant Peace has obviously handed the basic information on. So they have a bit of a head start, if you do turn out to be involved. They'll be here in half an hour or so. Why don't you go and get dressed, have some breakfast, whatever?"

The mention of breakfast reminded Merlyn that he hadn't eaten since lunchtime the day before. He darted down to the nearest newsagent-cum-cornershop and bought eggs, bacon and tomatoes. He put some rashers into one of his aunt's frying pans (he recognised it), then broke a couple of eggs in. When he got down from throwing some more clothes on he found the pan was awash with water and white goo from the bacon. He wondered whether Grandfather Cantelo would have found this unappetising mess "the essence of Englishness". Wishing he'd thought to buy bread he tipped the fried stuff on to a plate and eventually ate the results without relish. When Charlie arrived he introduced Superintendent Oddie and they went down the hall and into the sitting room. Deciding they were not about to conduct a seance or table-turning Merlyn opened the curtains. Charlie and Mike Oddie looked around, surprised if not exactly impressed.

"This is where Auntie entertained the mugs, is it?" Charlie asked.

"Clients. She treated it seriously, and so did they."

"Sorry. I'd forgotten it was all a cross between Gypsy Petulengro and the Citizens' Advice Bureau."

"Don't take any notice of him, Mr Docherty," said Oddie. "He doesn't do the hushed voice and deepest sympathy stuff unless there's really no option. Could we sit down and talk this over?"

"Please," said Merlyn, gesturing towards the easy chairs and the table.

"Anyone for Tarot?" Charlie asked. Then, sobering down, he said: "I've told the Superintendent all I know – that is, the state of play up until you came and talked over the book with Felicity. What's happened since? I gather you must be the accepted heir, the true half-Cantelo?"

"Yes, the Forensic Science Service has pronounced me who I said I was. No surprise to me, of course, though people *do* sometimes get nasty shocks as to who they are. I've been to see my real father and his family. I suspect it was a bit of a surprise to him to learn he was my father. If he's heard."

Both men looked at him.

"Come again? Why should that be?"

"I suspect he'd got the mad idea that I was really the result of an incestuous relationship between Grandfather Cantelo and his daughter Thora – my mother."

Mike Oddie whistled. Then he raised his eyebrows questioningly.

"I was named after him," explained Merlyn. "And Grandfather seems to have led a thoroughly disgraceful life in his later years, involving a lot of family covering-up. I've met – at a rather grim family party – a cousin of mine called Roderick Massey, born Cantelo. I've been wondering a bit about his paternity. He is mentioned in Aunt Clarissa's will, for no good reason I can think of, apart from that possibility. Clarissa was always drawn to people others shunned."

Oddie held up his hand.

"Wait. We're jumping several guns here. And we're in danger of concentrating on the family, and dark deeds in its past. Surely that's not the only possibility. The Cantelo clothing business was a very important part of the Leeds rag trade not so long ago. The answer could just as soon be in the family business as the family scandals."

Merlyn felt he had been pulled up short, and thought for a bit.

"Business matters? From thirty years ago, or longer? Isn't that unlikely?"

Oddie clung to his idea.

"You seem to be considering *family* matters from thirty years ago the motive force. Isn't that equally unlikely?"

Merlyn shook his head.

"No, because family matters *do* cause long shadows. The results live on. Jake, my father, has lived with his suspicions about my paternity for a long, long time. If Grandfather Cantelo is the father of Roderick Massey then it's less shocking than outright incest, but still pretty scandalous, and would have been pretty hurtful to his son at the time. Sleeping with Paul's wife, his daughter-in-law, would have been the talk of Headingley."

"*Would* have been – thirty years ago, and if people had known. It's still something people would shake their heads over, but still ... Is the family so dependent on a respectable reputation that anyone would act to keep something like that quiet?"

"All we're saying," put in Charlie, "is that it's much too early to put all our eggs in that particular basket."

"Fair enough," said Merlyn. "Still, I suppose you'll be

wanting to talk to all the family."

"Yes, in time. But first we've got to talk to the family of the dead boy, Terry Bates, then to any other boys involved last night. Joyriders hunt in packs as a rule. Probably the parents will swear they were at home all night, if necessary claiming to have checked their bedrooms every ten minutes. This is most likely a blind alley, but we have to go up it."

"Then we begin broadening out," said Oddie. Merlyn nodded — he was being told, not consulted. "That's when the Cantelo family comes into things. Perhaps you could tell us about them now, could you? Charlie will take down the details, because there are quite a lot of them, aren't there?"

"Definitely," said Merlyn with relish, rather enjoying the thought of handing them the problem. "By the standards of the time an enormous family – a Catholic one without the religion. Right, first the three boys. Hugh, definitely dead, with a daughter, Rosalind. Then Gerald, I think dead, although I've never bothered to ask, but after having fathered two sons, Malachi and Francis. A bit of a religious maniac, apparently, at least when the boys were growing up. Then Paul, who took off soon after the birth of his son Roderick, now known as Roderick Massey, after his stepfather. Got those?"

"Just a tick ... Right, got them," said Charlie.

"Now for the daughters. Emily married a man called Fowldes, and is the mother of Edward. Then Marigold, married to Stanley Sowden at a fairly advanced age, but became mother to Caroline. Then there was Clarissa, whom you know about. The youngest was Thora, my mother, and I'm her only surviving child. She died of breast cancer. That's the lot – simplicity itself!"

Charlie, still scribbling, didn't seem to think so.

"Do I need to go further down the tree? I presume there are great-grandchildren of the old man as well."

"Yes, one or two. All school age. You don't want to know."

"Right," said Oddie. "Well, that seems to stitch things up nicely, I think we can go about other business for the moment. By the way, I'm afraid your car is a write-off, sir."

"I can get another," said Merlyn, then added: "if I want to."

"Exactly, sir. Maybe you'd feel easier on public transport for the moment. Or on your own two feet."

"Maybe. I'll give it a try. We don't use feet much in Brussels. But you're quite right; the idea of getting another old banger doesn't appeal."

Merlyn let Oddie and Peace make their farewells, and watched them as they made their way down the front path and out of the gate. Somehow the idea of staying in and around the house that day seemed to appeal strongly.

* * *

Oddie and Peace found their encounter with the Bates family distressing and unenlightening. Terry's mother and father were both in the house on the Peabody Estate where he had lived, but they gathered in the course of the interview that his father was living with a new woman friend two streets away on the same estate. The parents seemed to have remained friends, or to have been brought together by grief. Grief there certainly was. Terry's ten-year-old sister and his mother both sobbed on and off, while his father looked straight ahead, seemingly into nothingness. His hand, though, was in his wife's.

"I can't take it in," said Mrs Bates, trying to gather herself together. "He were in bed when I went upstairs. Ten o'clock it were, or just after. He were in bed and fast asleep."

Oddie doubted that last bit, but it was neither here nor there whether it was true or not. By the early hours Terry was out on the streets and joyriding to his death.

"He'd had warnings for joyriding, hadn't he?" he asked.

His mother shrugged.

"They all do it, don't they? They're just lads."

She hadn't managed to shift to the past tense yet, the two policemen noticed. It would come slowly.

"Who is 'they all'?" asked Charlie. "Who were his mates?"

Mrs Bates shrugged again.

"I dunno. He doesn't talk about them."

"I think you do know," Charlie persisted. "We're just trying to save time. We'll have their names somewhere on our records, if we've got Terry's. And you can't get Terry into any more trouble."

"He thought the world of his mates. I wouldn't want to land them in for anything. They're nice lads."

"Mrs Bates, there may well be a charge of murder here, and I doubt if it will be one of Terry's mates who's charged. The car was tampered with, we think, and it's a fair bet that the intended victim was the car's owner, not your Terry."

There were people who would have taken this information as a signal to commence legal action on the car owner, but Mrs Bates was not one of them. She looked at Charlie horror-struck.

"You mean – what do you mean? Were there a bomb or owt like that? Like in Northern Ireland? Or had they got at the brakes?"

"The brakes, we think," said Oddie quietly.

"That's evil! And it was our Terry that got it! His mates were Billy Benson, Matthew Parsons and Jed Peterbridge," said his father suddenly. "They're the main ones. One or other o' them will have been out wi' Terry. Go easy on them. It's not them you want. They're good lads."

"It's not them we want," said Charlie.

But they got very little out of Terry's mates. Apparently only Jed Peterbridge had been with him, and he had seen nothing that caused him to have doubts about the car. Jed was in bed with a swollen foot and ankle and a pile of pornographic magazines which he didn't bother to hide.

"O' course I didn't see anyone tamperin' wi' the car. Think we're fuckin' crazy? The car were just outside the 'ouse, an' it were the oldest in the street. We just took it to ride it to the car park near Kirkstall Abbey an' 'ave a bit of a bonfire. If we'd 'a' seen anyone underneath we wouldn't 'a' gone near it, would us?"

No, of course they wouldn't, the policemen agreed. And that was that, really. Jed was even vague about when they'd stolen the car. They'd met up at midnight, at the corner of Jed's street, gone to a piece of waste ground down from the cricket and rugby stadium in Headingley and had "a few tinnies" together. At some point (Jed's indifference to time was magnificent and total) they'd gone in search of a car to hijack, and Terry (with a few illegal driving lessons from his father under his belt) had had no difficulty starting the car and driving off – he'd been doing this on and off since he was thirteen. When they got to the top of Kirkstall Lane Jed realised something was wrong. Terry was pressing the brake pedal to no effect. Dodgy brakes were familiar to habitual joyriders. Jed shouted "Get out" to Terry, opened his door, and threw himself out, badly spraining a foot. Terry went on, the car going faster and faster down the hill till it was out of sight. Jed, Terry's best mate, limped home.

To give him his due he seemed to have guilt feelings about this, and to have genuine grief at Terry's death – strong emotions he could only put into words with a struggle.

"I never knew he were goin' to die – how could I? We'd been in pile-ups before and both walked away. He were me mate – best mate I ever 'ad. I'll never 'ave another mate like Terry."

There was nothing to be done but slip quietly away and leave him to his thoughts. Charlie and Oddie got into their car, and Charlie said: "If the boys didn't tamper with the car for added kicks —"

"I don't think they did," said Oddie. "I don't think Jed was on drugs, and it's only hop-heads do that as a rule."

"Right. So if it wasn't them, the only real alternative is that this was aimed at Docherty."

"Aimed at Docherty by a Cantelo, do you think?"

"Most likely," said Charlie. "I'm not up in Common Market affairs these days. Could there be anything of interest there? It seems to have been his life for the last eight or ten years."

"Maybe. You said he'd had a lot to do with bringing the Eastern European countries in, didn't you?"

"Yes. What are you suggesting? Eastern Europe means Mafia?"

"It's something we might eventually have to look into. But I would have thought that a bullet in the street would be more in their line – less dodgy and uncertain than fixing brakes on an old car. But yes, I agree: first things first, and that means the Cantelo family."

They parked outside Millgarth and went into the area for members of the public. They were just starting through to the Station proper when they were hailed by the Duty Sergeant. They went over to his desk, and he spoke low.

"There's a lady waiting to talk to you, Superintendent. To both of you, actually. Lady over there."

He gestured towards a middle-aged woman, dressed in a smart but severe suit of charcoal grey. She was bespectacled, and looking rather dourly at them. Oddie went over to her, and she got up and held out her hand.

"Superintendent Oddie? I'm Rosalind Frere."

She hadn't looked at Charlie, but something told him she was a Cantelo. He nodded imperceptibly to Oddie.

"You wanted to speak to me, didn't you? Perhaps you'd like

to come along to my office."

Oddie led the way, his visitor walking with all the businesslike bustle of a high-flyer in business or politics. Charlie
walked silently beside her. Once in Oddie's office Rosalind
took the chair facing the desk and got straight down to business.

"I believe there's something been happening at number 15
Congreve Street." Oddie said nothing, but he nodded.
"You've been talking to Merlyn Docherty." Oddie nodded
again. "There's something you ought to know about that
man."

"Really?" Oddie ventured.

"You see my aunt, Clarissa Cantelo, was a spiritualist, a
medium – perhaps you have heard. Of course one doesn't take
that sort of thing seriously, not in this day and age —"

"But?"

"— but in her case there was a strong brain behind it.
Often she was wonderfully acute and accurate."

She halted, and seemed uncertain how to proceed.

"And?" asked Oddie.

"And one thing I think you ought to know is why she sent
Merlyn away when he was hardly more than a boy."

"And that was?"

"She was afraid. She sensed a terrible violence in him. She
thought he was going to murder someone."

"There!" said Rosalind Frere. "I can see I've surprised you."

Since both men had kept their expressions studiously neutral they wondered about her eyesight or her state of mind: perhaps she lived in such a settled condition of self-satisfaction that she always assumed she had produced the effect she had aimed to produce. But they also noticed a slight shaking of the hands that clutched an elegant bag. She was dressed-up, and she was nervous.

"That's a very damaging accusation you are making, Mrs Frere," said Oddie. "What is the basis of it?"

"Why, Aunt Clarissa herself, as I said. After Merlyn took off for Italy, and when family members started asking her where he'd gone and why he'd gone so quickly, without goodbyes or anything, that was what Auntie said. She'd got rid of him because she was just terrified about what might happen."

Oddie left a short pause.

"Was it said at the time that he'd gone to Italy? I understood the family was under the impression he was in India."

"India, Italy – I don't remember. I was only about thirteen at the time. And of course the important thing was that Aunt Clarissa was scared of him – that's what we talked about."

Oddie left another pause. No need to give her the impression they were jumping to her skipping rope.

"You first said Clarissa Cantelo was scared about what might happen. This could mean anything, including a threat *to,* not from, Merlyn Docherty."

"Oh no —"

"You then said she was scared of him, which makes it a lot more concrete. But was she so concrete? By 'scared of him' do you mean that she conceived the threat as directed at herself?"

"Well ... she was vague ... It could well have been, since he'd been living with her. On the other hand, it could have been some other member of the family, a girlfriend – anyone! Auntie was often vague about specifics: she might tell one of her clients that disaster would result from a certain course of action, but she'd be vague about what form it would take."

"That sounds like par for the course," said Charlie, "going by the horoscopes you read in the papers."

Rosalind bridled.

"Oh, you mustn't confuse Auntie with those frauds. Auntie believed in what she was doing and what she saw in the future."

"I see," said Oddie. "Though I don't suppose she was alone in that respect. Let's just stick to Merlyn Docherty for the moment, shall we? Now, you say his aunt had some kind of premonition that he might commit violence – even murder. Often premonitions like this are based on quite down-to-earth observations such as anyone might have. You for example, not too far from his own age. What are your memories of Merlyn Docherty at that time?"

Rosalind had clearly prepared herself for that question, and was relieved she had been asked it.

"Oh, *very* mixed up – Merlyn, I mean, not my memories. He was full of grudges and grievances, angers and resentments. Of course his poor mother had died when he was very young, and he didn't get on with his father, so in a way you could understand why he was like he was. There was real rage there – I'd say hatred."

"Hatred? Of anyone in particular?"

"Well, if there was anyone special it would be his father."

"So if you could have prophesied yourself, it would have been that all this suppressed violence would be directed at Jake Docherty?"

"I suppose so. But it was also very general. It could have

been directed at any of us – any of the Cantelos. I mean, the feelings of violence in him were sort of, well, *random* ones."

"Right ... And at this time, when he was here for eighteen months, living with his aunt, did you see a lot of Mr Docherty?"

"Well, quite a lot. I was often at Aunt Clarissa's, and we had both lost a parent, so —"

"You were close."

"Close*ish*."

"You'd lost your father, had you?" asked Charlie.

"That's right ... No, wait." She seemed genuinely to have to think. "No, he didn't die until 1985. But he was a top businessman, a really high-flyer, so we hardly ever saw him, my mother and I. So Merlyn wasn't the only one who was neglected, was he? I loved my father to bits, and when he was around he was a *super* father. To me it was very sad, but it was inevitable, given his work."

"So when he actually died, it didn't make all that much difference to you?"

"Not much, really," said Rosalind, after considering. "There was less money around, but we never *wanted*, never went short of anything, so I can't say that it mattered – or that I even noticed any lack of it. I've never been an extravagant sort of person."

"Do you remember the time when Docherty ... disappeared? Went away?"

"Oh yes," said Rosalind, a distinctly avid expression appearing on her face. "He had just done his GCE exams. I was going to do them in a year's time – or was it two years? Anyway I was interested, and would have talked them over with him, maybe even gone through the papers. But I never did, because he *did* disappear. I mean, no one was told he was going to take off like that. We were just told he was gone."

"Ye-e-es," said Oddie slowly. "Now, we've collected some

basic details on Mr Docherty since he came to see us soon after he arrived back in this country." Rosalind Frere seemed to start, but quickly recovered her composure. "He was born in 1966, so he presumably took his GCEs in 1982. He must have disappeared – or, as it turned out, simply emigrated to Italy – in the early summer of that year – June or July."

"I'm sure that's right," said Rosalind.

"So around that time the word was going around in the Cantelo family that Clarissa had sent him away because she feared his violent nature?"

"Yes."

"Now we need to know who we can check this up with. Sergeant Peace ..."

Charlie flipped back several pages in his notebook.

"Yes, now your father, Hugh Cantelo, is dead, Mrs Frere, as you've just told us. Living and fairly accessible are Marigold, Emily and the widower of Thora, Mr Docherty's father."

"*He* wouldn't have been told anything," said Rosalind.

"I see," said Charlie. "Two we don't know about are Paul and Gerald. Could you tell us anything about them?"

"Oh, I expect they're dead."

"You expect? Why do you expect that?"

Rosalind became quite brusque.

"Well, one usually hears *of* people, even if one doesn't hear *from* them, doesn't one?"

"Possibly one does," said Charlie, his mouth twitching. "But you haven't heard of either of your uncles since ... when?"

"Paul took off soon after Roderick was born – about 1978 or 1979 I would say. There was a divorce quite soon after, and his wife remarried. At that time he was living in Nevada. I've never heard anything of him since."

"And Gerald?"

"The last I heard of him would be later than that. He'd had religion for years — got it when he was in his twenties, after having a bent that way for quite some time, and was never good for anything after that. You could hardly have a casual chat with him without the Book of Revelations coming into it. You can guess how popular he was. Everyone had had the white horse up to *here*, and gave him a wide berth."

"I see. And when did he actually disappear – or take off, shall we say, and no one saw him again?"

"You make it sound almost suspicious. It wasn't. He took off, in your words. The boys were grown up by then, so it would be the mid-Eighties I should think. The last they heard he was part of a fundamentalist Christian group living on a caravan site in Skegness. The boys thought Good Riddance, and I don't blame them."

"And his wife?"

"She was even gladder than they were. She'd been a bit inclined to way-out religions herself when they met, but he cured her of it. She died last year – premature senility."

"Right," said Charlie, shutting his notebook. "That gives us more than enough to contact. We can think about the next generation when we've seen these."

"The next generation won't know anything," said Rosalind. "They were kept out of it."

But *you* know, thought Charlie.

"What are you actually going to ask these people?" demanded Rosalind.

"We would like confirmation that at the time of Mr Docherty's leaving Britain his aunt was afraid of him, or afraid of what he might do," said Oddie.

Rosalind nodded, apparently satisfied.

"It's a long time ago," she said, "but they'll remember *that*."

"Good ... But of course at the moment we are investigating a tampering with Mr Docherty's car, which has led to the death of a teenage joyrider. In other words, possibly a murderous attack *on*, not *by* Mr Docherty."

Rosalind's expression was scornful.

"Have you thought he might have done it himself?"

"No. Why do you think he would have done that?"

"To give substance to the idea that someone is trying to kill him – that someone being a member of the family."

"Rather dangerous, surely?" said Oddie courteously, but raising his eyebrows a fraction. "He couldn't have known that the car would be stolen by a joyrider. In the normal course of things he would have been the next person to drive it."

"Exactly. And he'd have kept it on level ground and in streets that were hardly used. Then the brakes would fail, he'd manage to stop it, and then call the police."

She looked at Oddie triumphantly.

"Well, it's a thought," said Oddie. "Definitely a thought."

"It was just bad luck for the thug who took it that he decided to drive it downhill," said Rosalind. "Though I can't say I have much sympathy for him."

Oddie decided he'd had enough. He got up, and Rosalind, after looking up at him for a few seconds realised that she was being told the interview was at an end.

"I must be going," she said. "At least you've been told everything now, which I'm sure you weren't before. The burden is off my mind."

"A policeman is rarely told everything early in a case," said Oddie, showing her through the door. "I shall be surprised if I have been now."

* * *

Merlyn took a quick walk with Dolly to the supermarket on the Otley Road, and had a better lunch than breakfast had been. Then he had an hour's siesta, relic of his years in Italy.

When he had woken and had a cup of tea he decided he had to breast the waves of the past and investigate the bedroom that had been his whenever he sought refuge from the drunken binges of his father, and then continuously for the years 1981 to '82.

He was glad he was alone. Even Danielle would have been a hindrance, because he remembered quite clearly that there was nothing of any distinction about the room, no clear impression that he had made on it. That would have puzzled or distressed Danielle. But to him it was natural and normal – as if he had realised he was merely camping out there, not setting up home in it.

He stood on the landing, swallowed, then threw open the door and put his hand round the jamb to turn on the light.

It was almost exactly as he had left it. The only difference was that the bed had been unmade, and the eiderdown draped over the bare mattress. Then, watched by Dolly from the door, he began a prowl around his old room. In the cupboard was football gear, in the drawers his flannels and white shirt for school cricket. Not much use in Italy, he had obviously thought when packing. Clothes he had already grown out of when he left were still in the wardrobe and drawers, along with the school uniform he no longer would have use for. His school satchel was under a chair, but it was empty. The early summer month when he had left had been a period of transition: exams were over, revision was useless, he had had a feeling that an end had been made. Even if he had stayed in Leeds, that summer would have marked an end to one part of his life: he remembered that he had decided, if he was going to continue his education, to go to a further education college, rather than continue at his present school. Perhaps that was why he was ripe for Clarissa's suggestion that he make a complete break.

The books told him more. No children's books. The Enid

Blytons and the Arthur Ransomes had been left in Sheffield. Perhaps they had been lapped up by Jake's second family, but more likely thrown out years before. There was the odd crime novel on the shelves – Christie, Ross Macdonald, P.D. James – and the beginnings of his adult taste in fiction: Dickens, Hardy, Waugh, Joyce Cary. He must be one of a tiny number of Cary readers left. Then he discovered on the shelves *Nostromo* and *Heart of Darkness*. Conrad had been a very recent discovery when he left Leeds, but one that had stayed with him. He found a little shelf of solid history tomes in paperback: Trevelyan's *Social History*, the Penguin histories of Great Britain, Dennis Mack Smith on Modern Italy. This last had been preparation for a new life once the idea had been mooted, he remembered, but too heavy to form part of his luggage.

Then he discovered in the cupboard a pile of exercise books, full of essays: Palmerston's foreign policy 1830-41; Mr Gradgrind's "political economy" (he had nearly been put off Dickens by having *Hard Times* as a set book for GCE). More interesting, he discovered underneath the improvised book-shelves a notebook with plans for his schoolwork, particularly for all the subjects where essays were involved: English Literature, History and French. He realised that even then he had a lawyer's caution, a desire to be well-prepared, an instinct to make any written work the product of considered and meticulous planning.

But in among the notes for essays he found memoranda of a more personal nature: not a diary by any means, but a record of some of the things that were worrying him that year leading up to the GCE – the autumn of 1981 to the summer of 1982. There was a note about the end of his relationship – really no more than a friendship – with Jenny Watson, and the bombshell of her pregnancy. "I bet it's Ben Eastlake whose responsible," the note ran, not too grammatically. Then there

was a note about his father. "It is now six months since I've
seen or heard from Jake. Well, if he doesn't give a dam, why
should I?" The sentiment didn't surprise him, though the
spelling did.

And then there were three notes relating to his Aunt
Clarissa, and the crisis that had led to his leaving the country.
He did not remember making the memoranda, but he remem-
bered the emotions and events they recorded. The first read:

> *February 23.* Today I got aunt to admit she was
> worried. I said "Is it the family?" and she just gave
> a nod. I asked "Which one of them are you wor-
> ried about?" and she answered "All of them."
> Then she shut up.

The second read:

> *April 3.* At last Aunt has said something else about
> the family, and what is worrying her. I asked her
> if it was about money, and she said: "It could be
> money, and it could be," she hesitated, "something
> else." I said that problems usually came down to
> money or sex, and she just said she wished she'd
> learned more about sex.

The third read:

> *May 30.* Aunt thinks I'm thretened by this family
> business. I said I didn't see how I could be involved,
> and she said "You are though. You're my hier." I
> didn't know this. I suppose if I wasn't around
> (*dead*) someone thinks they would inherit instead.

So there it all was, in blue-black and white: the reason he

had been sent abroad. There was a later entry, "Quite afraid, but definitely excited" which surely related to his feelings at the prospect. Also the confusion Clarissa felt at the time about – about what, precisely? There was hardly a hint about that. What was she afraid of, what was she fearing might happen? And why? But the question of money and the question of sex did seem to lead back to the last years of Grandfather Cantelo.

Merlyn shut the book and took it downstairs. It was tantalisingly scrappy, but yet suggestive enough to ponder on.

* * *

When Rosalind had left and Mike Oddie had opened the window to air the office symbolically of her high-octane personality, he and Charlie sat down to talk things over.

"What do you think of it all?" Charlie asked him.

"It could be true," he said cautiously.

"Yes, and crop circles are made by little green men scything them from space ships from Mars."

"No, wait. There could be scenarios that mean she was speaking the truth. One is that Clarissa was genuinely scared of her nephew. We only have his word for it that there was a loving relationship between them."

"They kept regular contact from 1980 until her death."

"We only have his word for that."

"He wouldn't have risked telling us that unless he had kept up pretty well with all that was going on in the Cantelo family."

"Plenty of people could have kept him up to speed on that. But the other possibility is maybe more interesting and likely: that is that she put this around to keep the Cantelos on-side, so as not to give them the impression that there was thought to be a threat that emanated from *them*."

"Hmmm," said Charlie, considering carefully. "That's

more like it. Wouldn't she have told Merlyn about doing that on one of their weekly phone calls?"

"Maybe. But since the idea of sending him abroad was to cut off all connection with the Cantelos, maybe she preferred to let him start his life all over again without reminding him of the past, particularly things likely to make him uneasy."

"Fair enough." After a moment Charlie came out with his doubts. "But I thought Rosalind was a pretty poor liar, and I still feel the whole thing was made up by her."

"I'd say the same, but that's impression, not evidence."

"Agreed. And it doesn't answer the question: why should she be involved?"

"Why? She's a member of the Cantelo family. What's your point?"

"She was younger than Merlyn, about fourteen when he took flight. She was vague about her age. If she was in the school year below his, which would account for her interest in his GCE papers, she'd have been fifteen then. About thirty-seven now, which seems about right. It's difficult to see her being involved at the time, though – no, it's more than diffi-cult, it's absurd. The idea that Merlyn had murderous inten-tions wouldn't even have been mentioned in her presence."

"Well, maybe her concern is more or less inherited from her father. No – more likely her mother," Oddie amended the thought. They both pondered for a moment on the situation in the family twenty years before.

"You know," said Charlie at last, "there's something odd here, because one gets the distinct sense of the Cantelos act-ing *together* on something. Not so much now – there seem to be lots of tensions and groupings – but back in the Eighties or earlier. And yet in other ways they seem to have been a very divided family, with little social or emotional connection even then. Would you agree?"

"Yes, I think so. The question is —"

"What brought them together. Exactly."

"I haven't the faintest glimmerings of a notion," said Oddie. "But – assuming we take all our information from Docherty at its face value – it's got to be something very important."

"Probably. Why do you say that, though?"

"It's got to be something that even now is worth killing him to keep concealed."

Chapter Fourteen
Big Business

Superintendent (soon to be ex-Superintendent) Oddie looked around him glumly. The room they were in was the firm's headquarters in the centre of Leeds – a new building at the end of the Headrow with lots of glass and light streaming through the windows. The furnishings had got rid of the stark look that had afflicted companies such as Witherspoon and Co. for thirty or more years, and they looked capacious, comfortable and – which perhaps was the point – expensive. They did not lighten Oddie's mood. Dotted around the long room were the top and toppish brass of Witherspoon's, the firm in question, and they were mingling with the applicants for the post of Director of Security – a sensitive position, granted that the firm manufactured armaments and sold them to anyone who could stump up the necessary. This was, of course, provided the deal could be squared with the government's ethical foreign policy (as it almost invariably could). It wasn't the top brass who deepened Mike's gloom. They seemed amiable enough on the surface (thin though that surface probably was). It was the ramshackle collection of men who were the applicants who depressed him. Many of them were known to him, had even been colleagues of his, and the number of them he would want on any detective enquiry he led could be numbered on the fingers of half a hand.

"Good luck," Charlie had said to him the day before.

"And what does that mean?" Oddie had asked.

"Not getting the job," said Charlie.

And, looking around, Mike was inclined to agree.

The majority of the presumably shortlisted applicants were senior police officers near to or past retirement age, and a dim, undistinguished lot they were.

"They're probably thinking the same about me," he thought.

But he knew in his heart he was not dim and undistinguished, and he knew in both his heart and his head that they were. Most of those whom he had had anything more than routine dealings with had given him more aggro than satisfaction, and of the three he had respect for one had a private life that ought to have put him beyond consideration, granted the dangers, in that particular post, of blackmail. The policemen of lower rank who had applied for the post displayed for the most part awareness of the fact that it was beyond all reasonable expectation on their part, so they probably were there mainly for the food and the booze, and perhaps for the experience. One or two were thugs, one or two were crooks, but most were reasonable and competent cops. Given the choice Oddie would have preferred a competent cop to the Lothario Superintendent any day, but he was not conducting the interviews, and he was willing to bet that those who were would go for rank, as something they could plausibly boast about.

Charlie's other piece of wisdom, proffered more than once over pints of bitter when they were on a case together, was to buy into a little specialised business.

"Run a shop selling model trains and planes, or one selling clocks, or cookery books, or jigsaws," he said. "Something where you can mug up the expertise quite quickly and give a service to enthusiasts and cranks, along with reminiscences of your most fascinating cases. Might not be heaven, but it would beat security work. Then when you *really* want to retire, you can sell it as a going concern."

The more he thought about it, the more he saw the company assembled in the long, light room, the better the advice sounded. Provided, of course, that he could make it a going concern.

"Hello. You're Superintendent Oddie, aren't you?"

Mike steeled himself and turned round. He had known there would be this sort of thing, and he had prepared himself mentally for it. The man was thirty-fiveish, immaculately blue-suited and smooth-haired, and horribly sleek.

"I'm Gabriel Witherspoon. A very minor twig on the family tree, but one of the people you'll be talking to today. I'm very much looking forward to hearing your ideas."

Like hell you are, thought Mike. But then he revised his opinion. He decided that he must be one of those shortlisted, and marked down as a definite prospect. Many of the others were there as make-weights, to demonstrate that this was a London Marathon among security jobs.

"Yes, I'm still a superintendent – for another couple of months," he said, shaking hands (immaculately dry, the other hand, and tanned to boot). "And I'll be interested to hear what you have to tell me about the job."

"Oh quite. Quite. Exchange of information and ideas, that's the thinking behind all this." He waved his hand at the people, the plates of savoury thingummibobs, the bottles. "You mustn't think of it as an ordinary job interview."

Except that at the end of the day one of us will be appointed, and twenty-five or so will be disappointed, Mike thought.

"And the other people here – the Witherspoon people I don't know – who are they?" he asked.

He omitted to mention that he *did* know some of the Witherspoon people, and had met them in his official capacity.

"They're all directors of the company. We had thought to have the present Director of Security along, but we were advised that that isn't the ticket any longer. Inhibits innovation, new thinking, radical approaches. No firm can afford to be a stick-in-the-mud these days, as I'm sure you know."

"Of course not," said Mike, with false heartiness.

"You won't find us a bunch of fuddy-duddies," said Gabriel Witherspoon. "And there's no ageism here either. In fact we range in age from my granddad, Tom Witherspoon over there, to young Andrew Cattermole, my nephew, who's twenty-five."

Mike seemed to sense a clenching of the teeth when the latter name was mentioned, as if not being a stick-in-the-mud had its limits where Gabriel Witherspoon was concerned, and appointing a 25-year old as a director definitely transgressed them.

He was glad when the smooth Gabriel moved away, sliding towards the superintendent with the thousand and three conquests. Mike disliked smoothness and sleekness – prejudice, perhaps, and typically Yorkshire ones, but they had been justified over and over by his experiences as a policeman.

He looked over towards the figure of Grandfather Witherspoon. He was a rather shambling man with an untidy moustache that could have been modelled on H.G. Wells's, and a distant, dreaming expression in his eyes, as if he had already started the process of detaching himself from his firm, his associates, perhaps from life itself. He had shunned all the little groups of people, interviewers and interviewees, and had sat himself by one of the small tables and was helping himself to the canapés, which were very good. A man who was reducing his life to the vital necessities, Oddie thought, and doing it without shame or embarrassment. And perhaps, like most old people, living on his memories rather than his present-day experiences.

He went over to him.

"The prawn ones are very tasty," he said, helping himself.

"And so are the blue cheese ones," the old man said. "I'm Tom Witherspoon."

"I know. And I'm Superintendent Mike Oddie."

"I know. What do you want?"

Mike knew the directness of old age, but he hedged.

"Well, I suppose I want a job here."

"You don't seem too certain. Wise man – you've got brains.

But what I meant was, why have you come over to talk to me?"

"You're very sharp."

"I'd be playing golf with all the other compulsorily retired businessmen if I wasn't. I still have my uses, though they are occasional, and my advice is ignored as often as followed. In my experience people want to talk to an eighty-year-old for one reason and one only: to tap his memory. They don't want the wisdom gained by running a business for fifty years, because it's not worth a bean in today's world, or so they think. So what area of my past do you want to talk about? I'm good on the early days, average on the middle ones, and quite hopeless on anything that happened yesterday or the day before. Everything is done by other people now, and I try to ignore or forget what they choose to do."

Mike opted for an equal directness.

"Cantelo. The shirt people."

There was a touch of cantankerousness in the old man's expression.

"I *know* they're the shirt people, or were. How many Cantelo families do you imagine there are in Leeds? ... Merlyn Cantelo ..."

"That's right."

"Funny bloke. In his day – his *good* days, when the firm was very prosperous – he was a sententious bugger, inclined to lecture you on what you should do in any particular set of circumstances, or what you should have done in some particular crisis or difficulty in your business that had come to his attention. Very hot on business ethics, the spirit of capitalist enterprise, the moral imperative to better yourself or stash away more money. Most people just switched off. I pitied the family rather. He had no sense of humour at all. They probably got that sort of stuff morning, noon and night – and God help them if *they* switched off! He would have found some ingenious way of making his displeasure known, and felt. He was that sort of man. He had to be in charge, and to be *felt* to be in charge."

"You might think that would unite the family against him."

"You might. But my impression is that they weren't united at all. Not that they were at sixes and sevens with each other all the time – that wasn't the case, and Cantelo would have stamped on it if there were signs of it happening ... No, it was just that they clearly didn't pull together. Each went his own way, and there was no affection for each other, no mutual loyalty, no support for each other in times of crisis or against their overbearing parent. I suppose Clarissa made some attempt to keep them together. Most people felt she was the best of the bunch."

"That's the clairvoyant?"

"You know perfectly well she was the clairvoyant. I suspect you know more about the family than I do. She must have been mad as a hatter – my reason or my prejudices tell me that – but she seemed perfectly sane, and rather a good woman. She looked after poor old Merlyn in his later years, when the rest had as little to do with him as possible. But it was uphill work, especially as the business was falling apart around his ears."

"What went wrong?"

The old man shrugged.

"Shirts changed, I suppose, and the firm didn't. Suddenly it was all stripes with white collars, Nehru shirts, caftans – God knows what. And the Cantelo shirt went on with its thick, warm material for Northern summers, and its big squares, and suddenly the only people who wanted them were people in Bradford in a serious rut. That's my guess. Maybe if he'd been younger he would have kept in touch with changing tastes, but Merlyn's mind was on other things."

Oddie handed him a plate of canapés and took one himself.

"And you know what the other things were, don't you?"

Tom Witherspoon nodded.

"I know what the rumours were."

"And the rumours said — what?"

"You know as well as I do. Girlies."

"And what sort of things were said about it at the time? What details got about, to fill in the general charge?"

Tom Witherspoon shifted uneasily in his chair.

"You know, I really don't like talking about it. At the time I may have had a bit of a snigger about it. When you're old yourself it's different. You know that all sorts of inhibitions – barriers we put up, so we don't do things that damage or embarrass us – lose their power to frighten us as we get older. Not that I want to chase young women, but ... you know. Old Man Cantelo's wife Elspeth died, he was lonely, he — well, he wanted them young, and went after them. Girls on the factory floor, secretaries ... prostitutes, it was said. How much of it was true, how much just talk that snowballed, I don't know."

Oddie left a second or two's pause.

"There was something else said, wasn't there?"

"You know it already," said the old man irritably. "Yes. There was talk about his own family. Do I need to say any more? It was all gossip – nothing but gossip."

"I think you'd be as good as anyone at sorting out the snowballing gossip from the bits that had the ring of truth."

"You're soft-soaping me, I know that, because I'm not senile yet." Witherspoon sighed. "There was talk that the behaviour had spilled over – so to speak – into his own family. I didn't give much credence to it at the time. Didn't give much thought to it, to tell you the truth. The old man was going a bit gaga, and inevitably malicious stories about him were accumulating. There was the odd story about him and Clarissa, who was keeping house for him, like I just said, and since most people liked her the stories were about her resisting him, locking her bedroom door, and so on. I wouldn't pay much heed to those, though if any of the other stories were true, it was only common sense in her to lock her door."

"What was the story that had, or seemed to have, most basis to it?" asked Oddie. There was silence again.

"This is about the return of that boy, isn't it?"

"Man. He's nearly forty now. Merlyn Docherty."

Witherspoon thought.

"Is there something ... *wrong* there? Is he the Docherty boy?"

"Yes he is. And his father is Jake Docherty."

"I never put any faith in those stories. They went round after the old man's death, and he'd have to have been at it with his own daughter long before his wife died, which seems to have been what set him off on the sexual rampage. That story was just whispered around some of the older members of the business community."

"But the story you thought might have something in it?"

"Well, just going on what happened ... I did think there might be something in the tales of Old Merlyn and his son Paul's wife. We knew the boys, you see, better than we knew the girls. Their father would sometimes take them to the factory, or bring them to dinners and social events. To see if they had managerial material, I suppose. And there was always tension between him and Paul, the youngest of the boys. Hugh set his sights higher than a middling-flourishing clothing firm in Leeds. Gerald was mad as a meat-axe. But Paul – he was ... interesting. Not a business brain, but highly strung, intelligent, sensitive. He and his wife had a son, he left them both almost immediately, and so far as I know he's somewhere in America. That's what really made the rumours go around. And the fact that Old Merlyn died just before Paul took off didn't stop them."

"And was that the only —?"

"I think they're going in for the pep talk," said Mr Witherspoon, getting up carefully and going towards the far door, where a crowd was gathering and passing through into the next room. "I'll pretend to go along and then nip away. I don't need pep talks at my age. And I think I've told you more than enough unsubstantiated rumours of yesteryear, don't you?"

"I'm grateful for your time."

"Stuff and nonsense. Time is what I've got plenty of, so long as it lasts. But I wish I understood what's behind all this. If this boy – man – is who he says he is, and if he's been left Clarissa's house and her money, as rumour suggests, I don't see there's any more for you to do. Let him enjoy it and be done with it."

"It's not quite as simple as that," said Oddie, moving cautiously along by his side. "His car was tampered with two nights ago, and a joyrider who took it was killed. I don't need to spell out the possibilities we have to consider."

The old man, walking beside him, shot him a glance.

"One of the Cantelos, are you thinking? Bad blood, and all that nonsense? Something suspicious about the old man's death, perhaps? I wouldn't envy you trying to investigate *that* twenty or more years on. And there were never any rumours about *that* at the time."

"I suspect everyone heaved a sigh of relief and went about their business," said Mike. "That applied to the family, but also to the business community as well, I imagine. He was an embarrassment."

"He was. A dirty joke with unpleasant overtones ..." He paused, as they neared the crowd slowly edging through the door into the next room, set out with rows of chairs. "You're not serious about this security job, are you?"

"I'm not sure. Anyway, it's a good trial balloon for job-hunting in the future. One of my colleagues thinks I should use my pay-off money to set myself up in a small business. Something specialised I could get interested in."

"Sounds like solid advice. I'm sure you know that *nothing*, not even daytime television, is more boring than security work. Tell me if you find anything interesting to specialise in. I might put some money into it – give me an interest. Nothing to interest me here now. I'm Tom Witherspoon, by the way. Oh — I told you. Known to the workers as Old Tom. Makes me sound a bit like Cantelo, doesn't it? Go on — go in. Bore yourself to death."

And he pottered off, apparently rather pleased with himself.

* * *

Merlyn had clung to the house in Congreve Street for thirty-six hours. One trip out to fetch a Chinese takeaway had been his only excursion, and then he had had to stop himself from looking over his shoulder the whole time. Dolly was happy to exercise herself, as obviously she had done in his aunt's last years, and anyway Merlyn didn't think she would be much use as a defender. Even if he'd felt more confident he didn't feel sure what he wanted to do outside the house. His instinct was to go and tell the family of the dead boy how sorry he was, but instinct also told him that a visit from him would only increase their pain. But by the second evening in the old house the urge to imprison himself was wearing out. The television news at ten was the same as that at six, and there was only Hindemith on Radio Three. Going to the window he saw that in the street outside Mr Robinson was coming through his gate for his late-night dog walk. Duke, his Yorkshire terrier, was following him as if this was a chore he went through in order to give his owner the requisite exercise. Merlyn put Dolly on her lead and went out to the front gate.

"Hello Merlyn. Don't worry about Duke and Dolly. She often comes and pays us a visit. Are you joining us?"

"If you don't mind."

"Not at all. But is it wise? There are a lot of rumours going around about your car."

"True ones, probably. It was interfered with. And some poor young blighter got what was intended for me."

"So I heard. You should be taking precautions, you know."

"I can't stay locked in the house for ever – let alone in a hotel room. B & B in Armley jail would be preferable. I'm keeping my eyes open – what more can I do?"

"Get police protection, that's what I'd demand."

"But it's what you wouldn't get." At that moment a police car passed along Cardigan Road, at the end of Congreve Street. "But they're doing what they can afford to. Mr Robinson, you've been around here a long time, haven't you?"

"All my life, boy. Born in Leeds General, brought back here a week later, and been here all my life."

"I remember you when I came to live with Aunt Clarissa. That was around 1980. Do you remember that time?"

"Remember it? Well, not specifically, but I suppose ... Would that be about when your grandfather died?"

"That happened a year or two earlier."

"So Clarissa had become mistress of the house and had set up in the crystal-ball reading business."

"Clairvoyant. That's right. I've just found a few little notes I made at the time. Auntie was obviously worried then, and worried about something connected to the family. You wouldn't have any idea what that could have been, would you?"

Mr Robinson stopped, the two dogs stopped, and all looked at Merlyn.

"You're not remembering well, young man. The Cantelos didn't fraternise with the neighbours. Beyond a 'good morning' or a few words about the weather, there was nothing passed, not till your aunt took over and things loosened up a bit. Your grandfather liked that house, and he needed a big one with the family he had, but he thought he was a mite above the area, and any social contacts he had must have been made at work, or perhaps with the Rotarians. You won't find anyone around here that knows much about Cantelo family affairs. We kept – we were kept – at a distance."

Merlyn's disappointment showed in his face.

"That's a bit of a blow. I can't ask one of the family because anyone and everyone could be implicated."

Mr Robinson considered.

"One of the ones who was too young to be in on anything at the time might have caught a whiff of something later on."

"They'd probably stay schtum because their parents were implicated."

"Possibly so. You seem to be thinking that they all might have been in it."

"That seems to have been Auntie's assumption."

"Have you thought of Renee?"

"Renee? Who's she?"

"I think you would find that she was helping at the refreshments after the funeral. I saw her going into the house half or three-quarters of an hour before the family started arriving back."

"Renee? The woman who came three mornings a week to do the heavy housework?"

"That's right. The last of a stable of servants. She was working there in your grandfather's last years, and she went on working for Clarissa until a year or two ago. Since then she's just come in 'to oblige' as she used to say, when Clarissa felt the need for her."

"Do you think she knew anything?"

"Don't know. But one thing I do know is she's a great talker. And a great observer too. Sometimes an outsider sees more of the game. Her name is Renee Osborne, and she lives in Kirkstall View. If I was you I'd get in touch."

Merlyn came down Kirkstall View next morning, with Dolly on a lead. The little dog was already showing signs that the walk had been longer than she cared for. Merlyn was looking for number eleven, where the telephone directory told him there was an Osborne, R. The number had obviously been too familiar to Clarissa to need entering in her little book of phone numbers, which was mostly filled up with clients, and their home and business numbers. The street began its downward descent to Abbey Road at number 29, and he followed it down as fast as Dolly's dilatoriness would allow. By the bus-stop halfway up a young woman with two young children was keeping up a one-sided battle with them.

"If you don't stop shoving Katie you'll get a smack. I mean it. Jerry, you're all over chocolate. You'll be sick on the bus, and then you'll know about it. And it'll be straight to bed when you get home. I mean it."

Why did incompetent mothers always say that, Merlyn wondered? Because the children had already twigged that their threats were meaningless, and they were making a desperate attempt to shore up their credibility? He passed a woman in her tiny patch of front garden dead-heading brown daffodils and blowsy, falling tulips. The spring bulbs were over, except for the odd bluebell, and it was time to prepare for bedding plants. He let himself through the low wrought-iron gate of number eleven and rang the doorbell.

"She's not in," came a shout. Looking up the road he saw it was the gardening woman two houses up. "She and Patsy've gone to Morrison's. They've bin gone half an hour, so they won't be long, not unless they've stayed for coffee."

"Oh ... right," said Merlyn. "I'll wait around ... Who's

Patsy?"

"Renee's daughter. Lives next door." She pointed to the terrace house between them. "Sam's out on a job – car broke down on the road to Shipley – otherwise he'd've driven them."

Merlyn nodded as if he knew who she was talking about, then went out again on to Kirkstall View and gave Dolly a desultory stroll she certainly did not relish. It was twenty minutes before he saw, coming from Abbey Road, two female figures, one elderly but spry, the other middle-aged. The older woman rang a vague bell in his mind: it could have been from his distant past living in Congreve Street, or from the more recent wake there, where there had been domestic help flitting between kitchen and dining room. He decided to let them go into their homes, if they were Renee and Patsy, but as they passed them Dolly started wagging her tail. The older woman turned and looked Merlyn in the face.

"That's Dolly, isn't it? Clarissa's Dolly. And you must be — I can't recall the name now. Getting old is horrible. Thora's lad. They said you'd come into everything."

Merlyn went up to her and shook her hand.

"Merlyn. Merlyn Docherty. I lived with Clarissa for a while."

"Of course you did. I remember that quite well. It's different when there's a boy in the house – more mess and dirt. But I didn't *see* much of you. Always at school, I suppose. But I mind your features, now I can get a look at you."

Merlyn rather doubted that. She was peering at him in a way that suggested that her eyesight was poor. She turned into her gate and held it open for him.

"Do you want me to come in, Mum?" said the other woman.

"No, love. No call for that. He'll just be wanting me to go and give the place a good clean. I can still do most of what I could do when you were a young-un, Merlyn, and there's not many 77-year-olds could say that, is there?"

She gave him a triumphant smile, opened the front door of her terraced house and led the way into the sitting room. Dolly was ecstatic at being done with walking, but improved the shining hour by an ecstasy of sniffing.

"There, look at her! And she's never been here before. I suppose she must be smelling me."

"Just noting things down to enlarge her catalogue I should think," said Merlyn. He decided to go along with the pretence that Renee had already furnished him with. "I was wondering if you could come round to Congreve Street for a day and give the ground floor a going over. You'll have to be a bit careful, in case there are important papers and things. But if you could just make it presentable, in case I should have callers, that's really all it needs."

She shot him a look that was almost roguish.

"Thinking of having a Cantelo family reunion? I don't reckon it will be all that well-attended." Merlyn laughed.

"Well, blood is thicker than water," he said. "But there's some of the family I wouldn't want to play host to."

"I can imagine. And some of them that you knew have disappeared long since."

"Who are they?" asked Merlyn, to get the conversation going. "I can think of Paul, but no one seemed to know where he was when I lived with Aunt Clarissa."

"Well, no one's seen Gerald for years, so far as I can make out. Not that anyone's advertising for him in the papers or anything. And they've not seen your Uncle Paul for even longer – not since soon after your grandfather died."

"His son Roderick seems to have been in contact with him recently."

"Really? If he *is* ... But you don't want to hear that old scandal."

"Actually I always find old scandal irresistible. It seems as if it was the boys who took flight, doesn't it? I wonder why."

"Well, there were ... Any road, that's neither here nor there. It's your Aunt Clarissa you'll be mourning, and a loss she is too, even if the family don't realise it. She was a good friend to me, and for many years too. I started working there in 1972, and I still went up now and then up to her death."

"Did she talk to you a lot? Confide in you?"

Again she shot him a glance. Maybe she was already suspecting that the request for domestic help was mainly a cover.

"Not so's you'd notice," she said. "Not like some, who'd tell you their whole life history, or who their husbands are sleeping with. You hear all sorts of things – you'd never believe it. Clarissa was a lady, and there was nothing of that. Just now and again I'd see that she was worried, and I'd say something, and she'd maybe come out with this and that – bits and pieces, you know."

"About the family, I suppose?"

"Well, yes. I'm talking about when her dad was alive. Later she had her clients, as you'll know, but she couldn't see them at home while her dad was living there. He'd have exploded and told them they were fools. And she never talked about her clients anyway – like a priest not revealing what he's told in confessional. So mostly what she talked about would be the family, if she talked at all. Some of them I met, though not often. Funny lot."

"Yes, we are, aren't we?"

"Oh, I wasn't including you, Mr Docherty."

"Merlyn."

"Well, Merlyn then ... You're different. And Clarissa always said that you were. But you could see most of them are a bit funny, and I saw it again at the funeral. They just make you feel ... uneasy."

"Really? At Clarissa's funeral? Of course I was seeing them for the first time in years."

"So was I, I can tell you. The Cantelos were never ones to go calling on each other. That was the first time I'd seen them together since Old Man Cantelo's funeral. They were just the same then."

"And they made you feel uneasy?"

She frowned, trying to pin it down in words she was used to.

"They couldn't do what people try to do at funerals. They couldn't pretend to be friendly, united in grief, that sort of thing. *Loving* would be even better, of course, but there was no question of that. They did all the surface stuff, smiling, shaking hands, asking how they'd been (because they obviously hadn't seen each other in years, mostly) but then it would wear thin, and there'd be these snide remarks, these boastings – about money, jobs, prestige – as if they were all in competition with each other. Tell you the truth, I thought it was childish. School playground stuff."

"Was it a sort of cover, do you think, or reflex action"

He saw he had disconcerted her with that last expression.

"Maybe a cover. Or maybe like going back to childhood. I thought then that all they were really thinking about was who got Clarissa's house and money. And that meant you, didn't it? So all the ones who had hopes turned on you, or said you weren't really you at all. Daft. Even I who didn't know you well could see it was you. And these days things like that can be proved scientifically, can't they?"

"They can, thank heavens, and they have been. But you said things had been the same at Grandfather Cantelo's funeral."

She nodded vigorously.

"The same in spades. Edgy? You wouldn't believe how edgy they all were, especially considering most of them were pleased as punch. Clarissa went round to speak to them all and she just couldn't understand. Everybody knew then that she was going to get the house, and the money was going to be divided among the daughters, who got a bit more than the sons, so what was eating each of them? And what made it stranger was that they'd seemed to be getting on better in the last months of their father's life, so what had gone wrong?"

"I'd never heard that they'd been getting on better."

"Probably because it didn't last. I had it from Caroline Sowden, who was a little mate of mine – still is, in a way. Caroline Chaunteley she is now – daft name. Everyone treats her like she isn't all there, but she's not so green as she's cabbage-looking."

"I'd forgotten that expression," said Merlyn, smiling. "But did it really apply to Caroline?"

"Did, and still does. I knew her then because she'd come to Congreve Street now and then, maybe with a message from her dad. But he was also my doctor. He and Marigold had a big house and surgery overlooking Kirkstall Abbey, and I'd sometimes see her and have a chat with her there. She told me at the time that there'd been a family meeting at their house, and others at the houses of her aunties and uncles. Emily was there, Paul, even Rosalind's father, as well as the Sowdens."

"Not Clarissa or Gerald?"

"Not so far as I know." She shook her head. "No one would ask Gerald if they hoped to have any sensible discussion."

"No," agreed Merlyn. "But if it was some kind of peace conference you'd have expected Clarissa to be at the heart of it."

"That's true. But we don't know it was anything like that. Anyway, whatever it was that was going on, they were back to normal by the time of the funeral. Paul for one stormed out, and all the rest could hardly bring themselves to talk to one another. It was something Clarissa just couldn't understand."

"Did she ever talk about it later?"

"Not for ages. But once, maybe two or three years ago, it

came up in conversation, and she just said: 'I never understood that, not for years.' I was going to ask what had been
behind it, but I looked at her and her eyes had that shut-down
look they sometimes had, and I kept my mouth buttoned. I
had to do that quite often, working in Congreve Street."

"You're thinking of Grandfather Cantelo and his young
girls, aren't you?" asked Merlyn. He thought immediately he
had made a mistake. She was too old to discuss something like
that readily. She merely tightened her lips.

"Least said, soonest mended. I didn't know anything
except the odd rumour, and I don't know any more now. But
it was an enormous embarrassment for the family, and I'd be
willing to bet the older generation was planning to do something about it."

"I talked about that with Mr Featherstone."

"Is that Clarissa's solicitor?"

"Yes. One of the possibilities the younger generation of the
family seem to have discussed was to have him declared mentally incapable of handling his own affairs."

"He wasn't," said Renee Osborne in a downright manner.
"I saw him regularly at that time. He was a bit funny – embarrassing, like – but he was perfectly clear in his mind, and particularly so about money."

"That's what I thought. Nobody mentioned him being
senile when I was living there, which was not long after he
died."

"I bet they didn't mention him and the young girls either."

"No, that's true. They didn't."

"In some people's mind the two things went together: one
was proof of the other. But in any case they would never have
dared to try to get him certified – that was the expression we
used in my day. Even the strong ones – Emily, Hugh, Clarissa
– they never stood up to him, especially not face to face. They
didn't have the guts when things came to a head. Even if

they'd sent a solicitor along to assess his mental state there'd have been the devil's own bust-up, and they'd probably all have been out of the will altogether. Because if the solicitor wasn't bent, there was no way he could have declared old Merlyn barmy."

"Which still leaves us with the question of why the Cantelos were meeting secretly together."

"Hmmm. Well, you won't get anything out of the older generation, since it's something they've kept secret for twenty-odd years. You might try the next generation."

"You said Caroline was sharper than she seems. I must say that comes as a bit of a surprise."

She pursed her lips.

"I don't think I said that. But she knows a lot more than she gives on about, hoards of things – knowledge, little scraps of information. I meet her in the supermarket now and then, and we always have a good chat, and I always get a feeling of 'You'd be surprised what I know'."

Merlyn considered this.

"She's well disposed towards me, so I could give her another try. Or perhaps someone new would do the trick better. I must say I was a bit afraid she was sizing me up as husband material. She seems to have had a crush on me when we were at school, though at the time she kept it deadly quiet."

"She keeps everything deadly quiet," explained Renee. "She's good at hiding things, storing them up. I think it makes her feel powerful, important. And she's got no particular feeling for her mother, by the way. She won't hold things back on her account, I don't think. And the same goes for your friend Edward Fowldes – he was your friend at school, wasn't he?"

"He was my best friend among the Cantelos."

"Have you talked to him?"

"No, I haven't. I don't quite know why. He was always a quiet, tactful, considerate boy. I suppose I thought Malachi a better bet ... And I suppose I felt rather rotten about trying to squeeze things out of someone I once liked."

"Worth trying, though."

"Yes, I think you're right. We must have another chat, Renee. There's all sorts of people we haven't really talked about. Young Roderick Massey, for example."

Those pursed lips came back.

"Never met him. Never heard Clarissa speak of him. Only heard about him from Caroline. I knew his ... Paul Cantelo. Flibbertigibbet sort of chap. No backbone."

"Seems he became some sort of writer, and a teacher in an American university ... Now, when could you come and do a day's work in the old house?"

"Pretty much as soon as you like." She obviously held her diary in her head. "Tomorrow I'd rather not, because Patsy and Sam have their Silver Wedding, and they're having a do at the Parkside Hotel. What about Thursday?"

"You won't have a hangover?"

"I will not. I wouldn't be so daft. So I'll see you on Thursday. Goodbye for now, Dolly."

Dolly gave a moderately enthusiastic wag, and signalled that she was ready for another of Merlyn's marathon walks. When the two of them had got through the front door and out of the gate they started back up Kirkstall View, and every step they took sent a little nerve in Merlyn's brain twitching with a reproach, over and over:

"You bloody fool. You forgot. You bloody fool. You forgot."

But it was a long time ago. And when he was at Clarissa's he had had little to do with the other Cantelos. Whatever the reason, he kicked himself for forgetting that interesting little fact: that Caroline's elderly father was a doctor.

* * *

"I got more out of her than out of any of the family," said Merlyn to Charlie and Oddie later that day. "Mr Robinson said to me that I should go for outsiders, and he was right."

He had taken a bus into town, feeling rather strange, and had gone along to Millgarth Police Headquarters, and was sitting in Oddie's office, with a view over the market and towards the expensive flats in The Calls, the old dockland quarter. How different Leeds was to the town he had known twenty years ago, he thought.

"That may be right up to a point," said Oddie. "The outsiders will talk more easily. But when it comes down to it, how much will they know? An outsider will have rumour, hearsay, gossip to retail. I heard a lot yesterday from one of Cantelo's fellow businessmen. But in the end you have to go to the heart of the matter in question. And that means getting a reliable, informed story from one of the people at the centre."

"That could only be one of the older Cantelos," said Merlyn.

"Maybe," put in Charlie. "We have no reliable evidence of a conspiracy aimed at old Merlyn by his children. Can you blame us that we're concentrating on the person who tampered with your car? That's a definite crime, whether or not it leads us to something else. Can you imagine us ever getting enough evidence to put six or seven Cantelo children or their wives and husbands into the dock charged with — what? — parricide? That's pretty much what you're thinking, isn't it?"

"Yes, that's what I've had in mind," admitted Merlyn.

"With this Marigold's husband as a lynch-pin, obediently signing the death certificate?"

"Yes, maybe."

Charlie's mouth was screwed wryly.

"I'm not saying it's nonsense. I'm just saying we haven't a hope in hell of putting together a case."

"On the other hand," said Oddie, "if that is behind the attempt on you, then of course we're interested."

"You mean that whoever it was that tampered with the car probably sees me as the main one who's going into all this, and sees getting rid of me as the main way of putting a stop to the investigation?"

"Yes, basically."

Merlyn pondered a moment.

"Rosalind came to see you, didn't she? She would know that getting rid of me wouldn't stop you going into all this."

"That wasn't what we talked about. She was much more interested in talking about you than about the family in general. She tried to convince us that your aunt was afraid of *you*, scared of your violence and what you might do."

Merlyn looked at them for a moment, then burst out laughing.

"Nice try, Rosalind!"

"Though now I remember it," Oddie went on, "when we were talking about who could confirm this new slant on things, she was insistent on asking us what we would be asking them."

"Why do you think that was?"

"Well, conceivably she could prime them on your aunt's supposed fear of you, but she seemed to want to make sure that we were not going into other matters where perhaps she couldn't be so sure of them not giving away things she wanted to have kept hidden: things like the death of your grandfather, for example."

Merlyn seized on the suggestion.

"If I'm right about that, and if Rosalind knows about it too, there's no reason why other members of her and my generation shouldn't know about it."

"No reason why they shouldn't, and none why they should."

"Point taken. But I think it's time to find out."

"I agree," said Charlie, who had been taking skeletal notes. "You've talked to Caroline, Rosalind, Roderick Massey, Malachi and Francis Cantelo – who else?"

"No one else of my generation, and Roderick only at a party – the sort of chat I've also had with one or two others: Marigold, Emily, Edward. Edward is one I think I should talk to again, and alone. He's one I'd like to do myself, at any rate first, before you get to him. He was a friend twenty years ago, and this may count for something. I think he is an honourable man, and he might tell me if he knows anything to the purpose."

"If he's an honourable man and knows something he should have told us as soon as he found out about it," Charlie pointed out.

"Not necessarily. He may not *know*, and what he does know may not be criminal, or he may have found it out so long after the event that he thought the time was past when it could be followed up. And of course he may be completely in the dark. But I do think that if the Cantelo parents were getting together, their children ought to have noticed that something out of the ordinary was going on. And from what Renee Osborne told me Caroline Chaunteley did. So should the rest of them."

"Why do I get the impression," asked Charlie, "that you want to talk to Edward because you'd like one of us to talk to Caroline?"

"Because I've already talked to her twice, because she had a crush on me when we were teenagers, and because I find her irritating and a bit embarrassing. But Renee says there's a lot more to her than people generally think. So it's just possible that a new broom might sweep her clean."

"And a new broom of her generation would be most effective, wouldn't it?" said Oddie cunningly.

"Undoubtedly," said Merlyn. Charlie sighed.

That evening Merlyn rang Brussels and told Danielle that he thought things might be coming to a head. He found it enormously refreshing to talk to someone who was intelligent, uncomplicated, and an outsider. He was beginning to get irritated by the Cantelos, and to cast around in his head for the words that best summed them up. He thought what most of them suffered from was congenital inward-looking antagonism.

"I'm getting the impression of a little group of people who weren't united by anything except being of the same family, and otherwise just squabbled with each other, ran each other down, or kept their distance from each other. I suppose the thing it most resembles is a political party."

"Well, you don't get anything more full of squabbles than a Belgian political party," said Danielle. "As you know. But these are all people you knew already, aren't they?"

"Some of them. But even when I *knew* them I didn't *understand* them. I was only sixteen at the time, remember."

"So you've been going around talking to them and finding out what really makes them tick, have you?"

"To some extent. My car was stolen by joyriders, so I'm not very mobile at the moment. But I've talked to the maid, for example – the woman who worked at Congreve Street while I was living there, and for years before and after. It was a view from outside, but very suggestive."

"I see. Suggestive of what?"

"Well, of the Cantelo family ganging up in an unlikely way."

"To do what?"

"To protect their interests."

"I see ... So tell me about your car being stolen."

It must have been something in his voice when he mentioned it. He had tried to be airy, perhaps tried too hard. He had known Danielle for two years, and she knew when he was lying, or when (more often) he was trying not to tell her something to avoid the need for lying. He took a deep breath.

"I'd better tell you," he said.

So he told her about the car, the tampered-with brakes, the dead boy. When he had finished, Danielle said, with steel in her voice.

"You're coming home. Now."

And they argued back and forth, Danielle threatened to come to Leeds to get him, and in the end Merlyn said:

"I'll get a flight on Sunday."

Chapter Sixteen
A Chield's Amang You Takin Notes

Charlie got out of his car and looked up at the house. Brick and stonedash, with the odd painted beam providing a timid nod to the distant past. The gate from the street was open, and he went through the little apron of front garden to the olive-green painted door. He was about to press the bell when he heard a voice from upstairs.

"If you aren't well enough to go to school you certainly aren't well enough to go swimming or skating. You can stay in bed till lunchtime, and then we'll see if you're well enough to come with me to the shops."

Charlie had had a vivid thumbnail sketch of Caroline Chaunteley from Merlyn, and the voice he heard didn't correspond with it. As he pressed the doorbell he heard a door shut inside, then steps coming rapidly down the stairs.

"Caroline Chaunteley?" he said to the face that opened the door.

"Yes. But I never buy —"

"And I never sell. You're very wise. It's always rubbish if it's sold at the door, and if it isn't it's something you don't want. But I'm not selling anything, as I say. I'm a police officer."

"Oh! I don't see why you —"

"Do you think I could come in?" Charlie asked, smiling his most innocent and beguiling grin. "It's about your cousin Merlyn Docherty, and it's a little bit private."

"Oh yes, then," Caroline began, and then turned into the hall. "He's such a nice man, and I don't see why ... ?"

"Don't see why what?" asked Charlie, following her through into the lounge.

"Everyone has been so beastly to him. Well, not ..."

"Not everyone? Who, then, mainly?"

"Well, Rosalind. And Emily. They're one of my cousins and one of my aunts. And my mother hasn't been particularly nice. She *seems* nice, but —"

"Not nice really?"

"Horrid, sometimes. Oh, I shouldn't —"

Charlie held up his hand, as if he was still directing traffic.

"I hope you'll be quite open with me, and tell me honestly what you think or feel. Will you do that? This could be a case of murder."

"Murder! Surely —"

"A young man died after he went joyriding in Mr Docherty's car. It had been tampered with."

"But wasn't it an old car? I mean, brakes on old cars —"

"Tampered with. Not worn down, but deliberately made a danger to the driver. No one could have known that the car would be taken by joyriders. So the question arises: why would anyone want to kill your cousin Merlyn?"

"I can't think of anyone."

"You just mentioned several people who had been beastly to him."

Caroline's eyes widened.

"Yes, but I mean *beastly*. It's just words, isn't it? I mean, it's not —"

"Murder. No, beastly is not murder." They were sitting down now, Charlie in a large comfortable chair beside the empty grate, Caroline on the farthest cushion of the sofa. Charlie bent forward.

"Mrs Chaunteley, I heard you just now talking to your child – daughter, is it? I have a daughter, much younger – not yet at school. I heard you, and you can talk to your child in proper sentences, forcefully, sensibly. I think you could talk to me like that if you tried, and if you could it would give me a much better idea of what you know. I think you do know something, and something important too. Why don't you close your eyes and imagine that I'm a child – an intelligent child who wants answers to his question, and thinks you have some of them. Could you try that?"

"I — I don't know. I could try."

"So, close them ... Now, tell me how this habit of not finishing sentences, leaving people to guess your meaning, came about. Did it start when you were a child?"

She swallowed, thought, and then gave a coherent, finished answer.

"Yes. It sort of grew, but I knew what I was doing. My parents loved each other, but didn't much care for me. I think I was an incumbrance, or if not that at least an irrelevance. Quite young I realised that they, and particularly my mother, had decided that I was stupid. And I found that, with that view of me, they often said things in front of me that they shouldn't – and *wouldn't* have, if they'd thought me quick and bright."

"So it suited you to confirm them in this impression?"

She left a pause, as if wondering whether to strip off one more garment, then said:

"Yes."

"Because you liked hearing things that they thought would pass completely over your head?"

"Yes." She was keeping her eyes tightly closed, and sometimes screwing up her face. "And often they did. Pass over my head, I mean. But I would remember those puzzling remarks later on – sometimes years later – and then they would make sense, because by then I'd gained the knowledge of the world that could explain them."

"What sort of things did you learn?"

"I learned that I was not a wanted child, at least as far as my mother was concerned. My father had insisted that I was not to be aborted. He was a widower, and his previous marriage was childless, and he didn't want another the same. But he was always extra-attentive to my mother, to show her she had not been replaced by me in his affections. To me he was loving, but only when we were alone."

"That must have been hurtful."

"Yes, it was."

"I want to turn now to the time when you were about twelve, when your Grandfather Cantelo died. Do you remember?"

"Oh yes."

"Why do you say that so confidently?"

There was quite a long silence. Since her eyes were still closed it was as if she was asleep.

"Because Grandfather's death was the most extraordinary thing that ever happened to me. I mean, really the most extraordinary thing I ever overheard."

"You overheard a lot?"

A secretive smile spread over her face.

"I always enjoyed listening, though if it was just Mother and Father there wasn't much of interest, and they *never* talked about me. But this was different – for a start because there were so many people there."

"A sort of party? Or a conference. Tell me about it."

"I was told in advance that there were a lot of people coming to the house – that was a couple of hours before they arrived, though in fact it must have been organised days in advance. I think they didn't want to arouse my curiosity. I was told to go to bed early. I was twelve, well past the age of being sent to bed, or so I thought, but I didn't make a fuss. It was convenient that they thought I was a little mouse who always did as she was told. My room looked out over the front of the house, so I saw everyone arrive."

"And who was that?"

"Aunt Emily and her husband, Uncle Hugh and Auntie Joan, Uncle Paul on his own, Auntie Edie, Malachi and Francis's mother, and Merlyn's father."

"Merlyn's father? Jake Docherty?"

"Yes. He was the only one I didn't know at all."

"How did you know it was him, then?"

"Because they called him Jake later. I'll tell you."

"Go on, then."

"Well, I left it a long time before I went down. I was sure Aunt Clarissa would be coming, and perhaps Uncle Gerald too, though I knew nobody in the family wanted to have much to do with him, and I thought Auntie Edie was there instead. But I felt sure Aunt Clarissa would come, because it seemed to be some kind of family council, some crisis meeting or peace conference. But she didn't come, so eventually I went down."

"Where were they meeting?"

"In the dining room. Nice long table for them to sit around. There was a wardrobe in the hall just beside the door, but I couldn't hide in it because it was only March, and a lot of people had coats on when they arrived which were put in there. I didn't want to be found among the coats and scarves, so I just stood by the door into the dining room and hoped I'd be able to scuttle into the kitchen if any of them got up to go. The floor in the dining room was parquet, so if someone just got up to go to the toilet I would be able to hear quite well."

"You'd got it all worked out, hadn't you?"

"Oh, I had. Father sometimes had 'good, long talks' with his better-off patients in the dining room. I used to listen to those if mother was out of the way. That's where I first learned what venereal disease was."

"You went in for self-education, I can see that."

Caroline giggled. She was now very relaxed, and had definitely opened her eyes.

"Anyway, when I got down to the hall and had taken up position, they were discussing Clarissa. 'Clarissa is out of it,' I heard my father say. 'That's beyond question.' There were one or two mutters of agreement, but then Uncle Hugh came in: 'I don't see why. Her interests are threatened as much as any of our interests.' But Auntie Edie came in at that point: 'She'd be the first to be suspected – inheriting the house, and having nursed and suffered all his rages and awfulness all this time.' Then Uncle Hugh came back: 'But if we do go in for some kind of ballot, we could fix it so that it's not her. Then we could make sure she was somewhere where she could be vouched for. That way she'd be inside the tent pissing out, not outside pissing in.' Aunt Emily said: 'Don't be crude, Hugh.' And he just muttered: 'We'd have less to fear – that's the main thing."

"So they talked of some kind of ballot, did they?" asked Charlie. "You're sure?"

"Quite sure. It's not something anyone would forget! It was bizarre. Anyway, my father asked: 'When did you last talk to Clarissa, Hugh?' 'Good Lord, I've no idea. I haven't *really* talked to her for years.' 'Then I can assure you,' my father said, 'that there is no way – *no way* – that she would go along with this. If we broached it to her she would go straight along to the police and spill the beans. End of plan. End of discussion. We have to set a time when she's fully occupied anyway, and get plenty of outside witnesses, not just family. That's the only way to make sure that she's out of it altogether.'"

"Interesting," said Charlie.

"Then they started talking about how 'it' was to be done. They never used any specific word for what it was. My father said the best way was probably a pillow covered with polythene. He said 'it' – the method – was quite difficult to spot at the best of times, and the polythene made it still more so. 'Not that the doctor will be looking all that closely,' he said, and there was a nervous little laugh from somebody. It made my blood run cold. No name had been mentioned, you see, for the victim. For a moment I thought they might be talking about me! It must have been a case of the unloved child, feeling everyone could have dispensed with their existence. I think I even started across the hall in terror. Then I remembered how they'd talked about Aunt Clarissa inheriting and having nursed him. There was only one person Aunt Clarissa could inherit from. So I crept back, knowing they were planning to kill Grandfather."

"It must have been terrifying for you," said Charlie.

"Relief more like!" Caroline said, opening her eyes wide and giggling. "Well, I suppose it was terrifying as well, to know I had a family full of potential murderers. But when I knew it was Grandfather Cantelo I don't think I felt shocked or anything. I didn't like Grandfather, I didn't like going to visit him, and I didn't like the way he talked to me, or touched me. I only went to Congreve Street when I knew Clarissa would be there as well. I think she thought I was stupid, as everyone else does, but she was always kind."

"So you went back and listened at the door?"

"Yes, for a while. They were back on to Clarissa. They thought they couldn't just rely on her going to whatever she had on on the night 'it' was going to be done. Someone had to go with her. It was Aunt Edie who volunteered. I didn't really know the voice, because everyone avoided Gerald Cantelo, but hers was the only woman's voice I wasn't certain of. She said she would not have the strength or the courage to do it, but this way she could play her part. Clarissa knew she was interested in the spiritualist case, and she'd like to go along to one of her séances. That was agreed, and Edie said she'd drive her there. Clarissa always felt that driving herself to a session dissipated her spiritual energies just when she needed them most. What a lot of nonsense it all was! So Edie said she felt sure Clarissa would accept the offer of a lift, and once she was at the séance or meeting or whatever it was, she would phone my mother, who would ring round to all the others in the group. That was when I realised," she added, looking straight at Charlie.

"What did you realise?"

"That no one was to know who had drawn the straw that marked them out as the murderer. My mother would have to ring round all of them to tell them that Clarissa was out of the way, and only that way could she be sure of speaking to the one who was going to do the job."

Charlie thought hard.

"It makes sense. Then none of them – or only one of them – could break under questioning. No one would know who actually did it except the one who did."

"Though of course they didn't expect questioning. In their minds it was just a remote possibility that needed to be faced up to."

"Though someone like your uncle Paul, who seems to have been consumed with rage at being cuckolded by his own father, would have presented a danger. Anyone not in full control would."

"That could apply to Merlyn's dad as well."

"They really were relying rather heavily on your father pulling it off. He was your grandfather's doctor, and he could get an easy-going colleague to countersign, and that would be the end of it. As it turned out that *was* the end of it."

"Ye-e-es."

Charlie noted the hesitation, but ignored it for the moment.

"So what happened then?"

"They started to talk about the next meeting, and the drawing of straws. I nearly slipped away, but it became clear that a row was developing, so I stayed a bit longer. There was the question of who would prepare the draw that was to select the murderer (they never used that word, of course). People seemed to think that my father was a good idea – he being a doctor seemed to put him above suspicion, and also he was only a member of the family by marriage, which seemed to Emily and others to be an advantage as well. Then I heard a voice I didn't know well – it must have been Jake Docherty – say: 'He may be a doctor, but he's also an amateur conjurer. I've been at a kids' party where he's done all kinds of tricks. Good ones they were too. He's got his part in this business, and an important part, and it should be left at that. We've got to have someone who isn't going to be suspected of fiddling the ballot.'

"Good heavens," said Charlie. "What a collection of people! I get the impression of a group that were disunited even as they were planning a joint action."

"That's right. There was no way of uniting the Cantelos."

"Was he right about your father as a conjuror?"

"Oh yes. Some of the happiest days of my childhood were spent watching my dad do his tricks. He was only an amateur, of course, but a brilliant one. I sometimes thought he only wanted a child so he would have a resident audience."

"So who was finally picked to prepare the draw?"

"They rejected my mother, and finally they picked on Paul. 'Does that satisfy you, Jake?' they asked, and he grunted a reply. So that was all agreed, they arranged a date for the next meeting – about ten days away, at Emily's – and a provisional date for when 'it' was to be done – about three weeks away. They agreed that Paul would arrange nine identical slips of paper, one of which would have an X on it. At the meeting at Emily's they would inspect the slips, fold them, put them in a bag, then each would draw one out. They wouldn't open them – they would simply go away and have no more contact with each other till after the death, and even then nothing would be said about what had been decided and what had happened. Simple! Easy-peasy!"

Charlie thought long and hard.

"Simple maybe. But you were uncertain a minute or two ago when I said your father would sign the death certificate and that would be the end of it."

"Well yes, a bit. He did sign the death certificate, but ... well, I don't think things went as he expected."

"Tell me about it."

"Ten days after that meeting at ours there was the meeting at Aunt Emily's – my father and mother went there, and made no secret of where they were going. I knew that another ten days or so after that, Grandfather was scheduled to die. No one had any contact with any of the others, so the only way I might have learnt the actual date was by overhearing a discussion between my parents about it. I never did. I don't think they talked about it, because they didn't *need* to. They knew, and kept quiet about it, even among themselves. But I did feel that I knew by signs – looks, tensions, nerviness – when it was getting near."

"So how did you know when it happened?"

"I'm coming to that. I knew when they knew. We were at dinner one evening when the cook came in – she came and cooked dinner for five evenings a week, and the other evenings were *grim* – and she whispered in my father's ear. I heard the words 'Mr Merlyn Cantelo', and my father burst out: 'But that's –' with an expression of total surprise on his face. That's when I knew things hadn't gone as expected."

"So what happened then?"

"He realised at once that his reaction was wrong. Grandfather had been ill for three or four months. No one, let alone a doctor, could be surprised at his death, even though there'd been a lot of talk about his getting better. Father looked at Mary, the cook, but she was too dim to register that something was not quite right. He should have looked at me. He got up and went round the table to my mother. 'Marigold,' he said, 'I'm afraid your father —' and she dabbed at her eyes and said, 'He's dead, isn't he?' and father said 'Yes. I must go to Congreve Street.' Then he left the house, mother went up to their bedroom, and when Mary cleared away the plates she said: 'It's been a terrible shock for your mum and dad, hasn't it?' and I just said: 'I suppose so.' It had been a shock up to a point."

"Did you ever find out what had gone wrong?"

"Not really. I just got ... indications. I was only twelve, but I was often lonely, and used to thinking things through on my own. I decided that the death had come on the wrong day – probably the day before it was supposed to, or two days before. Clarissa still had a good alibi — she was in a long meeting with two or three other Leeds clairvoyants — so that was taken care of. Father was told that grandfather had died, which was what he was expecting. It was the timing that surprised him."

"Right. But that's your deduction, isn't it? You never heard your parents discussing it?"

"No. The only thing I heard was a telephone conversation, and there you only get one side, don't you?"

"Of course. How much later was this?"

"Oh, maybe three or four days. Before the funeral anyway."

"Meanwhile your father had gone and signed the death certificate, had he?"

"Oh yes. Asphyxia is difficult to detect, and in any case he wasn't going to look for signs of it, was he, like he said at the meeting. It could have been a family member who had got the slip with X on it doing the murder a day or two early. The main thing was, he was dead, and things needed to be wrapped up so the whole thing could be forgotten."

"You think that was the important thing, rather than finding out what actually happened?"

"Oh yes. I feel sure that they were all meant to remain in

doubt anyway. Permanently. So that once the certificate had been signed and the undertakers had taken him away for cremation —"

"Cremation?"

"Yes. Grandfather was always keen to do the modern thing. He said cremation was 'more hygienic'. And if he hadn't said it, one of the family would have put the words into his mouth. Cremation was safer all round. So things turned out pretty much as they were meant to. The date he died was just a hiccup. That's what my dad was saying the only time I did overhear him talking about Grandfather's death."

"What was he saying?"

"He was talking to one of the family members involved in the plot, but I don't know which one. He said 'The important thing is, he's dead. Everyone accepts it was natural causes. Why should we or anyone else enquire any further? ... Leave it! The old man is dead, and that's what we wanted. Let there be an end to it. An end!' And he slammed the phone down. He thought I was at school, but I'd come home early, pretending to be still upset about Grandfather's death. Being there when nobody thought you were was much the best way of overhearing things, I found."

And she smiled at Charlie with her great, brown, liquid eyes which expressed the clear desire that he and she should come to know each other better.

Later, when he'd told all this to Merlyn Docherty, Charlie expressed his frustration.

"So the death could have been natural causes. It could have been done a day or two early by the one who picked the X slip. It could have been done early by another family member who wanted to have the satisfaction of doing it —"

"Paul, maybe," said Merlyn.

"Right. Or it could have been done by someone else altogether. And so far as I can see for all – or most – of the family it was left uncertain what had happened, and who had done it. They were in blissful ignorance, and happy to remain that way."

Chapter Seventeen
Best Friend

"Eddie?"

Merlyn knew it was Edward Fowldes by the voice, and Edward knew it was Merlyn. Eddie was the nearest Merlyn had come to closeness with anyone of his own generation in the eighteen months he had been in Leeds twenty years before.

"Merlyn! I've been wondering if you'd be in touch."

"I shouldn't have left it so long, but I've been rather ... busy since I got back."

"I heard about the car only yesterday. I didn't even know you'd moved into Congreve Street."

"Camping here, rather than living. I'm sure your mother will have heard that."

"Maybe. Mother and I are not that close."

"The story of the Cantelo family."

"True. Though as you say Mother probably knows all the news about you. Information of a certain kind does travel around. There is some kind of grapevine."

"Probably centred on Rosalind. She's been aggressive in a way I don't remember when I was living here before. The truth is she made very little impression on me then, apart from once making a suggestive advance."

"We regarded her as just a schoolkid, whereas you and I were about to start out in the big world. She's just grown up. And she had to fend for herself – emotionally and in other ways."

"You're probably right. Eddie, I wondered if you would like to see the old house again, maybe for the last time. We had some pretty good times here while I was in Leeds."

"We did," Eddie said. "I was always fond of Clarissa, like

most people. I wish now I'd gone to see her in her last years. People said she was senile, or the next thing, but —"

"— but you realise now that wasn't true. Quite right. She was no worse than a little bit odd and very vague. Would you like to come round? Then we could go for a meal or a drink."

"A drink would be fine. I've got faddy in my middle age, full of likes and dislikes about my food. It means I don't get much pleasure from a meal out."

So they arranged that Eddie would come round the next evening, and when they'd looked around the house a bit they'd go to the West End pub or the Vesper Gate for a drink. Merlyn wondered whether he ought to buy another old car for his last days in Leeds and to get him back to the Continent. On his aunt's telephone table there was a pad with a number on it and a note: "to get rid of the car" in a shaky hand. His aunt selling off her means of transport when she knew she would never use it again. He nearly rang the number, but then thought of having to inspect under the car every time he went for a drive, and decided that if he did buy one it would be at the last minute before he left the country. He spent the next day looking at the notes he had made when Charlie told him about his interview with Caroline. Merlyn had to admit that the policeman had got a lot more out of her than any amateur investigator could have. Since a sexual interest had obviously played a part in Caroline's response to Charlie, Merlyn felt glad he had not been given the task himself.

With Eddie the best approach was of "old-friends-newly-met-up", with a casual, maybe crab-like lead-up to the main subject. So when Eddie arrived Merlyn was prepared to start in on what had happened to old school-mates in the intervening years, but as it turned out they lighted directly on old times in the house as their topic of conversation. They went into the dining room first, but Eddie simply looked around it disparagingly.

"This was never a room of any importance in our time, was it? Anyway, I was here after the funeral."

"Of course you were," said Merlyn, turning back to the door. "You're right. This room's day was when your mother and mine were young."

"This room is more to the point," said Eddie, when they went into the sitting room that doubled as a clairvoyant's consulting room. "We used to be fascinated by the Tarot cards and the crystal ball and the whole paraphernalia."

"Now and then we'd listen outside the door and bust a gut trying not to roar with laughter."

Eddie laughed now.

"Fancy getting one's first ideas about sexual behaviour from confessions to a spiritualist!"

"Once Clarissa came out and caught us. We were convinced it was her second sight told her we were there."

"Whereas it was probably a creaking floorboard."

Merlyn brought the tea in from the kitchen and poured them two cups. He looked around the room.

"Pity none of the Cantelos came for a consultancy session."

"They never would!" said Eddie. "Gerald apart they were rationalists to a man – and woman. My mother may sound like a nineteenth-century Methodist, but she firmly believes in a cool and godless universe."

"And the duty of everyone to guide their conduct in life by the sacred rules of competition."

"Don't I know it!" said Eddie, his tone heartfelt. "My mother tried it on me, but I must be some kind of mutant: the Cantelo spirit of get up and grab passed me by."

"I got a strong sense of that spirit from the strange novel I mentioned to you at Caroline's party," said Merlyn. Eddie nodded.

"I went and had a look at it in the Leeds Library," he said.

"It was written by Paul, I feel quite sure."

"What makes you so sure?"

"It corresponds with everything I remember about him, and everything people have told me about him since he took off."

"For instance?"

"The fact that it really never landed the knock-out satirical punch, but got sidetracked into some not very interesting plot-lines, instead of concentrating on the family, and the effects of their upbringing on their relationships with each other."

"You've really read it," said Merlyn. "I'm afraid I only skimmed through it before I gave it back to Sergeant Peace."

"Then again, I had to go to the library to read it, because there aren't any copies in the family. That's a real sign of Paul's futility: it was obviously written with his siblings in mind, to have a good laugh over, and then he couldn't summon up the gumption to give them all copies. He was a man with a cause and a grievance, but he just let the book fester away on library shelves. I'm not surprised he's become a teacher of creative writing: 'those who can't, teach'."

"He felt bitter enough about Grandfather Cantelo, you'd have thought, to hand it round," said Merlyn.

"You're thinking of later, when he died. But it was written before that, when Paul was quite young – the early-Seventies, I think. By the time Paul was consumed with hatred for his father the book wasn't half strong enough. It didn't take in the *real* sins of his father in Paul's eyes."

"The girlies?"

"Exactly. Including girlies in his own family."

Merlyn nodded thoughtfully.

"It's odd, isn't it? Old Merlyn thought of himself as a thoroughly modern person, but he behaved like a spoiled landowner of the *ancien régime*, taking as his right whatever caught his fancy."

"That's right. But from the book he doesn't come across as much worse than someone in the grip of a theory, and one who totally lacked a sense of humour."

"Yes. More like your average politician than a wicked and exploiting captain of industry. Well, at least you've read it properly. One of very, very few who have done so I imagine."

"It was interesting, but it went off at half-cock. In the event it was Paul who was the bomb. By the time of grandfather's funeral he was consumed with rage and with delight that his father was dead. He went round at the wake saying all sorts of indiscreet things, including his satisfaction that he was dead. Not at all the sort of behaviour expected of you in Headingley."

"I see ..." Merlyn pondered. "You don't think Paul could have been got rid of, do you? I mean sent away. As being —" he nearly said, "dangerous", but that might have revealed all too much to Eddie, so he just said, "too much of an embarrassment."

"Could be. He took off within the month after grandfather died. Maybe someone slipped him the fare to the States and it did the trick."

Merlyn considered this and poured them both second cups.

"You know, old Cantelo had something else in common with a politician: a total lack of a sense of humour. Heredity's a funny thing, isn't it? How many of the Cantelos had or has a sense of humour?"

"Clarissa was the only one who had, that I know of," said Eddie. "Maybe your mother did, but I never knew her. It would have helped her, being married to Jake. As to the rest of that generation – not a funny bone among them."

"Shall we look upstairs?" asked Merlyn.

He switched on the lights in the hall, and they began up the fine oak staircase, with its jumble of family photographs, amateur watercolours, and even framed cartoons.

"I never realised what a splendid staircase this was," said Eddie. "From the 1870s or 80s, I would guess. This must have been a very impressive house when it was built, rather brought down by some of the houses built around it." They got to the landing, and he pointed to one of the six doors off from it. "That was Grandfather Cantelo's bedroom. I remember being taken to see him when he was very ill – maybe a month or two before he died. I was about fourteen or fifteen. I hated him. I could see that he despised me, and most of his family."

"What happened?"

"I staged a prolonged coughing fit, and he waved me away, like an absolute monarch. He deigned to talk to my mother – she was strong-minded enough for him – but most of the rest of us were beneath contempt."

"So his pride in his system of child-raising must have been dented by then?"

"I expect he rationalised it as some quirk of heredity rather than a failure of the system ..." Eddie threw a glance at Merlyn. "When I saw him he was at a low ebb. He got better after that."

"Got better? Really better?"

Eddie grimaced.

"Quite a lot better. Dangerously better. He was thinking of starting up a big new clothing business."

Merlyn was staggered, and showed it.

"How on earth could he do that?"

"With the money from the sale of Cantelo Shirts. It fetched a packet in 1975. The buyer knew it was a failure of design, a refusal to follow the trends. The basic structure and economic prospects of the firm were fine, and the workforce first rate. So there was money. Grandad wanted to start a new firm from scratch, at the age of seventy-eight."

"He'd have lost everything."

Eddie nodded.

"He would. Everyone would." With another significant glance Eddie led the way to Merlyn's old room. "Oh, I remember this place. We had a lot of real old chinwags here. School-work of course. And other things."

"Yes, other things," agreed Merlyn. He took up the exercise book which he had found the week before and flipped through the pages. "I found notes here about things that happened just before I left. Aunt had told me that she thought I was threatened by some kind of family business – that I might be targeted because I was her heir."

"Yes," said Eddie. "We talked about that at the time."

Merlyn was puzzled. Eddie seemed oddly embarrassed.

"Did we? I don't remember that. What did we say?"

"Only that it seemed some kind of financial thing. Clárissa suspected something, but she didn't know what it sprang from, what the motive was. She thought it might be money."

"That I might be got out of the way?"

"Yes. But she was very muddled. Clairvoyance certainly wasn't helping her ... I think I knew more than she did."

There was silence between them for a moment. This, Merlyn registered, was why Eddie was feeling guilty.

"I'm getting hints of a family conspiracy among our parents' generation," he said eventually.

"Yes." Eddie sighed. "It's something that has been around in the background for years and years – since Grandfather's death, in fact. Things somehow firm up as time goes by, but I'd heard whispers even when you were still here. That was from Caroline throwing hints, then retreating. She's an information flirt. She drops things into the conversation, then clams up or runs away. Perhaps I should have told you."

"Why didn't you?"

"Because my parents were involved. Even with very imperfect parents one is scared of losing them. It's the 'children, keep a hold on nurse for fear of finding something worse' syndrome."

"I can understand that, just about. Did rumour say who had actually killed Grandfather?"

"Rumour said and says that there was a secret ballot —"

"I know."

"But it also says he was killed, or died, before the agreed day, so none of the family was involved. That doesn't actually follow, you'll notice. You can call it wishful thinking, or stonewalling – whatever you like."

"Does rumour say who got the short straw, even if he or she never actually got to do the deed?"

Eddie sat thinking, then looked at his watch.

"Shall we go for that drink? If we go now it'll still be light enough to sit outside."

Merlyn nodded, conscious that this was not an outright refusal to tell, merely a sign that Eddie was not yet ready to, or was unwilling to do it in that house. They called for Dolly at the back and front doors, but she was out on her travels and had to be left behind. They walked down Kirkstall Lane and then along Morris Lane towards the Abbey and the Vesper Gate pub. Eddie pointed to a terrace of houses.

"Renee Osborne lives there. Remember her?"

"I should do. I was only talking to her a couple of days ago. She's coming tomorrow to give the house a good going-over."

"Really? Isn't she past it? Couldn't you have got a cleaning firm to do it?" Then he looked at Merlyn's face. "Sorry. Silly of me to ask. You're really after information rather than cleaning skills, I imagine. You went to the right place. They were really tied up with the Cantelos."

The Abbey was bathed in evening light. There were swans on the river, and cars exceeding the speed limit on the road above. It was a place caught incongruously between two worlds. They walked down across the deserted football and rugby pitches to the Vesper Gate and bought themselves two pints of beer. Most of the outside drinkers were coming in as a pinch invaded the evening air. Merlyn and Eddie took theirs outside, pleased that the near-deserted tables and the intermittent roar of traffic gave them a degree of privacy.

"You asked if there were rumours about who got the short straw," Eddie began in a low voice. "That, above all, there was absolute silence about. After all, they were not supposed to know. And in fact the chosen person could have done it – for reasons of his own – in advance."

"So it could be any of the nine?"

Eddie was clearly impressed by the accuracy of his information, but answered at once:

"I suspect eight. Caroline's father had his important role. It would have potentially compromised him and overburdened his conscience if he had been the perpetrator as well."

"You could be right. But eight is quite a number."

"All I have to go on is conjecture. My first thought was that it might be Paul."

"I never knew him. I have the impression of a nervous, impulsive, intellectual type of person."

"That's not far off. Inclined to go over the top, people said (the Cantelos, that is, who for the most part never went over the top). And he had, by all accounts, a really strong motive, quite apart from the prospect of losing his share of the family money."

"Yes. Cuckolded by his own father."

Eddie nodded, and was silent for some time.

"And then, immediately after the funeral, he disappeared. No one knew where he was. Then, months later, when it was clear that the death had been accepted by the police and everyone else as natural causes, he made contact from America, Arkansas of all remote and little-known places, and sued for divorce. Adding all those things together, there seemed to me to be a circumstantial case against him – not that he was *got* out of the way, but he panicked and fled."

"Why did you give up the idea of its being Paul?"

"I didn't. It's a possibility. But there are others, and fairly convincing ones too."

"Such as?"

"Malachi thought the one who got the X was Gerald's wife, his mother, and that she worked Gerald up to do it as a religious duty."

"You sound sceptical. I think I would be too. I heard she ruled herself out."

Eddie nodded.

"The American religious Right have some pretty fearsome direct action people. The British lot aren't like that: they're just ineffectual cranks waiting for the Day of Judgment or peddling some wild racial nonsense without the sort of venom of the political Right. I never heard anyone say Gerald was capable of taking on a squirrel in a bad mood."

Merlyn left a pause and then said: "So?" Eddie remained sunk in thought, looking into the depths of his mug for inspiration. Then, taking a small swig, he said:

"There was another person whose life was changed by Grandfather's death."

"Oh? Who?"

"Hugh. Rosalind's father. Bluff, good-looking, a hail-fellow-well-met type. At the time of his father's death he was working for BP, after a shortish spell working in the Cantelo shirt firm. The money he inherited from his father enabled him to buy into one of the London security firms then springing up, and soon after he went to work for British Telecom, just after it was set up, and soon he was hopping from branch to branch, onward and upward, up to the time when he died in a car smash."

"So he did well out of grandfather's death."

"Definitely. And you've only heard the half of it. The move to London involved the ditching of wife and family – Rosalind, that is – and the taking of a new and luscious dolly-bird wife with social cachet to boot. He lived a smart, fast lifestyle, and the responsibility for the car crash, in which five died, was entirely his. He was a slippery, voracious individual, all misleading façade. His daughter adored him. I would guess she saw him once a year, if that, after he wiped the dust of Leeds off his boots."

"All very interesting," said Merlyn. He grinned and said, because Eddie was an old friend he felt he could be direct with: "But only proving he's the sort of man you don't like."

Eddie smiled in return.

"The bookworm school-teacher loathing the smooth operator and envying him his worldly goods? Maybe so. Though you know I'm one of those teachers who's never wanted to be anything else, and the satisfaction I get when one of my flock reads *Great Expectations* and enjoys it warms me for weeks ... I did dislike him and his hearty manners, and I was sorry for Rosalind and still am: his neglect of her was cruel, and she's lived her life with a totally false picture of him which is her form of protection from reality. She's still defending his memory."

"I know. Do you think that that's behind her recent antics?"

"Like saying Aunt Clarissa believed you were a teenage psychotic killer in embryo. That's gone round on the rumour grapevine. I would guess so. How much she knows I'm not sure, but Rosalind is a compulsive gossip and information-hoarder, so it's a fair bet that she knows a good deal."

"And your money is on Uncle Hugh as the man who popped in and did the deed a day or two early?"

Eddie thought for a bit. Then he swilled down the last of his beer and stood up. "I don't need a taxi. I can walk home.

It's only ten minutes, and I feel like the exercise. But just to answer your question: No, my money is not on Hugh."

"Why not? After all you've just told me."

"Because they were a necessary preliminary. There's one thing I haven't touched on yet. It's not a fact, or a clue, just a trait of character. Dodgy evidence, quicksands stuff, but interesting, in my view."

"And that is?"

Eddie leaned forward, his hands on the table.

"Hugh had the reputation – at Cantelo's, BP, his London posts – of being the sort of man who leaves all the dirty work to his underlings. If there were redundancies he worked out the numbers and the identities, but left the announcements to his second-in-command. If there were dodgy dealings among the staff – fiddled expense accounts, underhand stuff with the firm's rivals – he'd do the investigations himself, but leave the confrontations and sackings to the same poor unfortunate right-hand man. Nothing was allowed to dent his breezy, cheery image. He liked his life to be like the Lord Mayor's procession, and left it to others to go round with the shovel afterwards."

Merlyn pondered, looking up at his old friend.

"So what you're saying is that, if he got the slip with X on it, he'd — what? Hire a hitman to do it? Somehow I can't see Leeds in the Seventies to have been teeming with willing hit-men."

"You'd be surprised ... That would be one possibility. There is another. Grandfather's life in his later years had left a trail of victims of one kind or another: people who had strong emotional reasons for wanting to be rid of him."

"True. Do you mean that if one of them didn't pull the right straw they'd have been willing to do it anyway because they so desperately *wanted* to do it? Are we back to Paul again, then? Or perhaps my father?"

"I think you're throwing the net too close to the ship," said Eddie. "There were all sorts of people outside the family circle who had similar sorts of motives."

"You mean he didn't confine his attentions to women in his own family?"

"What do you think? Why should he? He had nearly ten years as a widower. There were other affairs, rumoured and virtually acknowledged."

Merlyn considered this.

"Acknowledged *children* you mean?"

"At least one. One that I suspect, at any rate. Think about it, Merlyn. Think about it. I'm not making any direct accusations. I don't know enough. But try and make the connections yourself."

And raising his arm he strode up in the direction of Horsforth, his lean body seeming to form a sort of question mark.

Chapter Eighteen
Cleaning Up

Merlyn did not tidy or clean up the house in Congreve Street for Renee's visit the next day. His girlfriend Danielle had gone off into great gales of laughter over this instinct, which her commonsense Belgian attitudes revolted over. This had some-times meant important papers going missing and involving hours of searching, but in general he agreed with her, and so the next day he left everything pretty much where it was.

"I'm only camping out here," he told the old woman when she arrived, "so there's not much to do apart from hoovering and dusting. Just make the place so an asthmatic could come in without suffering an attack and I'll be happy."

She nodded, and went to the hall cupboard for the vacuum cleaner.

"How was your party last night?" Merlyn asked, as he fetched his jacket, wallet and papers on the case.

"Oh, nothing special. Just a few people along to drinks and things at Patsy and Sam's favourite local. Very nice eats they were, though – better than what Rosalind managed to get for the wake here. I like my food better than a lot of drink as I get older. It doesn't make you feel rotten afterwards. But people don't make much fuss about wedding anniversaries these days, do they?"

"Don't they? I'm virtually a foreigner, remember. I should have thought that if you manage to stay together for twenty-five years when everyone around you is splitting up, you deserve a bit of a celebration."

And raising his hand and saying "See you later" he went out of the house. He thought he had got most of what he needed from her in their last meeting. He didn't, however, leave Headingley for some considerable time, because there had been an accident and a traffic snarl-up on the Otley Road, and none of the town buses got through to Kirkstall Lane. It was nearly an hour before he got into town, and he was late for a meeting with Oddie and Charlie Peace which he had arranged in anticipation of there being something worth reporting from his meeting with Eddie.

They had coffee and rolls from the canteen. Merlyn decided that policemen did not seem to do themselves particularly well when it came to feeding and watering, and was surprised. Charlie and Oddie just stuffed it in, however, as if they were shoving coins into a parking meter. Merlyn told them about his meeting with Eddie, and what they'd talked about in the house and then at the Vesper Gate. The policemen were interested, but by the end they made it clear they were more than a little disgruntled.

"Why was he so enigmatic?" Charlie asked. "He complains about my Caroline being an information flirt, then he plays exactly the same game himself, with the same sort of tricks. She was forthcoming by comparison."

"That was sex," said Merlyn. "She was interested in you. I didn't have the same weapon for getting things out of Eddie."

"You had friendship, going back a long way," grumbled Charlie. "I would have thought that was a much more powerful weapon."

"I don't know about that," said Merlyn. "We talked about our friendship and what we did together, but a friendship that has had a twenty-year interruption isn't much of one, is it?"

"Why do you think he was so coy?" asked Oddie.

"Maybe the person he suspects is someone he loves, admires, owes some kind of loyalty to. Those emotions would be important to a man like Eddie."

"We're talking about the hitman – or woman – here," said Charlie. "Morally the man who hired him is the main villain, and surely Eddie need feel no loyalty or love for either of them."

"As far as Hugh Cantelo is concerned, certainly he feels

none at all. He obviously disliked and distrusted him when he was alive, and apparently with good grounds. But I think a more likely reason for Eddie's caution – yes, it came out as coyness, but I think it wasn't that – was that he has an idea who did it, but is far from sure. In that situation he preferred to leave it to me. If I had been prompted by him, there would be no satisfaction for him if I came up with the same name. If I had the same information as him but no prompting he would feel that his suspicions had been confirmed. Eddie's a sensitive, conscientious, morally aware type of person – very unusual in our family. He'd have scruples about throwing unsubstantiated allegations around."

They all thought about that.

"Makes sense," said Oddie. "I'd just like to say one thing. The whole business of the death of your grandfather is rather beside the point for us. I doubt if we could ever prove he was murdered, let alone who did it, so what joy is there in it for us? Only in as much as there may well be some connection with the dead boy Terry Bates, who got what was surely intended for you."

"I'm sure there is that connection," said Merlyn. "It happened after I'd been snooping around for some time, and when I became more vulnerable by moving to a private address, where before I'd been living in an efficient modern hotel."

"Right," said Charlie. "Not a very firm connection, but it'll do until we get something more substantial. The neighbours say you haven't been playing Kylie Minogue records at full blast through the night, and from the family there's nothing of more substance than Rosalind's very vague allegations about your aunt's suspicions."

"Just lies," said Merlyn.

"Probably. Or your aunt intentionally misleading the family."

Merlyn treated that suggestion with scepticism.

"I doubt it. She had her reputation as a clairvoyant to consider."

"So what do we have? Eddie's suggestion that the hitman could have been someone outside the family. That could have been misdirection on his part too."

"Agreed. But the suggestion does seem to fit in with Hugh's inclination to shuffle off responsibility, which is easily checked. The family was very vulnerable, once they had ganged up together. They were at the mercy of anyone who got cold feet, or someone temperamentally unreliable, like my father – who according to himself went ever more seriously off the rails in the years that followed."

"He could have blabbed after a couple of double Scotches in those years," Oddie pointed out.

"He could. Though if he was himself involved, as apparently he was, some form of self-protection would probably stop him doing that. Anyway, getting someone from outside the charmed – or charmless – circle makes sense. That could be a hitman hired for money —"

"They come surprisingly cheap, hitmen," said Charlie.

"— or it could have been someone with a really important grievance against the old man."

There was silence while they thought.

"I liked the idea of your uncle Paul, the one with the strong grievance," said Oddie, "but temperamental instability seems to rule him out. No one sensible would rope him in to do a job like that."

"No – I'd rather rope in Eddie's mother, Aunt Emily, given the choice between her and Paul. She'd certainly get the job done," said Merlyn, with a reluctant admiration.

"What we seem to be looking for is someone tough, strong-minded, reliable – a doer rather than a thinker or an organiser, and someone with a whiff of the primitive about them."

"The problem is," said Charlie, "that very few people from outside the family have come into the case so far. I wonder how old Rosalind's husband Barnett would have been at the time."

"Barnett?" said Merlyn, surprised. "But he would have had no connection with the family then. Rosalind would have been in her early teens."

"How do we know he had no connection? It may have been the connection that brought them together."

But they were interrupted by a call to Oddie about a body found in a council flat in Morley. That was the end of the conference: there was life, or at least death, going on in Leeds, and it took precedence over the death, twenty-odd years before, of the elderly businessman Merlyn Cantelo.

The present-day Merlyn took himself off, considered taking a taxi home, then took a bus instead from the bus station nearby. It too was delayed by a visit of minor royalty to Leeds, and by the time Merlyn got back to Congreve Street Renee had already finished her jobs around the house and gone home. He'd have to call round with her money. Old as she was, she looked to have done a good job. The carpets were looking brighter, the surfaces dust-free, the kitchen sparkling.

This house will fetch a fortune, he thought.

It was not a thought prompted by slavering cupidity. He lived in a city where property prices were still reasonable in spite of the sky-high wages paid to EU employees and European MPs. He was well-paid himself, and could join in the property rat-race when he and Danielle decided to marry and settle down. But the money from the old house in Congreve Street would certainly help him to settle comfortably – no, better than comfortably, he told himself.

He wandered round the house, room by room. Bright though the kitchen looked, the new owner would probably want it completely redone in a more modern style. Kitchens

tended to weaken the resolve of even the most fanatical con-
servationist. The size of both the sitting room and the dining
room would be an attraction, particularly as the central heating seemed efficient. He passed the telephone table in the hall
and saw that the top leaf of the pad had been tidied away – no
chance now of acquiring his aunt's old banger (somehow he
knew it would have been an old banger, because that was his
aunt's style of car) and taking it on a trip to Brussels before
consigning it to the knacker's yard.

The staircase, he could see, would be a wonderful selling
point: oak, supremely solid and confident, sheer Victorian
class. With all his aunt's bits and pieces, from family stuff to
sheer tat, removed, this part of the house could be genuinely
impressive. Upstairs, he looked again at the five bedrooms: all
but one were of a good size, and his aunt's and his grandfather's got good morning light. The bathroom was a period
piece – a large bath for the stretched-out luxury soak, an early
twentieth-century shower that gave waterfalls to stand under,
and hot towel-rails. Please God the new owner kept this room
as it was.

Something was niggling in the back of his mind.

"Try and make the connections yourself," Eddie had said.
Easier said than done. Had he got all the information that
Eddie himself had? He doubted it. He had been cut off from
the family's information network since soon after the death of
his grandfather. If Clarissa hadn't known something, he
would have had no chance of hearing of it.

As he made his way downstairs, like Eliza Doolittle making her entrance at the ball, the phone rang. Merlyn speeded
up and found that it was Charlie.

"Just an item of news," the policeman said. "We've got the
report of the SOCO people on the car. The brakes were certainly interfered with – a hole was made in the brake pipe. It
was a deadly piece of work, efficiently carried out."

"Interesting," said Merlyn.

"Very, we thought," agreed Charlie.

"I can't imagine Rosalind being a skilful car mechanic."

"Hardly any women before the present generation of young women would know their way around a car at all."

"Barnett, I suppose, might."

"Anyway, it's something to think about," said Charlie. "They took extensive DNA samples from the car and the area around it, but those will take a lot longer to be analysed."

"The case continues," said Merlyn, as they both rang off.

"Something to think about," Charlie had said. It was indeed. And Charlie's call had focused his attention back on cars.

Cleaning ladies did not tear off pages of a telephone notepad. All sorts of problems and difficulties could result if they did that, so it was more than their jobs were worth: those notepads were aides-memoires for action, reminders of numbers to ring, accounts of important points of earlier telephone conversations. A cleaner who went around destroying pages on a notepad could be in serious hot water.

Getting interested, he looked in wastepaper baskets, which were all empty, then in the dustbins. Nothing.

And then there were other things floating around in his mind: the fact that in the late Seventies Hugh Cantelo was working for BP; there was the car broken down on the road to Shipley; and he wondered about the workforce at Cantelo Shirts.

In the end there was no alternative but to sleep on it. He got to sleep quite easily, but his waking dream was an uneasy one. It was of an old man in bed, waving him away as if to say: "Put him in the Bastille", or "throw him into the Bosphorus". And as he paused at the bedroom door and turned back he saw the old man pull back the bedclothes and raise his nightshirt as if to expose himself. It was an uneasy sleep, and he had a shower next morning under that same generous stream of water he had thought about the night before, which refreshed him mightily. As he made his breakfast and ministered to Dolly's needs he wondered whether he was disturbed by his grandfather's rampaging sexuality in his last years – not just its inappropriate objects, but the fact of it. He also doubted whether old man Cantelo wore a nightshirt – unless of course the family firm marketed a line in them.

He had the ideal excuse for visiting Renee: she hadn't been paid for yesterday's work. He wondered whether to take Dolly, who wouldn't be of any help that he could imagine, and might even be a hindrance. Then he remembered that he had taken her before, and she might establish in Renee's mind the notion that this visit was of no more significance than that visit had been. He got her lead, endured her look of scepticism that said: "I hope I'm not going to be walked to death *this* time," then took her in his arms and went out the front door, locking it behind him.

He let Dolly down on to the pavement when he was beyond the Headingley Stadium area, and she seemed pleased to be out of the arms of someone who was clearly not skilled in the art of dog-carrying. When he got to Kirkstall View he looked for the woman who had been gardening on his previous visit, but obviously the tiny apron of front garden didn't need much work on it. He was sorry, because a talk with her could have been useful. He continued on down and rang the doorbell at number eleven.

"Oh, Mr Docherty —" began Renee, a sort of turban around her sparse hair, still not entirely ready for a new day. Merlyn switched to casual apologetic mode.

"I would have left your money yesterday if I'd known I was going to be so long," he said. Since Renee showed no signs of standing aside he managed to let fall the dog-lead as he fumbled in his pockets for the cash, and Dolly obligingly ran through the hall and into the little sitting room they had talked in before. Renee went to get her, and Merlyn followed as if he needed no invitation.

"Now, sit quietly until we've finished," he said to Dolly, who on occasion could decide to obey him. "It was eighteen we decided on, wasn't it? Here's twenty. I could see you did a lot beyond the call of duty: the place was looking very spick and span."

"Well, it only needed a going over," said Renee, not sitting down, "but it's very generous of you."

"The house must have brought back memories, I suppose," said Merlyn sinking into a chair. Renee reluctantly sat down too. Her face was now screwed up, seemingly involuntarily.

"Not so's you'd notice. I never had any particular feeling for the house. Just for your Aunt Clarissa. She was a lady there was not very many like."

"She was. That's how I felt about the place – it was her that drew me there. Still, I've just been looking around the house as a piece of merchandise – how much it will sell for? – without an ounce of sentiment. With Clarissa gone, there isn't really any call to feel sentimental about it."

"Pity you didn't come back and visit her, then," said Renee, with an unusual touch of tartness. Merlyn had the notion that she did not feel strongly about his supposed neglect of his aunt, just a dislike of his presence and a desire to get rid of him.

"She didn't want it. Absolutely forbade it. Wanted people to assume that I was dead. I brought it up quite often in our weekly telephone conversations, but she was adamant."

Renee's face had fallen. She felt she had been wrong-footed, and hastened to make amends.

"I'm sorry. I shouldn't have said what I did. It was uncalled-for. I didn't know you and she had kept in touch."

"We did. Quite enough to know she wasn't suffering from

Alzheimers, as some of the family pretend to think."

"Oh *them*," said Renee disgustedly. "They think what they want to think, and pretend it's the truth."

"I think you and I have pretty similar views of the Cantelos," said Merlyn. "Your daughter worked for us for a time, didn't she?"

There was the tiniest of pauses. But Renee was a sharp woman, and perhaps a cunning one, and she knew a longer pause would give something away, make Merlyn suspicious where maybe he was not already. She smiled a social smile.

"Of course – that was before your time at Congreve Street, wasn't it? Before you came to stay, anyway. She worked in the shirt factory for a bit. Quite well paid, but she didn't like it much. She preferred dealing with people. She went to work in the K-Supermarket, and she's done quite well. She's a supervisor now, and one of their longest-serving employees."

"Oh, that's very good. And having a stable marriage must help a lot. People keep chopping and changing these days, but it doesn't seem to make them any happier."

There was no answer for a bit, then Renee said bleakly: "I only had ten years. I don't know how things would have turned out if my Norman hadn't died."

"I get the impression Clarissa thought she was better off remaining unmarried," Merlyn said. "But that's the sort of thing none of us can say for sure, isn't it?"

Renee nodded.

"That's right. You can never know what would have happened if you'd done something different in the first place." There was a wistfulness in her voice. Merlyn looked at her and then stood up. It was time to be off.

"By the way, I'm thinking of buying an old car to get me back to Brussels and then get rid of it."

"Oh yes?" There was already a trace of defensiveness in the voice, which told Merlyn at lot.

"I thought – I can be a bit of a sentimentalist about some things, you know – that I might see if Aunt Clarissa's old car is still on the market."

Renee came back quickly: "She got rid of that a while ago. Six months maybe."

"That's right. There was a note about that on the telephone pad, but you seem to have tidied it away yesterday."

A tiny red spot appeared on her upper cheekbone.

"Oh no, I'd never have done that. It could have been important. A cleaner just cleans and tidies. She doesn't destroy things."

"But the page on the top – a note by Aunt Clarissa, to ring a number and get rid of the car – was there yesterday morning but gone yesterday evening."

Renee was not good at lying, or thinking quickly.

"Well ... it seems funny. But all sorts of members of the family and others have probably had the key to the house."

"I changed the locks."

"Well, maybe you just tore it off yourself – absent-minded like. I know I do that sometimes."

"But it wasn't in the wastepaper baskets or the dustbin ... Your son-in-law runs a garage, doesn't he?" There was silence. "One of your neighbours talked about his being out to a breakdown on the road to Shipley last time I came here. Could you tell me his telephone number, Renee?"

"It's 240 7658." The voice was lifeless. Merlyn felt sure it was the number on the pad.

"That was it. So Aunt Clarissa got rid of her car through your son-in-law's garage?"

"She may have done. What does it matter?"

"Maybe not at all. Except that you didn't want any connection between them to suggest things to me. Suggest what, I wonder?" Merlyn went to the window and looked out, up towards the next house. Then he became conscious of noise.

Of shouting. Of several voices raised and competing with each other in their decibels of vociferation.

"That's your daughter's house, isn't it? The next one up the road. There's some disturbance there."

Renee sighed.

"'Appen. They don't get on, our Patsy and Sam. They have our Gina living there with her two kids. That doesn't help."

"'Our Gina.' But not *his* Gina, I'd guess."

Renee looked at him viciously.

"Why can't you mind your own bleeding business?"

"I think this probably is my business."

"And what are you, then? A fucking marriage guidance counsellor?"

"Something like that, I suppose. I work for the Common Market."

"I tell you," Renee shrieked, "keep out of my family's business."

"At the moment they seem to be sharing it with the whole street."

As Renee shrank down in her chair, looking defeated, Merlyn left the little living room, pursued by Dolly, and out the front door. Once in the open air the noise from next door seemed unbearable, a symphony of competing cacophonies. He went out into the street and along the road to the next gate up. Further on up the hill the woman he had spoken to before was back in her garden.

"I wouldn't get involved," she shouted. "You might get hurt. They're at it regularly, just like this. They're violent people, especially him. They enjoy it."

Merlyn shook his head and pushed open the front door. The main noise was coming from the room to his right: a man's voice — big, loud and brutal. Words like "whore" and "scrubber" were being used, and being countered by shrill accusations.

"And what about that Jackie Marsden, then? Don't tell me you haven't been having it off with her!"

The subsidiary noise came from the kitchen. The young woman he had seen at the bus-stop had herded her two children in there, she apparently used to the family wars, they still young enough to be distressed by them.

"Stop whining, Katie. You should be used to it by now. It doesn't mean owt. Stop that whining now or you'll feel the back of my hand. And stop that, Jerry – stop clutching my legs like that. You know I don't like it. You're a big boy now. I'll set your granddad on to you, then you'll feel it. I mean it!"

Merlyn looked sadly at this latest example of the Cantelo inability to bring up children. Then he swivelled forty-five degrees and stood in the doorway, observer of a war-zone.

"You just grab any opportunity to have it off with Kevin. Like bleeding goats you are. Soon as I heard you'd invited him I knew what you were after, both of you. Silver wedding? More like plastic, and then you'd be overcharging. And then to find you'd actually booked a room for yourselves! Talk about bleeding brazen! Nothing like a bit of comfort, I suppose you thought."

"No, there's not. We're not like you. You'll show off everything you've got in the open air – think it's manly, don't you? Brings back your youth. I bet you and Jackie were at it in the bushes around the car park. I bet some of the cars coming and going saw a few sights!"

The expression on Sam's face suggested she had scored a bullseye.

"Well, what if we were? I'd spent two bleeding hours listening to that dimwit Kelly saying 'Kevin's a long time getting the drinks' and 'I hope that lobster didn't disagree with my Kevin's stomach'. Stupid cow! Some women don't have the brains of a stick-insect."

"We were never gone two hours!"

"One hour, fifty-two minutes, to be precise."

"Well, we had to get our money's-worth. I'd paid good money for that room."

"*You* had! You bleeding moron. You can't think much of yourself if you had to do the paying. Women! They've lost all pride. Well, this is it. This is the end of the road. We're finished, you and I. Finito. All washed up. Hail and farewell."

"Oh, I don't think so," said Merlyn, coming forward. "You enjoy it too much, don't you? Can't live with each other, and can't live without each other. And it's been like this pretty much since 1978, hasn't it?"

He came forward into the room. Sam swung round and saw him for the first time. His bulging eyes and outraged expression transferred themselves from his wife to the newcomer without strain or hesitation, and he continued clenching and unclenching his fists as if to emphasize his unchanging intention to get physical.

"And who the fucking 'ell are you? And how did you get in here?"

"Through the front door. And we have met. You sold me a car a week or two ago."

"I sell hundreds of fucking cars."

"I think you remember me, Sam. After all, I told you my name and my address. And you had reason to know where 15 Congreve Street was."

"It was years ago Renee worked there."

"Years ago. Those are the operative words, aren't they, Sam?"

Sam had stopped his grunting gestures of aggression and his fists were still. Either because the presence of a third party acted as a barrier, or because some instinct of self-preservation had become operational.

"Don't know what you mean."

"Years ago, when all this started. Back in the late Seventies, when Patsy worked for Cantelo and Co."

"I was only there a few months," put in his wife who was either being supportive or similarly self-preservational. "Didn't suit me there."

"No, you didn't like sitting over a machine all day, did you? Preferred being with people."

"That's right. I did. Still do."

"Still, you got together with one person while you were at Cantelo's, didn't you? And you went right to the top."

Patsy seemed about to say that she didn't know what he meant, but instead she locked her lips and looked away.

"Which might have been all very well, might even have been profitable, but you were – what? – engaged? Married? Just going with? With someone of a very combustible nature."

"Speak bloody English," said Sam.

"Violent. You've got a violent nature, Sam."

"This is all old stuff," the man said, his voice thickening in tone. "Dead as a doornail. Why come along now and rake it up?"

"Not dead as a doornail, Sam. Because the result of Cantelo's philanderings is out in the kitchen, isn't she? And I bet she knows all about her origins. She's probably used to it coming up in family rows since she was quite small and hardly understood."

The silence of the pair told him that was true.

"So what were you at the time? Married?"

"Engaged," said Patsy.

"And then the baby came along, little Gina. Wedding bells lined up at Saint Paul the Evangelist, I suppose? And then a nasty little hitch arose. I would guess it was a question of blood group, wasn't it? Little Gina was group A, and Sam started wondering why the baby should have a group which neither of her parents has. Does a bit of asking round among friends and finds out it's impossible she's his child, because he and you were — what? Say O and B. Am I on the right lines?"

They looked ahead stonily, but Merlyn noticed that Sam's shoulders were heaving, and his hands clenching and unclenching again. He also noticed that Patsy was looking at him wondering if the revelations that were being brought out into the open could be used to her advantage.

"And so, when he'd got the truth out of you, Patsy, by the usual method of thumping you till you told him, one or other of you did the decent thing and got a bit of money out of the old man. No one would blame you, and he'd hate a paternity suit, wouldn't he – an upright pillar of the community like old Cantelo?"

"You're way off the mark there," said Patsy. "He was stingy as hell. A measly thousand. Probably knew he hadn't long to live. Or not much of a good name left."

"Right. Too mean to arouse any gratitude, but then that probably wasn't on the cards in any case. So Sam was still fuming that he'd been cuckolded by a seventy-year-old when he was approached." He let the word sink in, then turned to him. "*Weren't you?*"

There was total silence, but the air around them seemed charged. Merlyn went on:

"It was a member of the Cantelo family. My money would be on Hugh. More or less in the trade, working for BP. Inevitably the story of Patsy's fall had got around in the little circle of the unhappy family, and they'd got to the point of deciding that something had to be done about the old man, and even to selecting who would be the one to do it. And Hugh, or whichever it was, thought he saw a way of getting the job all the family wanted done – or *nearly* all of it – by calling in help from outside. The family would be instant suspects, but you would be much less so, particularly as the pregnancy had been accepted as the result of your well-known relationship. Maybe Hugh threw in a generous inducement.

But maybe he didn't need to, because you so wanted to pay the old lecher back. He told you a time when Cantelo would be alone in the house, he established that you could get hold of Renee's key, and then he left it to you. And so you went, and you did it: you let yourself in, went quietly upstairs, and when you found old Merlyn Cantelo sleeping in his bed you took a pillow – or perhaps you'd brought one with you – and you suffocated him. Possibly he hardly even struggled. If he did he'd have been no match for you. Then you went and let yourself out. Job done – to your satisfaction, and also to the Cantelos'."

Sam stood there, a lowering, fuming presence.

"I'm saying nowt. This is nothing but fairy-tale stuff. Not a scrap of evidence. If the police were putting this to me I'd say the same: 'show me your proof'. And they wouldn't be able to."

Merlyn nodded slowly.

"No, I don't think they would. You did well, Sam. You got away with murder for twenty-five years, without a breath of suspicion. Renee certainly knew nothing about it, or she wouldn't have talked to me as she did last time I was round. There's a bit more than a breath of suspicion now, but I think you'll get away with it for the rest of your life."

"I can live with suspicion," said Sam, relaxing a little, "— 'specially from a jumped up civil service pen-pusher like you. Now just be shifting yourself. I've had enough of playing host to someone who's barged into my house to accuse me of murder."

"Right, I'll be making tracks," said Merlin, turning towards the door as if intending to do just that. "But I think you'll be playing host to other people shortly who'll be accusing you of murder. I'm pretty sure the police will be along soon."

"Oh? You're running the police force now, are you? Why should they question me about something that there's nothing to connect me with?"

"Oh, my grandfather's death won't be what they're interested in. At best that'll be a subsidiary matter. What they'll want to question you about will be the attempt on *my* life."

"Your life?" said Sam, an easy sneer coming over his face. "If I wanted to send you to kingdom come I could do it with a couple of karate chops."

"You probably could. But something a bit more indirect fitted the bill better, didn't it? Who more capable of fixing the brakes on a car than the man who had just sold it?"

"That's rubbish that is," said Sam, contemptuously, with a phony confidence. "You decided on the car, we did the paperwork, and you drove it away. I didn't have time to do any hanky-panky on the brakes."

"Not then, agreed. You came to Congreve Street at night, and did it then. Perfectly simple operation – a little hole in the brake pipe and hey-presto! Pity the wrong person came along and pinched it, poor bugger."

"So what proof will there be that I did that?"

"DNA, I wouldn't mind betting."

"DNA? Don't talk rubbish! I could have left DNA on that car any time, by working on it while it was in my used car lot."

He was sharp – with the brazen flyness of someone who is accustomed to treading the borderline between the legal and the criminal.

"And the car to the front of my car, and the car to the rear? They took samples from them too. And are you quite sure you didn't leave traces on them too? Oh, granted that fixing the brake pipe is a simple job, it's still the case that you're a bulky individual, and you didn't have the car on a hoist like you'd be used to. Are you sure you managed to do it without leaving traces on the other cars, on the road, the pavement? I very much doubt it!"

Sam stood uncertain, the aggression still palpably there,

but contending with an attempt to remember every little action he had taken on that night in Congreve Street.

"So I bet you touched things, left all sorts of little remembrances of your presence. Your vicious, brutal, vengeful presence. And that's what the police will be here soon to take you in for doing. You thought you were going to put a stop to me before my nosing around came anywhere near you. Instead you killed a poor bloody tearaway who'd never done you any harm, or anyone else much. And you'll go down for it, I promise you. Go down for a very long time."

There was a moment's pause, then the big man threw himself on Merlyn. As he tried to dodge and caught the attack on his left shoulder Merlyn heard a bark, then a yelp of pain from the man heading down to the floor, then the more surprising sensation of being joined in his attempt to hold him by first a dog, then by one woman, then a second, then a third. Sam Kettleby was being extinguished by his womenfolk. Dimly, as he pulled the man's hand behind his back in a half-nelson, Merlyn heard the voice of the woman in the garden next door speaking into her mobile to summon the police.

Chapter Nineteen
Getting On

A couple of hours later Merlyn and Charlie were heading for the White Horse pub, where they had first met. Oddie was off work that day, looking at a commercial property in the centre of Halifax. Charlie cast his eye balefully over the plates of thick shortcrust pastry enclosing a dribble of gravy and odd fragments of meat, advertised in the menus as steak and kidney pie, and ordered a sandwich. Clearly he had different standards once outside the police canteen, Merlyn decided, and ordered the same. They went over to a dark and unfrequented corner to go through the events of the day in hushed voices.

"So we have someone in custody – violent, thuggish, and what else?" Charlie asked. "I suspect you could have been badly hurt, if it wasn't for the dog and the women."

"I think you're right. Their help came as a big surprise. Never underestimate small dogs, and as for the women – well, I had put the wife down as in some way a willing participant in domestic violence, but in the event the chance of actually being rid of her husband at long last must have seemed too good to miss."

"Do you think the women knew? About the murder I mean."

"Not Renee, I feel sure of that. I expect she's learning of it now. But Patsy? Surely it must have come out in one of those rows."

"So what's ahead of her? A quickie divorce while he's safely stowed away in the jug?"

"I'd guess so. And quite possibly a swift transfer to a man called Kevin with a dim wife. We'd better pray he's not the same type as Sam. As to the daughter of the marriage, she's a sad case. I would guess she's felt her supposed father's hand all the time she's been growing up. What she needs is a long and exhaustive course on parenting, but she'll be the last person to acknowledge that she needs one."

"So how do we approach Sam Kettleby? Set one of our feisty women detectives on to questioning him? Lively, cheeky, argumentative, verging on the stroppy? That often works with ageing sexist thuggy types, which seems to be what he is."

"You're the expert. Sounds a promising approach to me."

"In a sense that's all academic. We'll never get him for the Cantelo murder, not after nearly a quarter of a century. And for the car business we'll just have to wait for the analysis of the DNA samples. If they fit, he could be sent down for nine years, which will probably mean four. But if the Forensic Service people don't come up trumps, he's out on the streets within a month or two, and back selling dodgy cars."

"If that happens it's best I'm out of the country. Which is what I intend to be anyway."

Charlie raised his eyebrows satirically.

"Back to Brussels? Doesn't being head of the Cantelo clan have any appeal to you at all?"

"Not the tiniest bit. And there is no clan: clans are about solidarity, sticking together, group protectiveness. The Cantelos may have come together to get rid of Daddy when his activities threatened their inheritance and their respectability, but it was a one-off phenomenon, and probably full of doubts, suspicions and potential betrayals and explosions. The Cantelos were brought up to compete, they were played off one against the other, and Grandfather Cantelo reaped a bitter harvest from that. Hugh may well not have done it, but morally he was as guilty as Sam Kettleby. And Rosalind realised this, and thought I was in danger of uncovering the secret."

"Oh sure. And with Sam too you feel Old Cantelo got his

just deserts – though we policemen aren't allowed to think like that these days, are we?"

"Yes, seducing the pick of the workforce is something unpleasantly nineteenth-century, isn't it? Millowners were pretty quick to claim their *droits-de-Seigneur*, in spite of their scorn of the aristocracy. It's disgusting because the girls had very few means of comeback, apart from demanding money for their silence. The women in his family had far more."

"They did," agreed Charlie. "They could tell their husbands, they could threaten him with a far worse stink than a machinist in a sweat shop could kick up."

"You know," said Merlyn thoughtfully, "though I realised from the start – in fact I knew it when I lived with Clarissa – that the Cantelos were a divided and unloving family, I've often thought of them, in the weeks since I came back here, as an entity: 'Why are the Cantelos doing this?' I thought often subconsciously, but the impulse was there. But 'the Cantelos' weren't doing anything, because they were never a family unit."

"Just individuals, acting as individuals."

"Yes. If I thought 'Why did Caroline invite Roderick to her little party?' when all the rest seemed to keep him out in the cold, then the answer lies in Caroline's character. She latches on to any man under forty, and she has a mischievous streak which means that she quite likes to create piquant and embarrassing situations."

"Why do you think your father got into the act?"

"The plot to murder old Merlyn? Pretty much the same emotions as Paul had: revenge for humiliation, though in his case it was retrospective. He didn't get the idea I wasn't his son till long after my birth."

"No, I meant why did he make contact with you when you came home, when he's been indifferent to you for years?"

"I suspect a similar Cantelo instinct to stir things up was

active there. Probably Malachi, after our dinner, rang him up. He has the same sort of instinct as Caroline – the instinct to cause mayhem, quite blithely and without scruple. He told him I was back, and poor old Jake maybe started thinking, maybe even got to feel slightly guilty. Anyway the feeling came over him that he had to check me out, see what I'd become, assuage any feelings that he'd been a bad father to me. In a lazy sort of way, and provided it doesn't inconvenience him in any way, Jake likes to feel that he's a pretty good bloke."

"So the family was going any which way but the same way – with Rosalind the most vocal and active, still trying to preserve the image of her beloved father who was in fact the nearest thing in the family to a con artist, and morally the murderer of his father to boot."

"That's about it. Though one should really share the moral guilt around. Someone said that murder seems to run in families. There was no series of murders in the Cantelo family, but the one that was contemplated involved almost all the family."

"Except your aunt."

"Exactly. Except Clarissa. She was *kept* out, ostensibly because as a major inheritor she would be the first to be suspected, but in fact because they knew she wouldn't consider for a moment going along with it."

"And when she began to get whiffs of what had been going on, she decided to get you out of the way because the financial motive that had led to the death of her father could very easily be transferred to you as her next heir."

"Yes. Stripped of the spiritualist trappings that she entertained in her mind, that was probably the essence of it. I don't resent or regret what she did for a moment. It gave me a new life, and a new self."

"Which you'll now go and resume?"

"Oh yes. I've made an appointment to get a Pet Passport

for Dolly. Thank God the old nonsense about quarantine is a thing of the past. The thing I'll do is put the house on the market, get the top price I can for it, and take refuge in darkest Brussels."

"And marry and have children and defy the curse of the Cantelos?"

"Yes. I don't for a moment believe in curses, do you?"

"Not for a moment," said Charlie.

"To put the matter at its most basic, I've learnt from the Cantelos a whole range of things not to do – in marriage as well as in bringing up children. I'm not going to go into the whole business of having a family with a thick, dark cloud hanging over me. The Cantelos are history. What happens now is up to me."

"True of you," said Charlie getting up, "and true of me. I've just heard I've got my inspectorship."

"Wonderful! Congratulations! The future is yours!" said Merlyn with a touch of irony.

"Not really. An inspector is just the superintendent's dogsbody, looking for a way of making his own mark."

"That's true of all promotions. Unless you stay happily on the lowest rung – which may be the sensible thing to do – that's how it is for everybody with ambitions."

"Well, I'll look forward to you being President of the European Union."

"That will be a job for politicians, if we ever get it. I'm not a politician. I'm a civil servant. One of the lower forms of human life."

They parted outside the White Horse. Charlie went back to Millgarth to arrange a celebratory dinner with Felicity – which, since they wanted Carola to be involved, turned out to be the better sort of fast food joint. Merlyn wandered through town and dropped into an estate agent's to start the process of ridding himself of the burden of the house in Congreve Street.

Then he popped into W.H. Smith to riffle through their section of continental newspapers to start the process of getting back into the work routine. He bought *Paris Match* and *Corriere della Serra*. The Italian Prime Minister, Silvio Berlusconi, was being childish again. Nothing new under the sun.

He wandered around the paperback shelves, looking for something to read on the journey, but in fact musing on the fate of the brood brought up by Grandfather Cantelo. He thought that his mother must have been the most normal of all. He found Clarissa and perhaps Paul were also likeable, but Clarissa had taken refuge in her dubious clairvoyancy business, and Paul's aspirations had led him far, but only geographically: he suspected that the creative writing professorship in Arkansas had very little to do with writing of any sort, either elevated or popular. *Family Business* had gone off at half cock because he had no faith in himself or his satiric gifts. Both these attractive scions of the family had been damaged individuals: Paul's target remained unhurt because Grandfather Cantelo was a bigger person than the flea-biting satirist who was his son: Grandfather did at least know about business, even if as a family man he was a disaster.

He shook the thoughts from him, paid for his papers and a Peter Robinson, and left the shop.

Out in the open area in the middle of Lands Lane a little knot of religious maniacs, led by a woman with a foghorn voice, was proclaiming its faith to passers-by, and to a few amused listeners whose expressions suggested they were encountering something out of *The Lost World*.

"You are the chosen of the Lord, his own Special People," bellowed the woman, "but he demands of you obedience to his laws, the will to do *His* will daily, hourly. Is that too much to ask?"

"A lot too much," said a middle-aged woman in the group

of spectators.

"No, not a lot too much! The very least He could ask! The God who made you, loves you when you do His will. But how do you think He feels when you trudge knee-high through the mire of adultery, perversion, vileness of all kinds —"

There was a pull on Merlyn's sleeve.

"You got the price of a cup of tea, mate?"

It was one of the little knot of believers: an old man, ill-shaven, with bright, sharp eyes.

"I might have," said Merlyn.

"I'm sorry to bother you, but I knew I could rely on you. You're the right sort, I can always tell. Have you ever thought of becoming a British Israelite?"

Suddenly the thought occurred to Merlyn that this might be Uncle Gerald, father of Malachi and Francis, lost long ago to the wilder shores of religion. For a moment he looked into the face with interest, intent on detecting signs of a Cantelo inheritance: the low forehead, the determined nose. He had almost physically to shake himself free of the impulse: what-ever need could he have for one more Cantelo relative? In this case a jostler for an eternal good place in the heavenly pecking order? None whatsoever. He must stop, from now, being obsessed with the Cantelo family. He rummaged in his pock-et for loose change.

"Here, have this," he said, handing the man a Euro.

He wheeled round and went in search of a travel agent to book his flight back to Brussels. Then he phoned Danielle and left a message on her answer machine. "See you tomorrow" was followed by "Marry me."